Fear No
EVIL

WHO IS ALEX CROSS?

PHYSICAL DESCRIPTION:
========================

Alex Cross is 6 foot 3 inches (190cm), and weighs 196 lbs (89 kg).
He is African American, with an athletic build.

FAMILY HISTORY:
==================

Cross was raised by his grandmother, Regina Cross Hope – known as Nana
Mama – following the death of his mother and his father's subsequent
descent into alcoholism. He moved to D.C. from Winston-Salem, North
Carolina, to live with Nana Mama when he was ten.

RELATIONSHIP HISTORY:
========================

Cross was previously married to Maria, mother to his children Damon and
Janelle, however she was tragically killed in a drive-by shooting. Cross
has another son, Alex Jr., with Christine Johnson. He is now married
to Detective Brianna (Bree) Stone, who was recently appointed Chief of
Detectives for the Metro Police Department.

EDUCATION:
=========

Cross has a PhD in psychology from Johns Hopkins University in Baltimore,
Maryland, with a special concentration in the field of abnormal
psychology and forensic psychology.

EMPLOYMENT:
==========

Cross works as a psychologist in a private practice, based in his home. He
also consults for the Major Case Squad of the Metro Police Department,
where he previously worked as a psychologist for the Homicide and Major
Crimes team.

PROFILE

A loving father, Cross is never happier than when spending time with
his family. He is also a dedicated member of his community and often
volunteers at his local parish and soup kitchen. When not working
in the practice or consulting for MPD, he enjoys playing classical
music on the piano, reading, and teaching his children how to box.

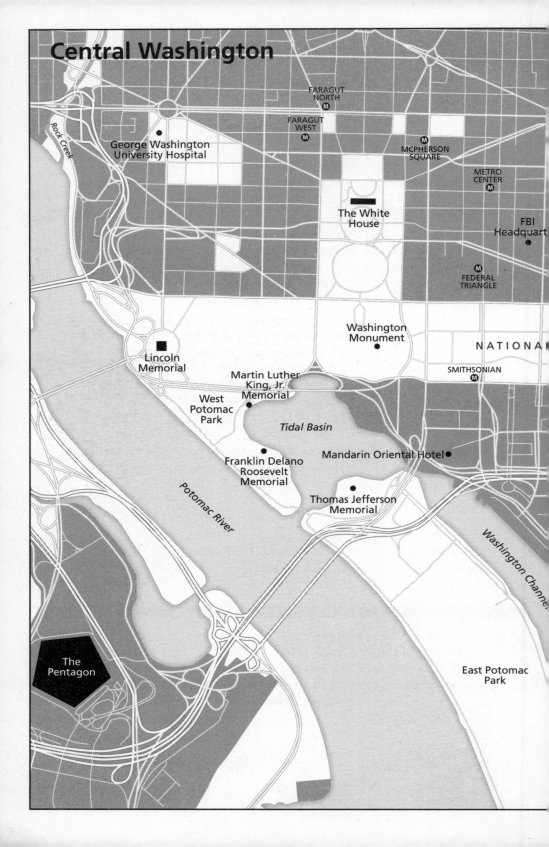

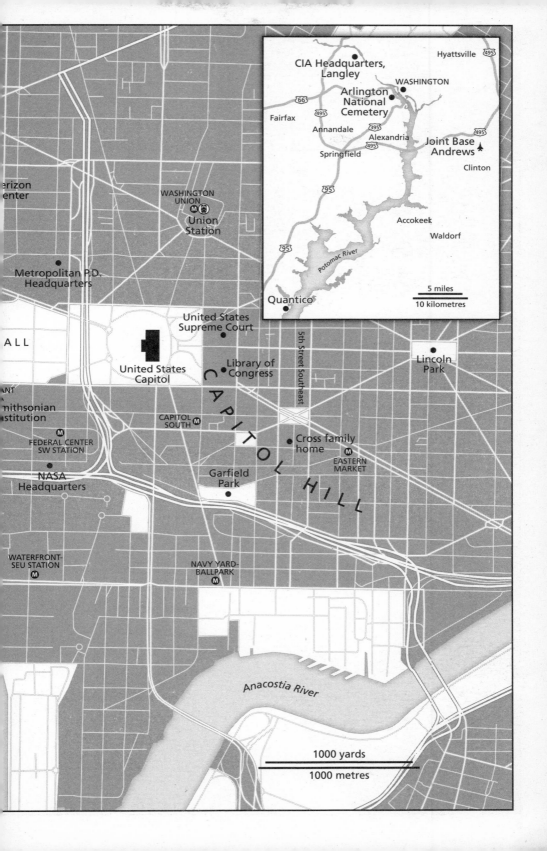

Hyattsville

CIA Headquarters,
Langley

WASHINGTON

Arlington
National
Cemetery

Fairfax

Annandale

Alexandria

Joint Base
Andrews

Springfield

Clinton

Accokeek

Waldorf

Potomac River

Quantico

5 miles

10 kilometres

WASHINGTON
UNION
Union
Station

Metropolitan P.D.
Headquarters

erizon
enter

ALL

United States
Supreme Court

Lincoln
Park

5th Street Southeast

United States
Capitol

Library of
Congress

CAPITOL
SOUTH

CAPITOL HILL

ANT

mithsonian
stitution

FEDERAL CENTER
SW STATION

Cross family
home

EASTERN
MARKET

NASA
Headquarters

Garfield
Park

WATERFRONT-
SEU STATION

NAVY YARD-
BALLPARK

Anacostia River

1000 yards

1000 metres

A list of titles by James Patterson appears at the
back of this book

Fear No
EVIL
JAMES
PATTERSON

CENTURY

1 3 5 7 9 10 8 6 4 2

Century
20 Vauxhall Bridge Road
London SW1V 2SA

Century is part of the Penguin Random House group of companies
whose addresses can be found at global.penguinrandomhouse.com

First published in Great Britain by Century in 2021

www.penguin.co.uk

A CIP catalogue record for this book is available from the British Library

ISBN 9781529125252
ISBN 9781529125269 (trade paperback edition)

Printed and bound in Great Britain by Clays Ltd, Elcograf S.p.A.

The authorised representative in the EEA is Penguin Random House Ireland,
Morrison Chambers, 32 Nassau Street, Dublin D02 YH68

Penguin Random House is committed to a sustainable future
for our business, our readers and our planet. This book is made
from Forest Stewardship Council® certified paper.

Fear No
EVIL

CHAPTER

1

Washington, DC
Late June

MATTHEW BUTLER COCKED HIS HEAD to one side, considering the big-boned blonde in front of him. She was handcuffed and shackled to a heavy oak chair bolted into the concrete floor beneath bright fluorescent lights.

If the woman was anxious about her predicament, she wasn't showing it in the least. She was as chill as the yoga outfit she wore. No sweat on her pale brow. Beneath her warm-up hoodie, her chest rose and fell calmly, each breath measured. Her shoulders were relaxed. Even her eyes looked soft.

Butler adjusted the strap of his shoulder holster.

"I know they've trained you for this sort of thing," he said in a voice with the slightest of Western twangs. "But your training won't work against me, Catherine. It never does."

A fit, balding man with a hawkish nose, Butler had

workman's hands and wore black jeans, Nike running shoes, and a dark blue polo shirt. He crossed his thick forearms when she smiled back at him with brilliant white teeth.

"Whoever you are, you are going to be destroyed for what you're doing," Catherine Hingham said. "When they find out—"

Butler cut her off. "You know, in my many years as a professional, Catherine, I have come to rather enjoy the delicate process of breaking into hearts and minds. They are very much interlinked, you know—hearts and minds—and I have found that one is almost always the key to the other."

"Langley will annihilate you," Hingham said, studying Butler as if she wanted to remember every line in his face.

"Your operators won't help you today," Butler said, gesturing at a pile of blank paper and a pen on the table before her. "Tell me the truth and we can all move on with our lives."

"I'll say it again: You have no jurisdiction over me."

Butler chuckled, gestured around the room. "Oh, but in here, I do."

"I want to see a lawyer, then."

"I'm sure," he said, sobering. "But we're talking about a serious threat to our national security, Catherine. A few rules of engagement can and will be broken in order to thwart that threat."

"I am not a national security threat," she said evenly. "I work for the Central Intelligence Agency, with the highest clearances, in support of my country's freedoms. Your freedoms as well."

"That's what makes your traitorous actions so hard to understand, Catherine."

Her face reddened and she shifted in her chair. "I am no traitor."

Butler took a step toward her. "The hell you're not. We know about the Maldives."

Hingham blinked, furrowed her brow. "The Maldives? Like, the islands in the Indian Ocean?"

"The same."

"I have no idea what you're talking about. I have never been to the Maldives. I've never even been to India."

"No?"

"Never. You can talk to my case officers about it."

"I plan to at some point," Butler said, taking another step toward her. He reached down to touch the back of her left hand before letting his finger trail across her wedding band and modest engagement ring. "Does he know? Your husband?"

"That I work for the CIA?" she said. "Yes. But he has zero idea what I actually do. Those are the rules. We play by them."

Butler sighed as he gently took hold of her left pinkie with his leathery hand, thumb on top.

"Do you know the surest way to sever the connection between the body and mind, and therefore the heart?"

"No," she said.

"Pain," Butler said. He gripped her little finger tight and levered his thumb sharply downward until he heard a bone snap.

2

CATHERINE HINGHAM SCREAMED IN AGONY, fighting against her restraints, then yelled at him, "You cannot do this! This is the United States of America and I'm a sworn officer of the Central—"

Butler broke her ring finger, then waited for her to stop screaming and crying.

"You have eight fingers left, Catherine," Butler said calmly. "I will break them all and if you still do not tell me what I want to know, I will have your five-year-old daughter brought here and I will begin breaking *her* tiny fingers one by one until you confess."

The CIA officer stared at him in disgust and horror. "Emily has cerebral palsy."

"I know."

"You wouldn't. It's…monstrous."

"It is," he said and sighed again. "And yet, because there is so much at stake, Catherine, I will break your little girl's fingers. But only if you make it necessary."

The CIA officer continued to stare at him for several moments. He gazed back at her evenly until her lower lip trembled and she hung her head.

"The costs," Hingham whispered hoarsely. "You have no idea what a child like Em…" She could not go on and broke down sobbing.

"The heart wins again," Butler said. He pushed the pile of blank pages in front of her. "Start writing. The Maldives. The numbered accounts. Their connections. All of it."

After a few moments, Catherine Hingham calmed enough to raise her head. "I need witness protection."

"I'll see what I can do," Butler said and held out the pen to her. "Now write."

The CIA officer reached out with both handcuffed hands shaking. She took the pen. "Please," she said. "My family doesn't deserve what will happen if—"

"Write," he said firmly. "And I'll see what I can do."

The CIA officer reluctantly began to scribble names, addresses, account numbers, and more. When she'd moved to a second page, Butler had seen enough to be satisfied.

He walked behind the CIA officer and nodded to a small camera mounted high in the corner of the room.

A gravelly male voice came through the tiny earbud Butler wore in his left ear. "Mmmm. Well done. When you have what we need, end the interview and file your report, please."

Butler nodded again before moving in front of Catherine Hingham. She set her pen down and pushed the pages across the table at him.

"That's it," she said in a hoarse voice. "Everything I know."

"Unlikely," Butler said, using the nail of his index finger to lift up the first sheet so he could scan the information she'd provided on page two. "But this looks useful enough for now. It will give us leverage. Was that so hard, Catherine?"

She relaxed a little and said, "Okay, then, I've given you what you wanted. Now I need a doctor to fix my hand. I need witness protection."

With his fingernail, Butler scooted the confession pages to the far right of the table. "You're a smart woman, Catherine. Well educated. Yale, if I remember. You should know your history better. We don't protect traitors in the United States of America. From Benedict Arnold on, they've all had to pay the price. And now, so will you."

The CIA officer looked confused and then terrified when Butler took a step back and drew a stubby pistol with a sound suppressor from his shoulder holster.

"No, please, my kids are—" she managed before he took aim and shot her between the eyes.

CHAPTER

3

FROM THE TIME WE'D MET as ten-year-olds, John Sampson, my best friend and long-term DC Metro Police partner, had been stoic, quiet, observant. Since his wife, Billie, had died, he'd become even more reserved and was now given to long bouts of brooding silence. I knew he was still wrestling with grief.

But that late-June morning, Big John was acting as wound up as a kid about to hit the front gates of Disney World as he bopped around my front room, where we'd laid out all our gear for a trip we'd been talking about taking for years.

"You think we'll see a grizzly?" Sampson asked, grinning at me.

"I'm hoping not," I said. "At least, not up close."

"They're in there, big-time. And wolves."

"And deer, elk, and cutthroat trout," I said. "I've been studying the brochure too."

Nana Mama, my ninety-something grandmother, came in wringing her hands and asked with worry in her voice, "Did I hear you say grizzly bears?"

Sampson glowed with excitement. "Nana, the Bob Marshall Wilderness has one of the densest concentrations of grizzlies in the lower forty-eight states. But don't worry. We'll have bear spray and sidearms. And cameras."

"I don't know why you couldn't choose a safer place to go on your manly trip."

"If it was safer, it wouldn't be manly," I said. "There's got to be a challenge."

"Glad I'm an old lady, then. Breakfast in five minutes." Nana Mama turned and shuffled away, shaking her head.

"Checklist?" Sampson said.

"I'm ready if you are."

We started going through every item we'd thought necessary for the twenty-nine-mile horseback trip deep into one of the last great wildernesses on earth and for the five-day raft ride we'd take out of the Bob Marshall on the South Fork of the Flathead River. An outfitter was providing the rafts, tents, food, and bear-proof storage equipment. Everything else had to fit into four rubberized dry bags we'd use on the river after he dropped us off.

We could have signed up for a fully guided affair, but Sampson wanted us to do a good part of the trip alone, and after some thought, I'd agreed. Six days deep in the backcountry of Montana would give Big John many chances to open up and talk, which is critical to the process of coping with tragic loss.

"How's Willow feeling about our little trip?" I asked.

Sampson smiled. "She doesn't like the idea of grizzly bears any more than Nana does, but she knows it will make me happy."

"Your little girl's always been wise beyond her years."

"Truth. Bree liking her job?"

Thinking of my smart, beautiful, and independent wife, I said, "She loves it. Got up early to be at the office. Something about a possible assignment in Paris."

"Paris! What a difference a career change makes."

"No kidding. It was like the gig was tailor-made for her."

"Maybe we should think about going into private-sector investigations too."

"Pay's better, for sure," I allowed.

Before he could reply, my seventeen-year-old daughter, Jannie, poked her head in and said, "Nana says your eggs are getting cold."

I put down my dry bag and went to the kitchen, where I found my youngest child, Ali, already finishing up his plate.

"Morning, sunshine," I said, giving him a hug. He ignored it, so I tickled him.

"C'mon, Dad!" He laughed, then groaned. "Why can't I go with you?"

"Because you're a kid and we don't know what we'll be facing."

"I can do it," he insisted.

Sampson said, "Ali, let your dad and me scope it out this year. If we think you're up to it, we'll bring you along on the next trip. Deal?"

Ali scrunched up his face and shrugged. "I guess. When do you leave?"

"First thing in the—"

My cell phone began to ring at the same time Sampson's chimed.

"No," John protested. "Don't answer that, Alex. We're supposed to be gone already!"

But when I saw the caller ID, I grimaced and knew I had to answer. "Commissioner Dennison," I said. "John Sampson and I were just heading out the door on vacation."

"Cancel it," said the commissioner of the Metro DC Police Department. "We've got a dead female, gunshot wound to the head, dumped in the garage under the International Spy Museum on L'Enfant Plaza. Her ID says she's—"

"Commissioner, with all due respect," I said, "we've been planning this trip for—"

"I don't care, Cross," he snapped. "Her ID says she's CIA. If you want to continue your contract with Metro, you'll get down there. And if Sampson wants to keep his job, he'll be with you."

I stared at the ceiling a second, looked at John, and shook my head.

"Okay, Commissioner. We're on our way."

CHAPTER

4

TENTH AVENUE IN SOUTHWEST DC goes under L'Enfant Plaza with a turnoff for monthly permit and public parking. The deceased, a big blonde in her late thirties with a gunshot wound to the head, was sitting upright in a corner of the third level of monthly permit parking.

A crude sign that said TRAITOR was hung around her neck.

"Someone had to have seen her get put here," I said. "Cameras, anyway."

Sampson nodded. "Maybe we *will* make our flight tomorrow morning."

Valerie Jackson, a Metro patrol officer, met us at a band of yellow tape she'd strung around the crime scene. The spy museum's director had discovered the victim when he arrived shortly after dawn.

"She has a CIA ID?" Sampson asked.

"Photo and everything. It's still on her lap. Catherine Hingham of the CIA."

We put on blue shoe covers and latex gloves before crossing to the deceased, who was dressed like a suburban mom out for a lunch date after yoga class. We saw how nasty the exit wound was, but we both noted how little blood there was around and behind her.

"She was moved here," Sampson said.

"I was just going to say the same thing," I said. "She was shot elsewhere, cleaned up a little, and put here as a message."

"To who?"

"Other traitors?"

We saw two black Suburbans drive in and park.

"Who the hell let them in?" Officer Jackson said, moving toward the cars. Six men and women in black windbreakers emerged. One guy with slicked-back blond hair and an attitude came straight to the yellow tape and ducked under it. When Officer Jackson tried to cut him off, he flashed an ID and kept coming.

"Dean Weaver, Detectives," he said. "Central Intelligence Agency."

"CIA?" Sampson said, pulling himself up to his full six foot nine inches and getting in the man's way.

"Good—you can hear, and you understand English," Weaver said, holding up his identification. "We'll be taking over the investigation from here. I want any and all evidence left in situ. And I ask that you kindly leave."

I shook my head. "Not a chance. Federal law prohibits the CIA from running investigations in the United States, so I'll have to ask you to leave *my* crime scene."

"And who are you?"

"Dr. Alex Cross, investigative consultant to Metro PD and the FBI. And if you don't leave, I'll be calling my liaison, Supervising Special Agent Ned Mahoney, who I'm sure would be glad to explain how the law works domestically."

The CIA officer looked ready to pop his cork but he kept it under control. "Catherine Hingham is—was—one of ours, Dr. Cross," he said with clenched fists. "Can I please at least identify her?"

"After you explain how you found out so fast," I said.

"I…can't say. It's…complicated."

Sampson smiled. "Must happen like that a lot in the spy business."

The CIA officer sighed. "You have no idea."

"Let him look, John," I said, and Sampson let Weaver walk a few more feet forward until he could see the body.

Weaver's shoulders slumped and he stood there glumly for several minutes, looking at her. "That's Catherine," he said when he turned around. "And I don't care what that sign says. She was no traitor."

"Thank you," Sampson said. "But again, we're going to have to ask you to leave."

"Don't you want to know about her?" Weaver asked.

"I thought you guys never talk about what you do."

"We don't, usually. This is different."

5

TONI ALSTON, ONE OF THE district's medical examiners, arrived along with two crime scene specialists. They began photographing the area as we stood off to the side, listening to the CIA officer describe Catherine Hingham as one of the smartest, most dedicated field operatives he'd ever worked with.

"Field operative?" I said. "She looks like a—"

"Suburban housewife or a schoolteacher," Weaver said. "That was the point. She used both those covers, among others."

According to Weaver, Catherine Hingham had been fluent in five languages and worked in a variety of deep undercover settings. All the while, she raised two children, one of whom was born with cerebral palsy.

"Most mothers would have resigned immediately," Weaver

said. "But Catherine's husband, Frank, is a speech pathologist and infinitely more qualified to be Emily's primary caregiver. Does he know yet?"

"Not that we're aware of," Sampson said. "And we'd appreciate being the ones to break the news to him."

"Where does he *think* she is?" I asked.

The CIA officer looked at me appraisingly. "Training in Los Angeles."

"Where was she really?"

"Until the day before yesterday, she was in Nogales, Mexico."

"Doing what?"

Weaver put up his hands. "Now, that I cannot discuss."

I said, "But given Nogales, we can assume what?"

"Assume nothing. She was on an assignment critical to national security and I'll have to leave it at that or risk prison time." He fished a card from his wallet. "But if you've got other questions, you can call me, day or night, and whatever I can tell you, I will."

"Was she one of yours?" I asked, taking the card. "Part of your team, like the others over by the Suburbans?"

Weaver cocked his head. "You are sharp, Dr. Cross. Yes, Catherine was one of mine and she entered the CIA with several of those officers. We were a team."

"Were you or any other members of your team also in Nogales?" Sampson asked.

The agent's eyes shifted; he blinked. "No. I wish we had been, but Catherine wanted to work this one solo."

"Was she corruptible? Financially? Ideologically?" I asked.

"No!" Weaver said sharply. "One hundred percent no. Catherine was...one of the good people—"

"Dr. Cross?" Toni Alston interrupted.

"Excuse me," I said and went over to the medical examiner.

Alston told me her preliminary examination indicated Hingham had died roughly thirty-six hours earlier from a single, small-caliber gunshot to the head. Her left pinkie and left ring finger were broken.

"Torture?" I asked.

"Possibly. Broken fingers must have been painful. But I'm not seeing any other marks on her so far," Alston said. "I'll know more once I get her back to my lab. And we found this in an inside pocket of her hoodie."

She went over and retrieved an evidence bag. Inside was a white letter-size envelope. Printed on it in a large, garish red font was one word: CONFESSION.

The text was so vivid, Weaver could see it from twenty feet away. "Confession?" he said, coming toward us. "I want to see that right now."

This time I stepped in front of him, my hands way out to my sides as if I were guarding him in a hoops game. "Mr. Weaver, that will not happen without some kind of waiver from the Department of Justice," I said. "There's nothing you or I can do without one. Now, please leave the crime scene or I'll have you forcibly removed."

The CIA officer wanted to paste me; I could see it in his eyes and the bunching of his muscles. But a cooler head prevailed. He nodded and said, "I'm going to see about that right now."

Weaver walked away, shooed the rest of his team back into the Suburbans, and left.

I was about to suggest we get hold of the parking lot's security cameras when my cell phone buzzed in my pocket.

When I saw the text on the screen, I felt instantly exposed. I looked all around and back to where the Suburbans had vanished.

"Alex?" Sampson said.

I held up a finger and then read the text again.

Top of the morning, Dr. C. It's been months, hasn't it? I know I've been playing catchup these last few days. Bree's left Metro PD behind her. How exciting! Jannie's entering her senior year soon. Damon's killing it at Davidson. Ali's becoming quite the young detective. And you're on the new case of the Traitor in the Parking Garage. I swear, if I take my eyes off you for a moment, Alex Cross, your entire life changes.—M

CHAPTER

6

ACROSS THE POTOMAC RIVER, in an Arlington office tower, Bree Stone knocked on the door to the conference room and entered. Five people waited for her at the table. Four were women, two in their late twenties and two in their forties. All were dressed for business. The lone male was silver-haired, craggily handsome, and dressed impeccably in a bespoke blue suit, starched white shirt, and red tie with teal polka dots.

"Bree Stone," he said in a British accent, standing to shake her hand. "Good to finally meet you in person."

"Desmond Slattery," she said, returning the smile. "When did you fly in?"

"I caught the red-eye from Heathrow," he said.

"And here you are, not a hair out of place."

"Got to keep the reputation clean," he said and chuckled.

The petite, fortyish brunette at the head of the table said, "Sit anywhere you'd like, Bree."

Elena Martin, the founder and president of Bluestone Group, was one of the smartest women Bree had ever met, a super-dynamo who needed less than five hours of sleep a night. A former analyst and investigator with the Defense Intelligence Agency, Martin was also an entrepreneurial visionary; after leaving the military, she quickly built Bluestone into one of the top private-security firms in the country by aggressively recruiting and hiring highly respected law enforcement professionals like Bree.

After taking a seat next to Slattery—a former inspector at Scotland Yard—Bree smiled at the other women at the table, whom she'd never seen before.

Elena Martin introduced the other woman in her forties as Patricia Nolan.

"Ms. Nolan is corporate counsel at Pegasus International," Elena Martin said. "Do you know the company?"

Bree shook her head.

Nolan smiled. "Not surprising. We're a hedge fund that prides itself on its low profile. We're incorporated in Delaware with offices on Wall Street and in Paris."

The president of Bluestone said to Bree, "I've told them you speak fluent French with a Caribbean accent."

Bree nodded. "My mother was from Saint Martin."

"I also told them you are one of our star investigators, and they wanted to meet you in person."

"I'm delighted, and I appreciate the confidence, Elena," Bree said. Nolan introduced her to the two younger women, and Bree reached across the table to shake their hands.

When she sat back, she glanced at Slattery and saw a

slightly sour look on his face. He obviously considered himself one of Bluestone's star investigators as well. For a second, Bree wondered why Slattery hadn't gotten this assignment, then pushed the thought aside. She smiled at the clients. "How can I be of service?"

Anna Tuttle, an attractive, sandy-blond young woman in a blue business suit, said, "You can help us get our son-of-a-bitch CEO fired."

Cassie Dane, a buxom redhead with porcelain-pale skin and ice-green eyes, said in a sweet Southern accent, "Or, better yet, put Philippe's ass in prison with men who will not be kind or gentle."

"There's something I should explain first, Ms. Stone," the corporate attorney said. "I am here at the request of the board of directors of Pegasus to determine whether our founder, CEO, and chairman Philippe Abelmar is guilty of sexual harassment—"

"He definitely is," Anna Tuttle said.

"And a serial abuser of women—"

"That too," Cassie Dane said, her cheeks reddening.

"And quite possibly an embezzler," Nolan said.

Tuttle looked a little disgusted as she nodded to Bree. "We appreciate Ms. Nolan being here, really, we do, but just so you understand, the rumors of sexual harassment have been flying around Philippe forever. And yet it wasn't until the suspicions about missing money surfaced that the Pegasus board decided to hire someone to investigate."

Nolan's jaw stiffened. "Philippe Abelmar is a powerful, charismatic man, and France is a different country with different moral views than our own. But I admit he held sway over the board despite the rumors about his inappropriate activities until they saw evidence that he may have siphoned off as much as four hundred million dollars."

"Four hundred million?" Bree said, her brows rising.

"See?" Tuttle said to Dane. "It's all anyone cares about."

The Southern belle pushed back a wayward lock of red hair and shrugged. "I honestly don't give a damn what finally drug 'em to the dance, Anna. I just want that man's testicles in a vise. And maybe some public shaming while we're at it."

Slattery winced at the testicles-in-a-vise comment before clearing his throat and looking at Pegasus's corporate counsel. "My specialty at Scotland Yard was economic crimes and forensic accounting. I'll be working the money end of things in Manhattan and London."

Tuttle said, "London's where I worked after Paris."

"Where we all worked after Paris, hon," Cassie Dane said.

CHAPTER

7

THE THREE WOMEN EXPLAINED TO Bree how it worked at Pegasus. Recruiters in the company's Wall Street offices tended to choose pretty Ivy League co-eds for their internship programs.

After a year of training in the science of modern finance, the young women were rotated to Paris, where Philippe Abelmar oversaw their continuing education in the art of making money.

Anna Tuttle said, "For six months it was all about the philosophy, beauty, and inherent goodness of capitalism. And the value of knowing numbers—whether we were up or down and how we were going to take advantage of subtle changes in the markets. If you were particularly bright, you were made special personal assistant to Philippe."

"Nothing to do with brightness and I know it," Cassie Dane said. She gestured at her chest, saying, "Sure, I went to Penn, but that pervo Frog just liked my girls."

Both women described the Paris office as a culture where conversations were often laced with sexual innuendo. Abelmar encouraged the behavior, believing that tension between coworkers was a good thing, especially if it was rarely or never relieved.

"He flirted with me for months," Anna Tuttle said. "I tried to keep it professional, but Philippe made it impossible. Being his personal assistant meant I was always at his side or on call—at work, at his apartment, or on his jet."

"Or the yacht in Cannes," Cassie Dane said. "That's where Philippe drugged me and then forcibly raped me after I'd worked for him for six months."

"For me it was also roughly six months, but at his Paris apartment," Anna Tuttle said. "He held me there several days. The things he did were…unspeakable."

Bree said, "Did you file police reports?"

Both women looked at each other, embarrassed.

"He filmed it all," Dane said. "He showed me a video where I was acting only a little drunk and giving him verbal consent to take off my clothes and make a recording. I have no memory of that. Zero. And I usually remember everything!"

"That's all it takes in France," Tuttle said. "Evidence of verbal consent between adults. Except Philippe didn't take chances. He has signed documents, release forms, although neither of us remembers signing anything."

"No one tested you for drugs?"

"If I had it to do over? I'd give a quart of blood to figure out what he stuck in my drink," Dane said. "But he told me he'd release the videos on a porn site. Ruin me."

"And then you were transferred out of the Paris office?"

Tuttle said, "No. That happened after Philippe black-mailed me into having sex with him until my year as his personal assistant was over."

"And a new one was chosen," Cassie Dane said.

Bree frowned. "You didn't try to warn the new personal assistant?"

Patricia Nolan said, "In their defense, Bree, they had no idea at the time there were other complaints about Philippe."

"But *you* knew?"

Nolan swallowed. "I've been with Pegasus only two years…but yes, I knew of Philippe's reputation, if not the specifics of his actions."

"Until the four hundred million went missing," Anna Tuttle said coldly. "Then you were all about it after Pegasus ignored me and then drove me out of finance."

"Same," Cassie Dane said.

"No one's sued?" Bree asked.

The corporate counsel said, "There were several attempts over the years. All of them were settled privately with significant payments made to the women."

Anna Tuttle said, "He shuts you up with threats to release videos or with lawyers or with money. Philippe's put him-self above the law because he can. Harvard undergraduate. Yale Law. Sorbonne for business school. Billionaire before he turned forty."

Cassie Dane pushed back that stubborn lock of red hair and gazed at Bree, smiling easily. "That's who we're up against, Ms. Bree Stone, fricking Goliath Pervo. So, girl to girl, please tell me true: Are you up for putting Goliath's nuts in a vise and then letting us turn the handle tight? Or is this all too much for you to see through?"

Bree smiled and looked at her boss. "When do I leave for Paris, Elena?"

Elena Martin nodded. "There's a business class seat for you on this evening's Air France flight out of Dulles. Be on it."

CHAPTER

8

TRAFFIC HAD SLOWED TO A CRAWL on the Beltway toward Dulles Airport. Bree kept checking her watch. I was still dealing with the aftershock of knowing that M was back in my life. Again.

M was the name I knew him by, though John Sampson referred to him off and on as Mastermind. Over the years, M had alternately helped and hindered us as we investigated various murders and criminal enterprises and his roles in them.

For a time, M had tried to make me believe that Kyle Craig, an old, dead nemesis of mine, was actually back among the living. He'd done it to mess with my head and with Sampson's.

And even though this had been going on for years, we still didn't understand his motivations, which was infuriating. M liked to taunt me, and I knew better than to respond to his texts.

But it was still bugging me.

"Alex, we haven't moved in five minutes," Bree said, breaking into my thoughts.

"We've got two hours to get there, and it's only six miles away," I said. "According to Waze, there's an accident about a mile up the road. We'll make it."

"I better make it. It's only my career and Bluestone's reputation at stake," Bree said. "Can't you throw up your bubble and turn on your siren?"

"Do it, Dad!" Ali cried from the back seat.

Jannie laughed. "I've never been in the car when you've done that, Dad."

I glanced in the rearview and said, "That's because I don't make a habit of using the bubble and siren to get around traffic jams on personal time."

Bree said, "If this goes on another fifteen minutes, I'll take the heat and do it myself."

Seeing I wasn't going to use the siren and lights, Ali and Jannie quickly got bored, put on their earbuds, and retreated into their phones. Bree started to do the same before I said, "You haven't asked me about my day."

She frowned. "Oh? I guess I didn't. I'm sorry. I was so preoccupied with packing for Paris."

"I get it."

"You've got my undivided attention for the next fourteen minutes. But if we haven't moved, then you're lighting up that siren."

"Deal," I said, then described the scene beneath the spy museum, the arrival of the CIA officers who'd worked with the deceased, and Sampson's and my subsequent trip to see Catherine Hingham's husband and two children.

We'd found Frank Hingham feeding lunch to Emily, their birdlike young daughter, in her large, elaborate wheelchair. He was awaiting the arrival of a nurse's aide so he could take their son, Luke, to a soccer game. After the aide arrived, we took Hingham aside and told him his wife had been found murdered, was last seen alive in Nogales, Mexico.

After glancing in the back seat to make sure our kids weren't listening, Bree asked, "How'd he react?"

"Like we'd put a spear through his heart," I said. "He literally fell down, crashed against his desk. He was shocked and then sobbing. He said he didn't know how he was going to do it."

"Do what?"

"Tell his kids, especially his daughter. Emily and her mom were very close."

"Did you get the family computers?"

"*And* we searched her office. Hingham gave us permission before taking his son to the soccer game. He said he'd tell Luke and Emily afterward at home."

"You let him go?"

"If you'd seen him, you'd know he wasn't involved."

"You mentioned a confession," Bree said. "You ask him about it?"

"Not yet," I said. "It felt like it might be too much, too soon for him."

"You've read it?"

"Scanned it. But we'll be taking a close look at the family finances before we talk to the husband again. Or a forensic accountant will."

Bree said, "I'm working with one of those on this case. He's a Brit, former Scotland Yard, looks like he walked out of *Downton Abbey*."

I laughed. "Your life *has* changed."

She looked at her watch, said, "Yes, it has, and that's fourteen minutes and we haven't moved twenty feet."

Knowing better than to argue, I leaned over, pulled out the bubble, slapped it on the roof, and threw the siren switch.

Ali and Jannie cheered when the siren started whooping and the bubble started flashing neon blue and red. The cars in front of us moved aside just enough to let me into the breakdown lane, where I hit the gas.

Bree clapped and smiled. "Now I am definitely on my way to Paris!"

I dropped her at the curb at Dulles fifteen minutes later. After hugging her goodbye, telling her I loved her, and wishing her good luck, I watched until she was inside, heading toward the check-in counter.

I'll admit it—as I got back in the car to take the kids home, there was a small part of me that was envious of Bree's new and exciting life. And another part that was a little worried about who my wife might be when she returned.

CHAPTER

9

THE FOLLOWING DAY, I CALLED Bree at six a.m. DC time, knowing it was noon in Paris and her plane should have landed a few hours earlier. She answered on the second ring.

"I just got out of the shower and was going to call you," she said.

"How's Paris?"

"I took a walk after checking into my hotel and it's as beautiful as my mother said."

"No problems with the language?"

"None. I fit right in. The cabdriver, the clerk at the front desk, and the waiter where I ate breakfast were all surprised I was from the U.S. with my accent."

"Bluestone picked the right detective. A full day in front of you?"

"Yes. I'm going to meet with the head of the Paris office. You?"

"Sampson and I are going to check out the forensics lab," I said and yawned.

"I love you."

"And I love you. Even from thousands of miles across the ocean."

"You're a sweet man, Alex Cross."

"I have my moments. Most of them with you."

"Aww," she said. "Have a good day, baby."

"And you have a perfect day in Paris, *chérie amour*."

Bree laughed. "You never fail to surprise me."

"And I hope I never will," I said. I hung up with a big smile that stayed plastered on my face long after we'd ended the call and I'd forced myself to get ready for the day.

Later that morning, John Sampson and I took the stairs down to Metro's forensics lab in department headquarters in downtown Washington, DC.

"We were supposed to be on a plane to Kalispell, Montana, right now," Sampson moaned. "We're supposed to be just hours away from the Bob Marshall Wilderness."

"No use fighting with reality, my friend," I said. "We'll get to Montana when we're supposed to get to Montana."

"Uh-huh," Sampson said. "You know it snows out there. A lot. We have only a few weeks before access shuts down for trips like ours. Last trip in is late August."

"I know and I appreciate your frustration," I said. "You need this trip."

"I do. Nothing wrong with that."

"It's just not going to be today," I said. I opened the door to the lab.

We went to the front counter and told the tech there that we were looking for Margaret Forester, the forensic documents specialist. The tech directed us to the right and down two doors.

We found Forester in a small room, sitting on a high stool at a tilted drafting table. A stout woman in her fifties with a shock of short ginger hair, the specialist wore a lab coat, safety goggles, a hairnet, and latex gloves, all designed to prevent contamination of the documents. She was peering through a large mounted magnifier at a single sheet of paper.

"That our confession, Margaret?" Sampson asked when she looked over at us after we shut the door.

"It's a doozy. FBI should be made aware of the contents ASAP."

"Can we read it?" I asked.

"Put on the gear on the hooks behind you first."

A few moments later we were clad similarly to Forester and standing on either side of her.

John asked, "Written under duress?"

She smiled at him. "You see the shaky handwriting."

I said, "We're sure she wrote it?"

The documents specialist said, "We got a sample of her handwriting from the CIA. Matches."

I began to study the confession in earnest.

My name is Catherine Hingham. I am an undercover field officer for the Central Intelligence Agency. For the past six years I have been part of an interdepartmental group working to disrupt the Alejandro drug cartel in Mexico and Latin America. I was part of a team that put Marco Alejandro behind bars two years ago. I was also corrupted by Alejandro and other members of the cartel.

To be specific, through intermediaries, cryptocurrencies, and offshore bank accounts to be identified later in my testimony, I received more than $1.75 million in bribes from the Alejandro cartel. In return, I provided the cartel with information about the multiagency investigation into their activities.

Even though Marco Alejandro is in prison for life, I broke the law and betrayed my country and my sworn oath. I take responsibility for my actions even though they were done for the sake of my daughter, Emily, who has severe cerebral palsy. The rising cost of Emily's ongoing care drove our family to the brink of bankruptcy and put my daughter's life in jeopardy. Everything I did, I did for her. I say this not as an excuse but as a fact.

I also state as fact that the Alejandro cartel was making similar payments to two members of the U.S. House Judiciary subcommittee on drug trafficking: Arturo San Miguel of New Mexico and Barbara Hayes of California. I helped facilitate the payments to them and will list their accounts.

I know that my role in this corruption and betrayal of my country has cost lives and for that I will be forever ashamed and dishonored. Accounts with all pertinent passwords are listed on the back of this page along with the names of others in intelligence and law enforcement who I believe have betrayed the public trust at the behest of the Alejandro cartel.

The document was signed simply *Catherine Hingham.*

On the back of the confession, the CIA field operative named agents of the U.S. Customs Service, the U.S. Border Patrol, the FBI, the DEA, the Treasury Department, and the Mexican national police who had succumbed to money or pressure or both. Catherine Hingham's confession was beyond explosive and seemed to suggest an elaborate effort by the Alejandro cartel to neutralize anyone who stood in its way, despite its kingpin's incarceration.

The information was so sensitive and the allegations so damning that after a second reading, we knew we would not be able to run the larger investigation called for by her shocking allegations.

After we took pictures of both sides of the statement and thanked Margaret Forester for her time, we went upstairs to explain the situation to Metro Chief Michaels and Police Commissioner Dennison.

Commissioner Dennison was something of a media hog, known to leak juicy items that bolstered his reputation. The trait was one of the reasons Bree had left her job as chief of detectives to join Bluestone Group. Indeed, as soon as we began to describe the contents of the confession, Dennison asked to see it, and I could tell that the commissioner was playing the publicity angles, imagining himself in the spotlight. Thankfully, Chief Michaels argued that any effort Metro Police might make as far as investigating members of federal law enforcement would be stonewalled and the FBI would end up seizing the case and eliminating our role.

"We need to turn it over to them, Commissioner, or we'll be kept in the dark in the long run," Michaels said. "This is bigger than Metro PD."

The commissioner bristled at the idea and remained noncommittal throughout the day, effectively wasting an opportunity for the FBI to get a nationwide investigation up and running with appropriate speed. It wasn't until around nine that evening that Chief Michaels texted us to let us know Dennison would contact his liaison with the Bureau first thing in the morning.

Neither of us were happy about the delay, but as Sampson had said, better late than never.

CHAPTER

10

Paris

BREE LEFT HER HOTEL ON the Rue Jean Goujon in the eighth arrondissement and walked through the streets as the French capital came alive that sultry summer day. Despite the building heat, when she reached a walkway above the Seine River, she saw people jogging everywhere.

And mobs of tourists. And young lovers holding hands as they strolled by. And two well-put-together older women walking arm in arm and wearing bright summer dresses, one carrying a baguette and the other three yellow roses. Both were giggling at some shared secret when Bree passed them.

She knew well that she was in Paris on a serious assignment that had big consequences for everyone involved. But she was still enjoying the elegance of the French capital and its people, who seemed more refined and yet more relaxed than the citizens of DC.

On her stroll earlier, Bree had been enchanted by her first glimpse of Paris. Now, as she walked toward Bluestone Group's offices, she felt herself falling head over heels in love with the city. She had to bring Alex. She had to show him—

Her phone buzzed with a text in French she mentally translated: *Bree Stone, this is Marianne Le Tour. For reasons I'll explain face to face, I'd prefer we meet away from Bluestone's offices. Please hail a cab or call an Uber and come to the following address. It is my favorite place for coffee and croissants.*

Twenty minutes later, Bree exited an Uber in front of Toujours Printemps—"Always Spring"—a café and patisserie on the Left Bank, not far from the École des Beaux-Arts. She entered and saw a woman in her fifties waving at her from the back of the café.

Bree smiled and walked toward Marianne Le Tour as the woman stood, revealing her height and her chic gray pantsuit. With every step Bree took, the head of Bluestone Group's Paris office grew more stunningly beautiful.

Le Tour's hair was short, lush, steel gray, and swept back. She had gently arched cheekbones and cream-colored, nearly flawless skin. But Bree decided that it must have been Le Tour's eyes that had gotten her jobs on the fashion runways of Paris and Milan at the age of sixteen. Her eyes were shaped like a cat's and sapphire blue, large, and sparkling. They danced all over Bree as the former model stepped forward to greet her with an air kiss and an *"Enchanté."*

Bree returned the greeting and, at Le Tour's gesture, took

a seat opposite her. It was only then that she realized that Le Tour held her head artfully to show only two-thirds of her face.

As if she could hear Bree's thoughts, Le Tour casually turned her head to reveal the faint, thin four-inch scar running from the right side of her jaw forward and down. Bree averted her eyes and in French asked, "What's good here?"

Le Tour seemed to appreciate Bree not mentioning the scar that had ended her career at twenty-two. She gave a dazzling smile and said, "Everything's good, but the croissants are world class. They snap open with absolute perfection. And the espresso is the best in Paris."

"Both, then," Bree said.

Le Tour waved to a waiter, who hustled over to take her order: a basket of pastries heavy on the croissants and two double espressos. When he'd gone, the head of Bluestone Paris said, "Are you wondering why we are meeting here?"

"Best croissants and espresso in Paris?"

"That, yes. But the real reason is that two years ago, our office did some work for the Pegasus Group and Philippe Abelmar. I'm concerned there may be lingering loyalties that could prove problematic for your investigation."

"What kind of work did Bluestone do for Pegasus?"

"We were asked to look into a data breach. Beyond that, I'm not at liberty to say, but I assure you it has nothing to do with the allegations at hand."

"So what kind of support can I expect?"

"Very little at first and certainly not from our cyber experts," Le Tour cautioned. "You can text me, of course, at any time and I can point you in the right direction."

"And if I get in hot water?"

Le Tour smiled and slid what looked like a one-euro coin across the table to her. "It's a beacon. Press the back once, hard, and I can track your location. If you press twice, it will send an SOS straight to my cell phone. At that point, secrecy and discretion be damned, and we will come to help you with everything we've got."

"Do I need a weapon?"

"And a license to carry it," Le Tour said, nodding to the Chanel shopping bag at her feet. She took a large envelope out of her purse and slid it across the table. "Here is your alias, and the license, passport, and papers supporting it. Under the cashmere sweater in the bag, you will find a small Beretta, a waist holster, and two full clips of nine-millimeter ammunition. Please use restraint. Any shooting attracts the anti-terror teams."

"Only in an emergency," Bree promised, opening the envelope and taking out the identity card. "'Bree St. Lucie of Saint Martin,'" she read.

"You've worked there setting up shell corporations for offshore bank accounts. You're here in Paris looking into opportunities."

Bree was impressed. "How did you make this all happen so fast?"

"One of the top commanders at La Crim, Paris's investigative police unit, cannot stand Philippe Abelmar. She wishes you the best of luck as you go hunting. So does a friend high up in the Sûreté."

"Could they help with a few other things?"

"What were you thinking?"

"Copies of past complaints against Abelmar."

"They're all sealed as far as I know."

"I guess we need to know just how much your source in La Crim hates Abelmar."

Le Tour's dazzling smile returned. "I think I'm going to like you, Bree Stone. In fact, I already know I do."

11

THE NEXT AFTERNOON, AS BREE was changing to go out for a run along the Seine, her phone buzzed, alerting her to a text from Marianne Le Tour that told her to check her Bluestone e-mail account and to use a VPN to cover her tracks.

Bree did just that on her laptop, opening an app Ali had shown her called TunnelBear that would keep her location and the IP address of her laptop disguised. Then she signed into her Bluestone account and found an e-mail from Le Tour that included a forwarded message from an address she did not recognize.

You have until six a.m. tomorrow to read these files, which will destroy themselves at that time. None of this information may be referred to in your investigation or used in a court of law or in your final report to the board. Good luck. As you'll see, he's scum.

Bree glanced at her running shoes, told herself she'd

run along the Seine tomorrow morning after the files self-destructed, got a Coke from the minibar, and clicked on the zip file at the bottom of the e-mail. After the file downloaded, she opened it to reveal twelve smaller files, each identified by a last name and a date. Anna Tuttle was there. So was Cassie Dane. But Bree started with the oldest file, from nearly twelve years before.

Three hours later, Bree finished screenshotting the file from the most recent complaint against Philippe Abelmar sealed by the French courts.

She felt dirtied by the overall experience and was appalled by the behavior described; her eyes burned from angry tears. If the statements contained in the complaints were true, Abelmar was as cunning, twisted, and repulsive a villain as any Alex had come across in his days with the FBI's Behavioral Analysis Unit.

She also suspected that the billionaire was buying off judges inside the French courts to cover his actions. Three of the judges had sealed two or more of the complaints and subsequent settlements, all of which featured gag orders and payments of between two and four hundred thousand euros to the young women whom the chairman of Pegasus had allegedly abused at various locations throughout France.

Another common denominator was a specific bistro in Batignolles, the quiet, village-like neighborhood in Paris's seventeenth arrondissement where Abelmar lived. He owned a sprawling penthouse that had undergone extensive renovations in the six years since he'd purchased it.

According to every one of the complaints, the founder of Pegasus often took his victims to Canard de Flaque, or Puddle Duck, his favorite local restaurant. He ate there three or four times a week when he was in Paris. Several of the women believed they'd been drugged at the bistro, then escorted to his nearby home, where they lost all memory and their nightmares began.

What don't I know? Bree typed in a separate document. She often asked that question during an investigation. It helped her focus on where she wanted to look next.

She typed, *The judges and what Abelmar has on them? Layout of A's apartment?*

Bree stopped, went to her secure in-house Bluestone e-mail account, and sent a message to Marianne Le Tour asking for any and all information on the three judges who'd done most of the sealing. She also asked for a copy of whatever plans Abelmar had filed with the city regarding the renovation of his apartment.

After Bree sent her e-mail, she returned to her list, only to have her stomach growl. She checked her watch. Five after eight. She should eat.

She thought of the cases she'd read and realized she knew just the spot for her second night out in the City of Light.

CHAPTER

12

Sherman Oaks, California

CROUCHING IN THE PITCH-DARK on the lip of a brush-choked and dusty urban canyon, Matthew Butler peered through his latest toy—a Leupold four-power infrared monocular that made anything with a heat signature show up in shades of yellow, orange, and red.

Butler had the device aimed across the canyon at the back of a four-thousand-square-foot Mission-style home set on half an acre of lush garden. There was a kidney-shaped pool with a little waterfall feeding it and a terrace beyond with double doors that opened into the kitchen.

He had the layout of the house downloaded on his phone, but he had already committed to memory the blueprint and a real estate agent's video tour of the house. He believed he could walk the place blindfolded and not bump into a chair.

"Rear's clear," Butler murmured quietly, knowing the tiny Bluetooth mike taped to his throat would pick it up.

"Front clear," he heard a woman say through the receiver taped to the upper edge of his jawbone.

"Left flank clear," a man said.

"Right clear too," a second male said.

"Target?"

"Hasn't moved in four hours, Cap. Deep sleeper."

Butler checked his watch: 2:47 a.m. "Sunrise in three hours," he said. "It's enough time."

"I'm ready," the woman said.

"Ready," the men said.

"Launch," said Butler, raising the monocular again. He scrambled over the side of the canyon onto a coyote trail he'd scouted and walked the day before, clipping any bramble or thorny vine that might trip him up.

In five minutes, he was up and over the lip of the far side of the canyon and crouched behind two fan palms about forty yards from the terrace doors.

"Go, Cort," he said. "Go, JP."

Figures appeared from the vegetation on both sides of the house, crouching and crab-walking toward the rear corners of the building, which were equipped with motion sensors and cameras. But these men—Dale Cortland and J. P. Vincente—carried thin rectangular shields coated with a mirror-like finish over their heads. The motion detectors might be triggered, but if they were, the cameras would pick up only a reflection of the lights, glares that shimmered and moved.

The pair reached junction boxes at the corners of the house and began disabling the cameras and overriding the security system.

"Clear," Vincente said about ten minutes later.

"Same," Cortland said.

Butler broke from behind the fan palms, said, "Go, Purdy. Go, Big DD."

A small hooded figure ran in from the left—Alison Purdy, the burglar, was already working her magic on the door locks before Butler reached her side. A fourth figure, David "Big DD" Dawkins, came lumbering around the corner carrying a combat shotgun just as the door locks gave way. A huge African-American man who'd played defensive end for Baylor before joining the military, Dawkins was as skilled as any on Butler's handpicked team, especially with a weapon in his hands. But his primary role in these situations was to use his sheer size, presence, and growl of a voice to intimidate the hell out of people.

Dawkins was also, after Purdy, the best creeper Butler had. Despite his six-foot-six frame and the two hundred and eighty pounds of muscle packed onto it, Big DD was surprisingly quiet when he moved.

Purdy pushed the door open and entered with Dawkins following, both of them peering through infrared monoculars. Butler put his to his right eye, drew his .45, held it in his left hand, and went inside, with Cortland and Vincente covering their six.

They crossed through a great room, kitchen on the right, and went down the hallway to a staircase. Purdy began climbing it, gun held before her, green tritium sight glowing. Dawkins was right on her heels, shotgun at port arms, with Butler bringing up the rear. Upstairs, they took positions flanking the doors to the master suite. Purdy lowered and stowed her monocular.

Butler kept his infrared optic up, along with the .45. He nodded at the burglar; she ever so slowly turned the knob and pushed the door open.

Butler could see the target sleeping, glowing there on the king bed, not ten feet in front of him. He followed Purdy inside, and Big DD went to the main light switch.

Butler aimed at the center of the sleeping man's mass. "Your show, Purds."

"Go," Purdy said.

Butler lowered the monocular, squinted. The lights came on.

The man on the bed stopped breathing, then erupted like a snake in full strike, hurling himself to his right and off the side of the bed, buck naked. He was Caucasian and almost as big as Dawkins.

"Going for his gun," Butler said.

"Got him," Purdy said, leaping onto the bed and aiming her gun at the naked guy on the floor frantically trying to open his pistol vault.

The vault opened. She fired.

The air gun drove a drug dart into the man's upper back; Dawkins leaped over the bed and pinned the man's arm to the carpet with one massive foot, his head to the floor with the shotgun muzzle.

"Don't move, Special Agent White," Big DD growled. "You'll feel better in ten seconds or so."

"Who sent you?" White said, the drug starting to hit him. "What do you want?"

"The truth, Agent White," Butler said. "The truth will set you free."

CHAPTER

13

Washington, DC

MY YOUNGEST CHILD, ALI, WAS toying with his breakfast at our kitchen counter. I'd gotten up to make pancakes and sausage links, special for him. He usually wolfed them down with maple syrup.

"Thinking about camp?" I asked.

Ali didn't reply. I walked over and tapped him on the shoulder. He startled and spun around, wide-eyed.

"Gosh, Dad!" he cried. "Why'd you do that? You scared me!"

"Sorry," I said, holding up my palms. "I asked if you were thinking about camp. And you didn't answer me."

"Oh," he said. "I...I was just thinking about stuff."

I was about to ask what stuff when Jannie came into the kitchen, looked at Ali's plate, and said, "Where's Nana Mama?"

"Sleeping in. I'm short-order cook this morning."

"Can I have more protein with the pancakes? Eggs?"

"Coming right up," I said. "Two? Scrambled?"

"Yes, please," she said and rummaged in a kitchen drawer for the remote.

Ali took a few bites of his pancakes, then began to eat in earnest while I cracked Jannie's eggs and she turned on the local news. I was whisking them when the weather forecast ended.

Joanne Weld, the anchor, said, "Our own Bob Dickerson has more on last week's attempted arson at Maury Elementary School in Southeast. Bob?"

Ali looked up and stared at the screen, which cut to a bald man in his forties standing outside a schoolyard and nodding seriously at the camera.

"Joanne, it turns out that police, fire investigators, and DC educational authorities believe the arson was the work of the same hooded figure who vandalized three other elementary schools in Southeast—Brent, Ludlow-Taylor, and Ketcham—over the past few months."

The reporter gestured to a burned structure visible behind him. "Security cams at Maury caught the arsonist on the way to splash gas over a temporary classroom annex built at the back of the school last year. The annex, which was constructed of wood rather than brick, housed four classrooms, and the entire structure was lost in the blaze."

The shot jumped to a still from security video that showed a slight, bent-over person wearing dark clothes, a camo hood, and a face mask and carrying a gas can.

In a voice-over, Dickerson said, "The same individual has shown up on several security cameras. Still, authorities say they have not been able to identify the suspect and are asking for the public's help in finding this person before another school in Southeast is vandalized or burned or both."

Jannie said, "Ali, was your school vandalized?"

My young son stopped staring at the screen and looked at his sister. "Not that I know of. I mean, it gets tagged sometimes, but they clean it off. Hey, Dad?"

I looked up from the frying pan. "Ali?"

"How come he didn't say what kind of vandalism it was at the other schools?"

"Not enough time, probably. And they figured the arson was worse than the vandalism."

"Oh," he said, returning to his breakfast while I spooned Jannie's eggs onto her plate.

"Five minutes, Ali?"

He chewed and swallowed. "You don't have to take me, Dad. I know the way."

"I like taking you," I said. "It's more for me than you."

Ali shrugged and quietly went back to eating. And he stayed quiet even as he put his plate and fork in the dishwasher and retrieved his knapsack.

"You got everything for swimming? Soccer?"

He nodded with little enthusiasm. "Everything they said I needed."

"You were the one who asked to go to sports camp," I reminded him. "And now you sound like you'd rather go lie on a bed of nails."

"No," he said, forcing a smile. "I really do want to go. It'll be fun."

"You said a lot of your friends will be there," Jannie said.

"That's true. Can we go now, Dad?"

I followed my boy outside and up the sidewalk in silence.

It was hot but relatively dry for late June, a rare blessing in Washington, DC, and I was regretting not going for an early run as we walked toward the parking lot where the camp bus would pick up Ali and other kids from the neighborhood.

"Dad?" Ali said as the parking lot came in sight. "Can I ask you a question?"

"Shoot."

"When you investigate, you put together a timeline, right?"

"Usually. Especially if there's a team of detectives involved, because you want everyone on the same page, acting on the same shared set of proven facts. That's how investigations are run and how mysteries are solved."

"But you look for the things that are in common, right? I mean, like, if the vandalism was the same kind of vandalism?"

"Sure," I said. "And you try to keep track of what's different."

He nodded and fell quiet. Ali's mind had always whirled with obsessions. He found something he was interested in and then learned everything he could about it until his attention waned and a new, more powerful curiosity took over.

I had the feeling he was becoming obsessed with the arsonist and vandal who was targeting elementary schools in Southeast.

Ali stayed quiet until we reached the lot and he saw several of his buddies already there, talking and laughing. Then he brightened, hugged me goodbye, and ran over to them, his cares gone, one of the jokers again. I watched them horse around for several moments, knowing that these times were precious and that I needed to remember Ali like this, at this age. He would not always be my baby boy, my—

My cell phone buzzed. A text from Sampson. Someone leaked Hingham's confession. The story's up on the Washington Post website.

"Dennison," I said, groaning. "You are one stupid, self-serving SOB!"

My cell phone buzzed again. A new message, this one from FBI Supervising Special Agent Ned Mahoney, my old partner at the Bureau and the best law enforcement mind I knew.

Need to meet ASAP. Story about Hingham's confession blowing up. We're taking over and need to be at speed pronto.

CHAPTER

14

Paris

BREE EXITED A TAXI IN the Batignolles neighborhood, which was more subdued than the area around her hotel, with blocks of matching and beautifully maintained nineteenth-century apartment buildings that had boutiques and shops on the ground floors.

She spotted the hand-painted sign for the Canard de Flaque bistro at the end of the block and walked toward it, aware of the appreciative looks she was getting from men passing her. And why not? Bree had always looked ten years younger than her actual age, and she was wearing one of two evening outfits she'd packed for the trip: a pearl-colored silk blouse with a plunging neckline, tight charcoal slacks, and black leather high heels that clicked on the sidewalk. The clutch purse was the perfect size to hold the small Beretta and the euro-coin beacon, which she'd activated and slid into an inner pocket of the bag before leaving her hotel.

Seeing herself in the window reflection of the bistro door, Bree decided that the Tahitian pearl earrings and necklace Alex had given her on their anniversary were the perfect accessories for this outfit, which was much more feminine and provocative than the sort of thing she usually wore. Exactly what she wanted. She pushed open the door, stepped inside, and took in the bistro and its patrons in a sweeping glance.

Canard de Flaque was laid out in an L shape, with an eight-stool bar to her right. There were long, narrow mirrors on the walls between the windows, six low-backed, tufted-leather booths along the interior wall, and ten tables in the remaining space. It was elegant without being overly formal, and almost every seat was occupied.

"Do you have a reservation, madame?" asked the maître d' in English. He wore a nameplate on his lapel that said HENRI and apparently had a sharp nose for strangers.

"I don't, Henri," Bree said in French.

He replied in French, with a pained expression, "I'm afraid to disappoint you, madame. As beautiful as you are, Puddle Duck is booked solid."

Back home, Bree might have been irritated at the "as beautiful as you are" comment. But here in Paris, in Philippe Abelmar's favorite eatery, she smiled and put her left hand gently on Henri's forearm so he could see she wore no wedding ring.

"I don't mind sitting at the bar if there's space," she purred. "I've heard so many good things about the food here. It would be a shame to go somewhere else."

The maître d' broke into a happy grin. He picked up a

menu and said, "The bar I can do for you, madame. And where did you learn to speak French so well and with such an interesting accent?"

"In Saint Martin, in the Caribbean, where my mom taught French."

"Fantastic," he said, turning toward the bar. "You are visiting?"

"And exploring my options," Bree said.

"Well, then, I wish you luck," he said and gestured to the stool on the near end of the dark mahogany bar. "Please sit, madame."

Bree slid onto the stool next to a young woman with shoulder-length raven-black hair who was hunched over with her finger in her ear, talking on a cell phone in harsh whispers.

Smiling at the maître d', Bree said, "Thank you, Henri. You're very kind."

"My pleasure," he said, bobbing his head and handing her the menu before moving quickly back to his station near the door.

"Can I get you something to drink while you look at the menu, madame?" said the bartender, a tall, gaunt woman in her late thirties. She had a long narrow nose and moved in an awkward manner that reminded Bree of a crane.

"Champagne, Carole," Bree said, reading her nameplate.

The bartender smiled, made a half bow. "Oui, madame."

Bree looked in the mirror behind the bar and noted that the seat next to the young woman on the phone was empty. The other five bar stools were occupied by two women and three men who all seemed to know one another. Bree realized that if she pivoted to her right, she would be able to see the rest of the bistro and its patrons, even those in the booths along the inner wall, which were reflected in narrow mirrors.

Bree acted curious and relaxed as she turned on the stool to see the mirrors better. In less than ten seconds, she determined that unless he'd undergone radical plastic surgery, Philippe Abelmar was not in Canard de Flaque this evening.

As she was turning back to her champagne and the menu, she heard a man say, "Enough with the phone, Valentina. I need your undivided attention, please."

Bree glanced in the mirror behind the bar and saw that the seat next to the young woman was now occupied—by the same calm, assured, and well-dressed embezzler and sexual predator she'd come to Puddle Duck to hunt.

CHAPTER

15

PHILIPPE ABELMAR HAD A SALT-AND-PEPPER beard that complemented his slicked-back silver hair and piercing blue-gray eyes. His blue linen blazer and starched white shirt set off his deep tan.

Valentina, the raven-haired young woman next to Bree, raised her head, put her phone to her chest, and said in an Aussie accent: "It's my mum, Philippe."

"It always is," he shot back. "And she does not pay you, *chérie.* I do."

Bree acted interested in the entrées as she felt the tension rising next to her.

Valentina cleared her throat, then raised the phone and said, "Mum. I have to go."

Bree glanced up and saw Valentina set her phone on the bar top. "Your wish is my command. Again," Valentina said.

"Better," Abelmar said softly, tilting his head. "You are beautiful when angry."

"I'm not angry, Philippe. I'm tired. I've not had a day off in months."

"A week shy of six months. And yet, when have you learned more about the world? About finance?"

"I'm grateful. I tell you so every day. But you can't expect me to cut myself off from my mum while I work for you."

"Why not? You are my personal assistant for one year. Twelve months of your life. After that, you can talk to Mummy day and night for all I care."

The bartender came over to Bree. "Have you decided?"

"What's your favorite?" Bree asked.

"The veal."

"And the chef's specialty?"

Carole glanced to her right.

Philippe Abelmar said, "At Canard? The duck, of course."

Bree looked around to find the billionaire gazing at her from behind Valentina's shoulder.

"It's fantastic," he said. "But I warn you, it can become an addiction."

She smiled, said, "Thank you."

"My pleasure," he said.

"The duck," Bree said to the bartender, who nodded to her and to the billionaire.

Valentina said, "Philippe, may I please be excused for the evening? I won't make it through dinner without falling asleep."

Seeming to know he had an audience now, Abelmar said, "Of course, my dear. I am not that hungry tonight anyway.

Come, I'll get you a cab. And you can have the whole day off tomorrow to sleep and recharge."

Bree glanced in the mirror and saw genuine relief in the young woman's face and body posture as she got off her stool. The financier was getting up as well.

Bree turned to them. "Thank you for the recommendation."

The billionaire's personal assistant gave her an exhausted smile. Abelmar replied with warmth, "You are most welcome. *Bon appétit*, madame."

"*Bonsoir*, monsieur," she said cheerily. She pivoted away and watched in the mirror as they made their apologies to Henri and left.

Bree wanted to ask for a piece of paper and a pen so she could write down everything she could remember about the incident. Instead, she waited several long moments, then retrieved the phone Le Tour had given her, opened a note app, and began typing with her thumbs. She wrote that she'd gone to Canard hoping to see Abelmar in his element and that, to her surprise, she'd ended up interacting with him and his newest personal assistant.

They would remember her. Wouldn't they?

Valentina seemed exhausted, so maybe not. But unless the financier had a facial-recognition problem, he would know Bree if he saw her again.

Was that good? Or bad?

Bree was still trying to decide when her dinner arrived. She set the phone down and ate. Abelmar was right. The duck—in a reduced shiitake mushroom, garlic, and white wine sauce—was fantastic, the sort of meal you'd come back for again and again.

She felt full and satisfied when she finished but succumbed

to temptation and ordered the crème brûlée, which Carole the bartender also recommended. Bree glanced at her watch and saw it was close to ten, which was almost four p.m. in Washington, DC. She'd try calling Alex when she got back to her hotel room.

Scanning through her notes, Bree realized she hadn't described the argument between Abelmar and his PA.

PA Valentina? Bree wrote. *Australian? Complained tired. A.: listening, but cold. V.: she hadn't had a day off in months. A. cited benefits of what V. was learning. V. grateful, but…*

The crème brûlée arrived just as Bree started to feel like she'd missed something. She thanked the bartender, took a bite of the dessert, and barely registered how delicious it was because she realized just then what she'd missed.

After Valentina complained about not having had a day off in months, Abelmar had corrected her: *A week shy of six months.* That's what he'd said. *A week shy of—*

Bree felt her stomach turn over. The majority of the women she'd read about in the files reported that Abelmar first drugged and raped them on camera shortly before or just after they'd been working for him for six months.

A week shy of six months. And poor, tired, beautiful Valentina has no idea.

CHAPTER

16

SAY WHAT YOU WILL ABOUT the FBI, there is no organization finer when it comes to putting together a team of crack investigators and getting them in the field fast and with purpose.

To my mind, there was no one at the Bureau who could orchestrate and deploy this kind of far-reaching investigation better than my former partner Special Agent in Charge Ned Mahoney. Ned's ability to digest information and harness it to drive a probe was simply remarkable.

Indeed, after Sampson and I briefed him on our initial investigation and our conversation with Catherine Hingham's husband, Mahoney quickly drafted twelve veteran agents, set up a war room, and organized the probe around four of the allegations in the signed testimony left with her body.

- Allegations of corruption in federal law enforcement and intelligence agencies by the Alejandro drug cartel
- Allegations of corruption of two U.S. congresspersons by the Alejandro cartel
- Allegations of corruption against specific named members of U.S. law enforcement by the Alejandro cartel
- Allegations of corruption by Catherine Hingham against herself

"What else?" Mahoney asked after these were written along the top of a large, long whiteboard he'd had hung on the wall of the space the FBI gave us.

Sampson said, "Links from Hingham to those other named law enforcement personnel. How did she know they were corrupt? What's the connection?"

"I get it," Mahoney said, writing that on the board. "Other people of interest?"

I said, "Dean Weaver, Hingham's supervising field officer at the CIA."

"And the rest of his team," Sampson said. "They showed up at the crime scene and tried to take over. We still don't understand how they knew she'd been killed before she had even been identified."

"However they found out, they're CIA and can't operate in the United States."

"Exactly what we told them," Sampson said.

I said, "Put Marco Alejandro up there on the suspects list."

"Marco's out of the picture," Mahoney said. "He's been buried inside a supermax for the past eleven months. No communication whatsoever."

"Then who's running the cartel?"

"I'll get the latest from DEA intel."

"If that intel's not tainted," Sampson said. "Hingham said there was broad, interdepartmental corruption because of the cartel. So who do we trust?"

Ned said, "We trust the evidence and follow it. Especially the money trails, to wherever and whomever they lead."

My phone buzzed in my pocket. I got it out, saw it was Bree, and answered. "I wondered when I'd hear from you," I said, holding up a finger and exiting the war room for the hallway. "What time is it there?"

"Around eleven," she said. "I'm tired but wired."

"Sleep will find you. How's the case?"

"I can't give you the details, but I'd like your advice on something."

"Go ahead."

"What if you knew something really bad was about to happen to someone inside an investigation, but if you warned the person, you would lose the opportunity to potentially catch a really bad guy in the midst of a really bad act? Something not even money and power could make go away?"

"As Margaret Forester might say, that's a doozy."

"Margaret Forester?"

"The documents expert in the Metro lab?"

"Oh," she said and yawned. "Of course. And, yes, this is a doozy."

"What's the time frame of the bad act going down?"

"Next two weeks?"

"How bad an act?"

"The kind that would violate and damage someone physically and mentally for years to come."

"That's a hard one. I mean, if your goal is to prevent this kind of thing from ever happening again."

"You understand my predicament."

"Any chance you could recruit the person in danger, tell them what you know and hope they come to your side of the fight?"

"I've thought of that," Bree said. "The problem is, I can't use everything I know, because most of it is under seal by corrupt judges."

"Then lever the judges," I said.

"That's tomorrow," Bree said. "How are you? The kids? Nana?"

"I'm fine. Working with Ned and Sampson on the Hingham case. Nana's been sleeping in a lot. Jannie's Jannie. Damon's off on his backpacking trip with his college buddies. And Ali's becoming obsessed with the arson case."

"Okay."

"It sounds like he's investigating. Or wants to be."

She fell silent after that and I knew why. We tried to shield our children from some of the difficult things we saw and did in the course of our police work. "Bree?"

"I hope you're not encouraging that."

"I'm trying to stay neutral."

"As long as he's not putting himself in danger, Alex."

I looked at my watch. "He was at sports camp all day and should be home by now, getting ready for dinner."

"Just the same. I don't want him in over his head."

Mahoney came out the door and motioned me back into the war room.

"Ned wants me and you need sleep," I said.

"I do. And I love you."

"I love you too and I'll give your predicament some more thought."

I hung up and crossed to Mahoney, who stood impatiently in the doorway.

"We've got a second victim, a second confession," he said quietly. "One of ours. I want you and me on the scene ASAP."

"Okay. Where are we going?"

"Los Angeles. Go pack a bag. I'll meet you at Reagan National in an hour."

17

SAMPSON SLAPPED THE BUBBLE ON the roof of his squad car, lit up the sirens, and drove me from FBI headquarters to my home in under eight minutes.

He double-parked with the lights flashing and followed me up the porch stairs, saying, "Damn, I wish I were going with you."

"And I wish you were coming with me, but fatherhood matters most," I said as we went inside.

"It does. Thanks for reminding me."

"You sure you have time to get me to the airport?"

"Jannie's supposed to be babysitting Willow until seven."

We went into the kitchen, where Nana Mama was frying panko-crusted rabbit in onions, garlic, and chili oil.

"That smells unbelievable, Nana," Sampson said.

My ninety-something grandmother grinned. "I'll send you home with some for you and Willow for dinner."

I told her I had to pack to go to Los Angeles on short notice. I started to turn away, then asked where Ali was. She told me he'd called from the house of one of his sports-camp buddies and would be home for dinner.

I ran upstairs and threw underwear, socks, three shirts, two ties, two pairs of pants, and a dark blazer in a suitcase. After a moment's consideration, I grabbed my passport, in case we had to go to Mexico. I tossed in my toothbrush and a few other items, then took the luggage downstairs. Anything else I needed, I'd buy.

"John!" I said. "Let's go."

Sampson didn't answer. I could hear Nana Mama talking to him in concern. I dropped my bag and went back to the kitchen to find my oldest friend sitting at our table, forehead in hand, staring at his phone screen.

"He won't tell me what's wrong," my grandmother said.

"John?" I said.

Sampson finally looked at me, the anguish plain throughout his face. "M is watching, isn't he, Alex? M's still playing us all the time, isn't he?"

I took the phone from him and read the text message he'd received less than a minute before.

Dear John,

My apologies for not writing sooner to extend my sincere condolences about the passing of your wife, the ever-vivacious Billie. I was always impressed by her. So tiny and yet such a force of nature. You wouldn't think that something as small as a tick could kill a person like Billie, would you?

I know I wouldn't have thought that.

You see, John, your late wife did not die of Lyme disease. I know because I killed her and I thought now was the right time to tell you. How sad it was to watch her dwindle away, day after day after day.

Am I sorry your sweet Billie had to succumb? No, not really.

Billie's death was necessary, John. Everything I do is necessary and you and Cross need to believe that in a real way.

Because the ball is in your court now.

The clock is ticking.

Make a move.

Or I will.

—M

Sampson got to his feet, his eyes haunted, and said angrily, "He's trying to throw me, upset me. Billie died of a heart attack caused by Lyme disease."

"Was that the official result of the autopsy?" I asked quietly.

"There wasn't one, remember?" he said. "Because of all the hospital stays, the ME decided it wasn't necessary. And it wasn't. She died of Lyme's."

"Then I agree. M is trying to throw you."

"And he's watching us. It's time for that to stop."

"Who's watching us?" Nana Mama asked.

"We're about to make sure no one is, Nana," I said and looked at my watch.

Sampson turned stoic again. "I'll be back for the rabbit, Nana. I have to get Alex to the airport."

Outside, as we went to John's double-parked squad car with the bubble still flashing blue, he said, "I want my house swept top to bottom for bugs and cameras. And there's got to be some way to make sure there are no cameras trained on our homes."

"I'll ask Ned on the plane," I said.

When we got in the car, I saw Big John's hands were shaking.

"Want me to drive?"

"No," he said.

"M *is* trying to throw you."

The anguish was back on Sampson's face as he put the car in gear and said, "I know, but I've got to make sure. I owe that to Billie, that and so much more."

Before I could answer, he flipped on the siren and peeled away from the curb.

CHAPTER

18

Los Angeles

MAHONEY AND I TOUCHED DOWN in LAX around ten that evening, local time. We had spent the flight learning about the latest law enforcement victim to be found with a white envelope marked CONFESSION.

According to his personnel files, the deceased, FBI Special Agent Mason White, was a fourteen-year veteran of the Bureau with a solid record and a reputation outside work as a devoted husband and father of three kids. The pictures we pulled up on social media depicted thirty-nine-year-old White as a model citizen, loving hubby, and doting dad to his nine-year-old son and five-year-old twin daughters. White was born and raised in Provo, Utah, and had played offensive line on the Brigham Young football team before applying to the Bureau.

According to officers on the scene, White's wife had

returned home from a visit to San Diego, first stopping to drop off the kids with her parents in Pasadena. She'd entered the house around noon to find her husband dead, lashed naked to a chair, the sealed confession on a table beside him.

She'd become hysterical and called her husband's FBI boss, Patrick Loughlin, instead of 911. Loughlin, the supervising special agent of the FBI's LA office, had heard about the FBI's investigation of Hingham. He ordered agents to White's house and had them seal the crime scene pending our arrival.

Loughlin was waiting at the gate when Mahoney and I came off our flight. To be honest, with his flattened nose and callused hands, he looked more like a street heavy than a supervising special agent. An East Boston native, Loughlin had been a Boston patrol cop who'd gotten his college and law degrees at night. He'd been the oldest recruit in Ned's FBI Academy class at Quantico, but despite his age, he'd won both the physical and academic awards at graduation.

"Frickin' LA traffic's a nightmare," Loughlin said, his Boston accent still thick. "If we went by car, it'd be two hours. We'll take the chopper. Perk of the job, huh?"

Minutes later, we were flying in an FBI helicopter over the Staples Center and then the Hollywood Hills before sweeping out over the San Fernando Valley, which glimmered with millions of lights.

"You knew Special Agent White well," I said.

"A Boy Scout if ever there was one," Loughlin said. "A Mormon, for frick's sake. I got no idea what he's done to confess to."

"You haven't read it?" Mahoney said.

"This is your case, Ned," Loughlin said, holding up his palms. "I learned to respect jurisdictional boundaries my first day on the job as a cop, walking a beat around Fenway at a hundred fricking degrees in the—"

The pilot put the chopper in a tight, downward spiral then landed in the cul-de-sac right in front of White's property. The LA media had gotten wind of the case. There were several satellite trucks parked back down the road and reporters standing at the barricades.

Many of them seemed to recognize Loughlin as he exited because they ran forward in a crouch beneath the rotor wash. When he stood up, they began yelling questions at him, wondering why the FBI was there instead of local law enforcement.

"Isn't it obvious?" Loughlin shouted back. "An FBI agent is the victim. Use your brains for once, will ya? You have them, don't ya?"

Then he walked away, leaving the reporters slack-jawed. We followed him up the driveway as he griped, "Worst part of the frickin' job, talking to reporters. Not one of those bozos knows how to listen. But can they talk! Just like hens, always squawking."

I was barely listening, too impressed by Special Agent White's home. And the grounds too were beautiful, even at night.

"Did you know he lived this way, Pat?" Mahoney asked.

"Honestly, I didn't," Loughlin said. "But I did hear more than once that the wife's family has a lot of dough."

I asked, "Where is she? The wife?"

"Under protection at her parents' place in Pasadena. Poor thing was ripped apart when we spoke."

"We'll need to talk with her."

"First thing in the a.m. Tonight, I want you both to see White in situ before we put him on ice pending autopsy."

An agent at the door gave us blue booties, latex gloves, and hairnets before we entered. The furnishings were high end. You could see it within two steps. No money had been spared building or decorating this house.

"I could afford the bathroom in this place," Loughlin said. "Maybe a closet too. That's about it, though."

The agent led us into the great-room area where Mason White was still tied to a ladder-back chair. A sheet had been laid over his lap.

But the first thing I saw was White's bulging eyes and the wire garrote cinched so tight around his neck, it had cut arteries. The room reeked of blood and other body fluids expelled as he died.

"He's a big boy," I said, circling the corpse. "Look at the neck on him. Have to be someone awful strong to do that to a former offensive lineman. And what's that wound low on the left side of his torso?"

An FBI forensics tech said, "A puncture. Looks like it was done with, like, a thin knitting needle."

"Or a hypodermic dart from a high-powered air gun," I said. "Look at the bruising around it."

The tech stepped forward and peered at the bruise and hole. "Might explain it too."

Mahoney said, "Has the scene been photographed?"

"Yes, but not processed," the tech said.

Mahoney picked up the envelope marked CONFESSION / FBI EYES ONLY.

"I think we qualify," Loughlin said.

Ned nodded, cut the flap with the blade of his pocket-knife, and extracted four handwritten pages. The three of us studied them.

I wasn't two paragraphs down page one when Loughlin said, "Jesus H. Christ of Latter-Day Saints. Is this for frickin' real? A Mormon assassin?"

CHAPTER

19

Paris

BREE ENTERED THE CROWDED Toujours Printemps café and patisserie on the Left Bank the morning after she'd gone to the Canard de Flaque. Marianne Le Tour was seated at the same table, dressed in basic black, her eyes locked on an iPad.

The head of Bluestone Paris was so engrossed, it wasn't until Bree pulled back her chair that Le Tour startled and looked up. "Bree!"

"Marianne," Bree said, sliding into the seat. Le Tour was studying her like she was an interesting art object.

"I just saw the data from the GPS chip. Where you went last night."

"That's why I turned it on," Bree said and smiled as the waiter arrived.

They ordered cafés au lait and croissants this time. When the waiter left, Le Tour leaned across the table. In a voice that sounded both upset and admiring, she said, "You went straight to Canard? It's like his dining room."

"Exactly. I wanted to observe him in an environment where he feels comfortable."

Her eyebrows raised. "And did you see him? Abelmar?"

"He was sitting two stools down from me at the bar," Bree said. She described the scene in detail, including his interaction with his latest personal assistant, Valentina. "I believe she's being set up to be his next victim."

Le Tour frowned and crossed her arms. "You do not know that."

"I'm sorry. Did *you* read those sealed files?"

The head of Bluestone Paris shrank back a little and shook her head.

"Most of his victims mentioned the restaurant," Bree said. "Several said they believed they were drugged at Canard before—"

Le Tour held up her hands. "No details. Those files are still sealed here and I do not wish to lose my investigative license."

"I understand."

Le Tour sighed. "But *I* do not understand men like this. I have never met Abelmar, but I have seen his pictures. He is quite handsome."

"Ruggedly handsome and insanely rich," Bree agreed. "You're right. It doesn't make sense, until you realize that it's not really about sex. It's about domination and power, the fact that he can use these women, discard them, pay them off if need be. But most of all, I think he likes it because he gets away with it."

The head of Bluestone Paris thought about that, then

asked, "What will the board of Pegasus need in order to make its decision?"

"My report," Bree said. "When I'm done investigating."

The waiter returned with their breakfast. After he left, Bree said, "We also have someone in the London office working on Abelmar's financials."

"Really?" Le Tour said, perking up. "Desmond Slattery?"

"Yes. You know him?"

"We met just last year," Le Tour said and Bree thought her cheeks flushed a little. "He's quite the character. Scotland Yard. Man's man."

"If your idea of a man's man is someone who wears Savile Row bespoke suits."

"And wears them well," Le Tour said and laughed a little girlishly.

Bree grinned at her. "Shall I tell Des you say hello the next time I talk to him?"

"Don't you dare." Le Tour smiled, then went to her purse. "Here, you e-mailed me about these last night." She pushed a thumb drive across the table. "Profiles of the judges."

Bree took the thumb drive and put it in her pocket, impressed. "That was fast."

"We have several freelance researchers and hackers on speed-dial."

"Helpful."

"Extremely," she said and checked her watch. "I have one still trying to find copies of the blueprints for Abelmar's remodel. Can you tell me why you want to see them without giving me any details?"

Bree hesitated. "I'm trying to confirm the existence of secret rooms."

Le Tour winced, drank her coffee. "Is there anything else I can do for you?"

"Put someone other than me in Canard tonight and tell me what he does."

The head of Bluestone Paris shook her head. "That I cannot do. If I put one of my own in there, it will soon be common knowledge in the office that we are looking at Abelmar. And I do not think you want Abelmar knowing that. Correct?"

Bree thought about that. "For now," she said. "But at a certain point, I've found it can help a great deal to let a target know you're watching him."

CHAPTER

20

Los Angeles

I DREAMED OF BREE IN PARIS.

She was in some dimly lit jazz club, sipping from a champagne glass and looking like a bombshell in stiletto heels and a sleek, formfitting black dress with a slit high up the right thigh. She was alone at a table near the stage but kept glancing over her shoulder toward the shadowy back of the club, as if she were expecting someone. A quartet and a single singer came onto the stage.

The drummer sat at his kit and stomped several times on his bass drum. Then he stomped on it some more, then again and again.

That's when I startled awake and realized someone was pounding on my hotel-room door. I lurched out of bed, peered through the keyhole, and saw Ned Mahoney standing there in workout gear.

I opened the door. "I'm bagging the gym, Ned, I didn't sleep well last—"

"I just got a call from Pat Loughlin," Mahoney said. "They've lost communication with the two agents guarding the widow White and her family out in Pasadena. He's coming to get us in ten minutes."

I set a world record for showering, shaving, and dressing, grabbed a to-go cup of coffee in the lobby, and went out the front door just as LA Supervising Special Agent Loughlin pulled up in a black Suburban. Mahoney came out the door behind me, puffing and staring at me as if he couldn't believe I'd beaten him.

"It's a talent," I said and climbed in the back.

The second Mahoney shut the passenger-side front door, Loughlin pulled away. "We need this like a thumb in the eye," he said. "I'm thinking we could be in for a frickin' shitshow."

"When was the last time you had contact with the two agents?" I asked.

"Half past three this morning," Loughlin said. "Supposed to check in again at five thirty. When they didn't, they got called. When they didn't answer, I got called. I called their personal phones. When they didn't answer, I called Ned."

"No one's knocked?" Mahoney asked.

"Sheriff's deputy rang the bell at the front gate of the estate."

"Estate?"

"Correct," Loughlin said. "No answer. I told her to stand down, wait for us."

We'd stayed at a hotel in Burbank, so it didn't take long for us to get to the old and tony neighborhood in Pasadena.

An LA County Sheriff's patrol car sat idling ahead of us on the street where Amelia White's parents lived and where the FBI agent's widow had retreated with her children in a time of grief and crisis.

The deputy told us no one had gone in or out of the gate since she'd arrived, and that was nearly forty-five minutes ago. Loughlin thanked her and pulled over to park.

"I have no frickin' idea what we're dealing with here, so let's play it by the book. Everyone in armor. I have four vests in the trunk."

After studying the place on Google Earth, we walked up to a gate in the seven-foot ivy-covered wall that surrounded the three-acre estate of the widow's father, Jeffrey Reising, who'd made a fortune in the aerospace industry. The gate was built of steel covered with planks of whitewashed barn board, and the lower right corner featured a small placard with the name and phone number of a security company.

Loughlin rang the bell at the intercom, got no answer, then called the security company, identified himself, and asked if they'd had any alarms at the Reising residence during the night. When the dispatcher replied in the negative, he asked her to unlock the front gate and disarm the system.

Two minutes later, there was a click, and the gate swung open.

CHAPTER

21

Washington, DC

JOHN SAMPSON WATCHED HIS seven-year-old daughter, Willow, finish her breakfast, feeling as if it were one of the most moving acts he'd ever seen, filled with meaning, tinged with joy and sadness.

He could see his late wife, Billie, in Willow's face and in many of her gestures and habits, like having her two sunny-side-up eggs cut up in a bowl so she could use a spoon to eat them. And waiting until she'd emptied the bowl before drinking her juice. And then setting her juice glass on the table and proclaiming, "That hit the spot!"

"Every time," Sampson said when she stood up, grinning at him, her arms thrown over her head.

A big man, a reserved man, Sampson felt his heart melt when his daughter ran to him and he scooped her up in his arms, hugging and kissing her as she giggled.

"I love you, Daddy," Willow said when he finally put her down.

"I love you too, sweet thing," he said. "Are you ready to go?"

"Just have to brush my teeth," she said. "My bag's ready by the door."

"Good girl," he said.

Willow skipped down the hall and into her bedroom.

He stared after her. *How tiny she is. And yet her spirit seems ten times her size. Just like her mother.*

Sampson's chest felt heavy and heavier still when he remembered M's text from the day before. After he dropped off Willow, he'd see about having the house swept for bugs and cameras, and he'd have his cell phone checked while he was at it.

To get his mind off the idea that he was being monitored, he thought about his long-awaited and long-delayed trip to Montana.

He'd talked with the wife of the man they'd hired to take him and Alex and their gear into the Bob Marshall Wilderness. Sampson had apologized for the postponement and explained that they were in law enforcement and unable to predict the demands on their time. She was fine about it and said they still had at least eight weeks of good weather left and to notify her when they could be on their way.

"Another tooth's loose, Daddy," Willow said. "It feels funny."

She had her mouth open as she walked to him. He knelt, looked, and sure enough, one of her lower incisors moved when she pushed her tongue against it.

"I imagine it does," he said. "But you have a few more

days before it will come out, and in the meantime, you can tell your friends at camp that you're going to get a visit from the tooth fairy soon."

Willow liked that idea and retrieved her little school pack. He held her hand as they walked the three blocks to the church Billie had attended. The church offered a day camp, and Willow seemed to enjoy it.

"What's on deck today?" he asked, though he already knew because he'd signed all the permission slips in her pack.

Willow said, "I told you, Daddy. It's a field trip. We're going to a state park with a lake today. And on the last day of camp we're going to a beach. We're going to have a sandcastle contest."

"That sounds fun."

"Mom liked building sandcastles," she said matter-of-factly.

Sampson saw mental snapshots of his late wife on her knees at the beach, delighted with life, showing a younger Willow how to keep the sand just wet enough to hold its shape but not so wet it fell apart. "She did like sandcastles, didn't she?" he said.

"Mom liked everything."

"And everybody," Sampson said, his heart aching. "Your mother never met a stranger in her entire life."

"I liked that about her."

"I loved that about her," Sampson said. They arrived at the church, where several of the senior counselors were herding a group of kids Willow's age onto two yellow buses. "Go on, now. Mom would want you to have so much fun today that you'll feel like you couldn't have any more fun if you tried! And I want that too."

Willow laughed. "Will you be here to pick me up?"

"Either me or Jannie," he said and hugged her and kissed her again.

Sampson watched his young daughter climb on the bus—so tiny and yet so strong—get to a seat at a window near the back, and wave to him. Feeling his heart melt again, he waved back. He turned and started to go, moving around several other mothers and fathers walking their excited little kids to the buses.

There were more campers coming by car. They crowded the street in front of the church and were causing a mild traffic jam. Several drivers to the left and right of the knot began to honk their horns, one of them so insistently that Sampson paused and peered down the street.

From a young age, Sampson had known he had excellent eyesight. Doctors in army boot camp had confirmed that he was blessed with 20/12 vision, which meant that an object that people with normal vision saw clearly at twelve feet, he could see clearly at twenty feet.

The doctors also called him a "super-recognizer" because he had a near photographic memory for faces. Sampson couldn't always attach a name to a face, but he could almost always tell you where he'd seen the face and why he remembered it.

So the moment Sampson saw the man in jeans and a black T-shirt leaning against a tree across the street and down the block, he knew who he was looking at: Hayden Brooker. He had not seen the man in nearly fifteen years, but Brooker's face was etched deeply into his memory.

Sampson had known him in the army. Brooker had been

a Delta Force operator with a reputation as a stone-cold killer. The last rumor Sampson had heard from mutual acquaintances was that after mustering out, Brooker had joined the CIA.

As an assassin.

22

Los Angeles

WITH GUNS DRAWN, NED MAHONEY and I followed Patrick Loughlin through the open gate and into the estate belonging to the parents of the murdered FBI agent's widow.

Built of rust-colored pavers, the driveway climbed steeply beneath the shade of giant palms. Terraced gardens with flowers abloom broke the lower grounds into tiers on both sides of the drive, which crested onto a flat area with more meticulously maintained gardens.

A riot of birds of paradise flowers surrounded a flowing fountain in the circle in front of the Reisings' house, a rambling, white Cape with green trim and wings off both sides. Birds sang in the jacaranda trees, and somewhere chimes moved on the breeze.

"Ahh, Jaysus, no!" Loughlin cried and hurried toward a body sprawled in the driveway between the fountain and the front door. Male. Late thirties. Blue suit and tie. He had been shot between the eyes.

Loughlin's face twisted and paled. "Special Agent Carlos Deeds. Nine-year veteran of the Bureau. Young wife. Two kids. Jaysus fricking—"

"We've got another, Pat," Mahoney said, gesturing across the lawn to the left of the drive where a woman lay facedown.

Deeds's partner, Special Agent Madeline Cruise. She'd been shot high in the back.

"Someone's paying for this," Loughlin said hoarsely. "I promise you that."

"Call it in?" Mahoney asked.

The LA supervising special agent cleared his throat and said, "Let's see the sorry lot of it before we call in the cavalry."

We entered in full combat mode, guns up, sweeping back and forth as we went through the nineteen rooms in the mansion. We found Amelia White's father, Jeffrey Reising, in his home office, dead of two gunshot wounds to the face. In the upstairs master bedroom, Reising's wife, Jane, looked to have been executed with a single shot to the forehead as she slept.

We all kept it together until we found their three grand-children, nine-year-old Ricky and the five-year-old twins, Kate and Anne, all dead in their beds, their throats slit.

Loughlin, who'd been a cop since the age of twenty, broke down. Mahoney, a twenty-four-year agent, had to lean against a wall.

I'd been a homicide investigator for most of my adult life but lurched to a bathroom and puked up my breakfast. I entered the kitchen a few minutes later, and it turned out to be a blessing that I had an empty stomach.

Amelia White had been gagged, stripped naked, and lashed to a ladder-back chair. The condition of her body—the cuts, bruising, and broken bones—all suggested that the disgraced FBI agent's wife had been tortured before her throat was mercifully slit.

Someone had dipped a rolled-up section of that morning's *Los Angeles Times* in the blood pooled on the floor and used it to scrawl these words on the wall behind her:

LAS FAMILIAS MUERTAS NO CUENTAN CUENTOS.

"'Dead families tell no tales,'" Mahoney translated.

"Frickin' bastards!" Loughlin said, gesturing to the bloody newspaper that had been left on the floor, unfolded to show the story of Special Agent White's murder and his extraordinary confession to being an assassin for the Alejandro drug cartel.

I said, "Alejandro cartel hitmen did this."

"They're front and center in my book too," Loughlin said. "No souls. Pure evil to do this to her and...her children. Jaysus."

"This massacre isn't just payback," Mahoney said. "It's a warning to anyone else who might be tempted to confess their sins."

"A warning straight from that supermax in Colorado," I said.

Loughlin shook his head. "I talked to the warden at the Florence penitentiary yesterday. Marco Alejandro has been held there one hundred percent incommunicado for nearly a year. No interaction with other prisoners. No visitors. No mail. No internet. Nada. It was part of his sentence. The judge wanted Marco to remain in silence a full year to contemplate the carnage he'd caused."

"I don't think the silence is complete," I said. "The brutality here has got Marco written all over it. Somehow, he's aware of what's going on. Somehow, he's in communication with his people. He ordered this."

"Maybe," Mahoney said. "Or maybe Marco's successor in Mexico did."

CHAPTER

23

Paris

BREE SAT ALONE IN THE third row of crowded tables outside Les Deux Palais, a café across the boulevard from the tall iron-and-gilt fence and gates that protect the courtyard of the Palais de Justice de Paris.

The palace of justice, or couthouse, was heavily guarded. One police van idled on the sidewalk on the other side of the boulevard. A second van was parked behind the fence in the courtyard. Six armed officers with bulletproof vests manned the two gates.

It was hot for five thirty in the afternoon. Bree was drinking her third soda water with lime as employees began to stream out the courthouse gates.

She had an excellent view of them from her position. She checked the photos of the three judges on her burn phone against several of the employees leaving but saw none of them in the first big wave going home for the evening, which wasn't terribly surprising. The judges might be corrupt, but they still had to keep up appearances.

Bree figured it would be sometime between six thirty and seven before she caught sight of any of them. Then again, one judge was all she needed for what she had in mind for the Three Musketeers, as she'd taken to calling them.

C'mon, guys. All for one and one for all.

Bree thumbed the screen on the burn phone and connected to the internet through a VPN. She called up WhatsApp and scrolled until she had the names of the three judges in front of her.

Eeny, meeny, miny, Bree thought. *Who's it going to be?*

She opened her note-taking app, found the message she'd drafted earlier in the day, and read it for the tenth time, trying to gauge what its potential impact would be.

Bree remembered that she'd told Marianne Le Tour that she wanted to keep Philippe Abelmar unaware of the investigation for the time being. But after studying the profiles of the judges, she'd decided to at least raise *their* anxiety levels a little. And if they contacted Abelmar? So much the better.

By a quarter to seven, the unusual heat that had gripped Paris was easing, and Bree was considering the possibility that judges didn't use the main entrance to leave at the end of the day. She should go back to her hotel, get changed, and—

A woman exited the main entrance of the courthouse carrying two briefcases. In her late forties with ash-blond hair, she wore a blue skirt and jacket, a cream blouse, and a red silk scarf. Before the woman started down the stairs to the courtyard, Bree had confirmed her ID.

Adele Marchant, you get to be the first contestant on the—

Two men in dark business suits came out of the doors behind Judge Marchant. The one on the left was older, in his sixties, and portly, with an embarrassing shock of overly dyed black hair. His friend was taller, slighter, in his fifties, and bald. They were also carrying heavy attaché cases.

Bree thumbed for the photos and saw it was true—Judges Claude Alsace and Domenic Les Freres were leaving at the same time as Judge Marchant.

Judge Alsace, the portly one, was calling to Marchant now. She turned as he and Judge Les Freres climbed down the stairs to her, smiling and laughing.

Bree hadn't considered what might happen if she could tap the paranoia of all three at once instead of doing it one by one, the slow build. But the idea instantly appealed to her. She thumbed back to her note app, copied what she'd written, and went to WhatsApp.

After glancing up to make sure the trio of judges were still there, Bree selected their private cell numbers, made them a group, pasted her message, then looked up again.

The judges were no longer together. All three were walking to their separate cars parked in the courtyard.

Perfect, Bree thought and thumbed the Send button. She watched anxiously, hoping that it went through before—

Judge Marchant set her attaché cases down by her car and got out her phone to look at it. By his car, Judge Alsace did the same. Only Judge Les Freres opened his car door and got in.

Even from across the boulevard, even looking through the iron-and-gilt fence, Bree saw Judge Alsace lean against his car as if he were suddenly unsteady. Judge Marchant went dead still and then hunched over, one hand across her mouth, looking at her phone and shaking her head.

Then the judge picked up her head and gazed around as if hunting for the sender. Three rows back in the crowded tables outside the café, Bree felt confident but turned in another direction for a full minute.

When she looked back, Judge Alsace and Judge Marchant both stood outside Judge Les Freres's car and were speaking with him through the window. It was hard to see, but Bree was sure Les Freres also had his phone in his hand.

That got their attention, Bree thought. She got up and went into the café's restroom. There, she pulled the battery and SIM card from the burn phone, pocketed them, then broke the phone and dumped it in the trash beneath used paper towels. She would dispose of the battery and the SIM elsewhere.

By the time she returned to her table, the judges and their cars were gone. She wasn't worried. She had a better than decent hunch about where they might all be going.

And it wasn't home.

CHAPTER

24

Washington, DC

EARLY THAT AFTERNOON ON THE East Coast, Sampson entered the DC Office of the Chief Medical Examiner on E Street and asked at the front counter for Lauren Pickett, an assistant ME he'd known for years.

While he waited, he kept returning to Billie's church in his mind, kept seeing Hayden Brooker, his arms folded, legs crossed at the ankles, leaning against a tree, and staring at Sampson in amusement until a delivery van rolled to a stop, blocking his view. When it moved, Brooker had vanished.

But it was him. Sampson had no doubt about it. Same facial structure, same shaggy haircut, same *I hate the world and want to kill it* expression.

Did he want me to see him there at the church? Was he there to watch me and Willow? And why now? Why after all these years?

Before Sampson could further ponder Brooker's reappearance in his life, Lauren Pickett appeared. "John Sampson, what a pleasant surprise."

Dr. Pickett was a little older than Sampson, late forties, very attractive, and very smart. They'd worked together on multiple cases and he had always enjoyed her company.

"Sorry to come by without touching base first," he said. "Is there somewhere private we can talk?"

"Absolutely," Pickett said. "My office is free."

She led him back through a warren of cubicles to her office, which had photographs on the wall of her many adventure trips. Sampson saw her on a fishing boat in Panama, on an elephant in India, and carrying a heavy backpack in spectacular mountain terrain.

"That's the Bob Marshall Wilderness, isn't it?" he said.

Dr. Pickett smiled. "One of the most awe-inspiring places I have ever been. Really helped me heal."

"I remember you saying that. Alex Cross and I were supposed to be in the Bob right now. We were going to go in on horses with all our gear and rafts and float out the South Fork of the Flathead River. Six-day trip, mostly self-guided."

She sighed dreamily. "Sounds amazing. You had to postpone?"

"For a number of reasons," he said, a little deflated as he sat in a chair across from her. "I'd been hoping to do some of that healing you've talked about."

"How are you, John?" Pickett asked with sincere concern. "What's it been, a year now?"

"Thirteen months," Sampson said. "And I'm still working it out."

"And I expect you will be for a while yet. I know when

Don passed, it was a good two years before I could look at anything without the filter of his death. That trip to the Bob Marshall was at month twenty-four. I found peace in that wilderness."

"If I'm going to find some of that peace, I'll need your help."

"Anything, John. You know that," the assistant ME said and sat forward.

Sampson told her that he, Alex, and others in law enforcement had never made much noise about an unidentified criminal they'd known of for years, someone who often operated at the periphery of their investigations. Sending them messages. Taking false credit for heinous crimes. Claiming innocence in crimes he'd clearly committed. Taunting them about their lack of investigative skills.

"He calls himself M. I call him Mastermind. He wrote me yesterday."

Sampson handed her his phone with the message from M up on the screen.

Pickett frowned, took it, sat back and began to read. Sampson kept looking from the assistant ME to that picture of her in the Bob, wondering anxiously if he was ever going to get to that place himself.

"What kind of human sends a message like this?" Dr. Pickett said, looking grim as she handed him back his phone.

"Alex says he's a brilliant psychopath," Sampson said. "We believe he's been involved in mass murders, multiple kidnappings, and high-stakes rip-offs, among other crimes."

"He claims he killed Billie. That she didn't die of Lyme's. You believe that?"

"That's what I'm here to find out, Lauren. There wasn't an

autopsy because she'd been sick with Lyme's and the heart condition it caused for so long. Remember?"

The ME took a deep breath and said softly, "You want Billie's body exhumed, John? Is that what you're here for? Is that what you want?"

Sampson felt gutted. "It's the last thing I want, Lauren. But not knowing will keep gnawing at me until I bring Billie up from her grave and make sure. I might as well do it now and get it over with."

He choked out the last few words and hung his head. "I know M is making use of my pain. I believe in my heart that Billie died of Lyme's. But I feel like I have no choice but to live through more suffering to make absolutely sure it wasn't murder." He raised his head. "And I'd like to have her body cremated after that. It's what I think she originally wanted."

Pickett got up, came around her desk, and put her hand on his shoulder.

"You are a good man, John. No one should have to go through this kind of mental torture, especially you. But I agree with you. I will find out what it's going to take to make an exhumation happen in as dignified a way as possible. I will handle the case myself. Your Billie will be well taken care of, I promise you that."

CHAPTER
25

Paris

ACROSS THE ATLANTIC, IT WAS almost nine p.m. when Bree climbed out of her taxi wearing her only other outfit suitable for an evening at a swank bistro like Canard de Flaque. Her pencil skirt was black, above the knee, and tight-fitting. The silk top featured a colorful pattern and was equally flattering. Gray hose and lipstick-red pumps completed the look.

She glanced sidelong at her reflection in a storefront window, smiled, and thought, *Bree St. Lucie. Strolling along. Dressed to kill. Ready to see what havoc she's caused.*

At the front door to Puddle Duck, she hesitated, concerned about spending too much time in one place. But what choice did she have?

Bree opened the door and went inside; she saw Henri look up and smile.

"Madame," he said. "You honor us two days in a row with your presence."

Bree grinned. "It's the duck."

"It always is," Henri replied. "The bar? I have the same spot available."

"That would be perfect, thank you, Henri."

"My great pleasure, madame." He grabbed a menu and led her to the stool at the far end of the bar, closest to the dining area and booths.

Crossing the room and sliding into her seat, Bree avoided the temptation to scan the crowd. She took the menu, thanked Henri, and smiled at Carole, the bartender, who appeared in front of her.

"Champagne?" Carole asked.

"The same as last time, please. Thank you, Carole."

Bree pretended to consider the menu while taking occasional slow glances in the mirror as if checking her makeup. By the time the flute of champagne arrived, Bree knew that five of the other bar stools were taken.

To her left, on the stools Abelmar and his assistant had occupied the previous evening, a cute couple in their fifties were flirting. The next two stools were empty. Another couple and an older woman occupied the far three.

Only after Bree had taken a sip of the champagne and smacked her lips approvingly did Carole move off, at which point Bree dared to glance in the bar mirror at the tables in the dining room. Most of them were filled with happy, chic patrons.

Philippe Abelmar was not among them. She waited, sipping her champagne, before casually twisting her stool toward the long narrow mirrors between the big windows.

As she did, the front door to Canard opened. A big, muscular man with a shaved head entered; he was wearing a black V-neck T-shirt, black slacks, and black loafers. He gestured at the bar. Henri nodded. He walked over by himself, took the fourth stool, and got out his phone.

Abelmar was not in any of the booths that she could see. But there was one still empty. As she noted it, the billionaire entered, alone, glancing at his phone and appearing highly distracted.

Henri led Abelmar to the empty booth, and he sat, disappearing from Bree's view. Bree took a few more sips of champagne, told the bartender she'd like to start with escargots, and then twisted to look at the narrow mirrors.

Abelmar was on his phone in the booth, gesturing wildly, obviously having an animated conversation. Although she was dying to know to whom he was talking and whether it was about the note she'd sent to the three judges, Bree reminded herself that the man was a business tycoon with enterprises all over the world. *He could easily be upset about something completely different.*

She'd no sooner had that thought when Judge Adele Marchant entered the bistro, dressed more casually than she'd been earlier. She worried a ring on her right hand.

Judge Claude Alsace waddled in a moment later in his suit, sans tie, his hands clenched in fists and his pudgy jaw set tight. Judge Domenic Les Freres, who followed him, had abandoned both his tie and jacket. His white shirt was open two buttons and he was sweating so much, he could have opened a few more.

Eeny, meeny, miny, Bree thought as Henri led the three

judges toward Abelmar, who stood to greet them. *And now moe. This couldn't get better. Could it?*

The foursome disappeared into the booth. Bree ordered the duck and another glass of champagne before casually looking over at the mirror and the reflection of the booth where the billionaire and the judges were all huddled, speaking intensely.

Bree had a clear view of Judge Marchant's distraught face. Judge Les Freres waved his phone angrily at Abelmar. Judge Alsace had his head down, as if he found the white tablecloth fascinating.

When Bree turned back, Carole set down her second flute of champagne, along with a sliced baguette and a plate of six escargots cooked in butter, minced garlic, and shallots that made her groan twice with pleasure. She knew sopping up the butter with the bread was not the most couth thing she could do in a restaurant of this caliber, but she did it anyway after the couple beside her departed.

Bree noticed in the mirror that the big guy a few stools down was smiling and chuckling at her. She looked over at him. "What's so funny?"

Still smiling, he bobbed his chin toward the escargot plate and in a pleasant growl said, "I do the same when I eat here. The sauce is just too good to pass up, and they bake the bread here every afternoon."

Bree smiled, relaxed. "The duck is incredible too. I had it last night."

"The duck," he said, putting his hand over his heart. "Already put in my order."

Henri the maître d' led two women in their early thirties to the bar. They took seats next to the big guy and immediately engaged him in conversation, which suited Bree, as Carole had just placed her duck dinner before her.

The dish was even better than Bree remembered, each bite an intoxicating brew of flavors that shocked, morphed, and lingered on the tongue.

She was so absorbed in her meal, she almost forgot why she was there. After eating more of the succulent meat, she set down her knife and fork and casually pivoted in her chair. To her surprise, the judges no longer seemed upset. They were all grinning and clinking glasses of red wine.

And Abelmar?

He was full of good cheer as well, laughing as he turned to peer across the room at the same mirror Bree was looking at.

Their eyes locked.

Abelmar's grin crumbled and fell away.

26

BREE TRIED TO ACT AS IF she hadn't noticed the billionaire look-ing at her, but her heart was pounding as she pivoted back to her meal and scolded herself for being so blatant.

Had Abelmar recognized her? Or did he merely think he'd been recognized?

He's something of a celebrity, right? Bree thought as she forced herself to pick up her utensils. *He must get people gawking at him. And we did talk last night. Sort of.*

Bree kept her attention on her plate and focused on enjoying the rest of her entrée, the taste of which seemed to evolve as it cooled, giving the sauce a more caramelized consistency that made the way it lingered on the tongue even more remarkable. In her peripheral vision she saw Judge Marchant leaving.

Bree looked over. Judge Alsace and Judge Les Freres were

following their colleague and acting as if they didn't have a care in the world.

"How's the duck?" Carole asked.

Bree turned back to the bartender. "I won't tell my ninety-year-old grandmother-in-law, who is an incredible cook, but this may be the best meal of my entire life."

"The veal is excellent too."

"Tomorrow night," Bree promised.

"Same dessert? Crème brûlée?"

"Please, and with a decaf espresso?"

The bartender nodded and walked off.

The big bald guy signed his check and left.

Bree took another bite of the duck, savoring it, before sensing something in her periphery. She pivoted slightly in her seat.

Philippe Abelmar was standing beside her and studying her with some amusement. "The duck again?"

"I could not resist," she said, trying not to act taken aback by his sudden presence.

"I warned you that the duck can be an addiction," the billionaire said.

"I'm beginning to understand that."

His eyes danced and flickered over her face and chest as he said, "Do you know how an African lion keeps his dominance over a pride of lionesses?"

She thought about that. "Constantly fights other lions?"

"Not if he's smart," Abelmar said. "Not if he wants to live a long life. If he wants that, then he is actually sedentary much of the time, lying about in the shade with a bellyful of meat his lionesses have killed for him. But even then, in that sated state, the lion is still alert to anything new or out of

107

place. The merest whiff of a threat and he acts, goes to the source of danger immediately and confronts it."

"He protects his perimeter."

Abelmar smiled and nodded. "That's right. And if he needs to fight, he attacks right then, without hesitation. But more often than not, just the power, speed, and aggressiveness of the dominant lion is enough to send all inferior threats running without so much as a bite or a scratch."

"Is that why you came up to talk to me?" she asked, frowning. "You considered me an inferior threat?"

"You?" he said and he laughed in a rather nice way. "No. I came because I wanted to see if you liked the duck and because you are a very beautiful woman."

Bree smiled and said, "I appreciate that." She held out her hand.

He hesitated and then smiled and took it. "Philippe."

"Bree," she said.

"Your accent is…interesting," he said, letting go of her hand.

"Saint Martin," she said.

"Are you here on vacation or business?"

"A little of both."

"Your business?"

Bree paused before saying, "I work for a law firm in Saint Martin. We set up shell companies for people interested in moving their business or their money offshore."

Abelmar cocked his head, raised his eyebrows, and said, "Saint Martin. Who knew?"

"It's overlooked," she said. "But I still love it."

"You are doing this—building shell companies—for someone here in Paris?"

"I'm talking with prospective clients."

He thought about that, reached into his jacket pocket, and retrieved his business card. "I may be interested. Call my office. Come see me and we'll talk, Madame…"

"St. Lucie," she said, taking his card with feigned curiosity. "Bree St. Lucie."

CHAPTER

27

Pasadena

AS SOON AS WE UNDERSTOOD the scope and the motivation behind the murders at the home of Amelia White's parents, I went outside and phoned Sampson to bring him up to speed while Loughlin called in an army to process the scene and Mahoney arranged to put multiple heavily armed agents around the late Catherine Hingham's home in Alexandria, Virginia.

We didn't want more retribution killings on our hands if we could help it.

After I'd described Special Agent White's confession and the massacre of his family to John, he told me about seeing a man outside Billie's church whom he recognized from years before. John always had an incredible memory for faces.

"Who is it this time?" I asked.

"I ever tell you about a guy named Hayden Brooker?" Sampson said. "I knew him in the army?"

"You did two tours, John. You knew a lot of people."

"Brooker was Delta Force. Snuck into hooches. Slit throats."

I flashed on Amelia White and her children and felt nauseated as I said, "I remember now. You called him Master Sergeant Psycho."

"Never to his face, man," Sampson said, sounding horrified at that idea. "Brooker was stone-cold deadly. Scared the crap out of everyone. I never wanted to cross him."

"You sure it was him outside the church?"

"Positive," he said. "Little grayer, little paunchier, but it was Brooker. No doubt about it and no idea why he was there. On a different topic, I signed the documents to have Billie's body exhumed. I don't want to—I know M is just exploiting her death—but I have to do it."

"That's a lot on your plate for one day," I said, feeling for the guy. "And I understand your reasons completely. Keep me posted. About all of it. Love you, man."

"Same to you. How's Bree?"

"Haven't heard from her yet today but praying she stays safe."

"From here as well, brother," Sampson said and hung up.

While Loughlin oversaw the criminologists and agents arriving by the minute, Mahoney and I located the password to the Reisings' elaborate security system, which included alarms and multiple cameras mounted high around the exterior of the house. We accessed the system, backed up the video recordings, and watched the feeds at high speed, but we saw nothing on the grounds after eleven p.m., when the two now-dead FBI agents had walked the perimeter.

"That's impossible," Mahoney said, gesturing at the feed from over the front door. "Agent Deeds died right there. We never see him. We never see anything."

"Not true," I said. "Watch this." I tapped the feed that overlooked the pool. "Keep your eye on the potted plants. Wait for it."

Thirty seconds later, a rodent bolted from the vegetation and scampered across the pool deck.

"What is that?" Mahoney asked.

"Tree rat," Loughlin said.

"He does it every two minutes," I said.

"The tree rat does?" Mahoney said, incredulous.

"Definitely. I think they hacked into the system and by-passed the actual cameras. We're looking at a loop inserted into the recording, probably from before they attacked. Every feed's showing a loop."

"Well, they can't have done it to every camera in the neighborhood," Loughlin said. "We'll pick them up."

While the LA SAC assigned agents to canvass the area and request all security-camera footage, Mahoney and I tried to figure out how the killers had entered the estate and house without tripping alarms. We found no obvious footprints in the irrigated garden soil anywhere around the base of the high wall surrounding the estate.

But then I noticed that the moist earth in the northwest corner was slightly depressed in an area two feet wide by three feet long. When I got down on my hands and knees, I saw several dozen coarse fibers, each two to three inches, sticking up from the mud.

I picked up a few and stared at them and then at the nearby plants. "I have no idea what these are, but they shouldn't be here," I said, showing them to Mahoney.

Ned turned up the magnification on his phone camera and aimed it at the fibers. "I know what those are," he said within seconds.

"You do?"

"I have an old coco doormat out in the breezeway at my place at the beach. It's made from coconut fibers and tends to shed as it ages. Popular in Mexico."

I looked up at the wall. "So, after they hack the security system, the cartel hit men climb the wall, toss down a coco doormat, and drop down on it. Then they jump to the grass and cross to the house."

I pointed to the closest window and the closest door. "There or there."

We went to them and examined them closely. It wasn't until Mahoney did that nifty trick with his phone camera again that we saw the tiny nicks around the doorknob and the dead bolt.

We brought Loughlin out and showed him the evidence and told him our theory.

"After they come over the wall, one or more of them comes here," Mahoney said. "Picks the lock while two, maybe three others circle on Deeds and Cruise. Shoot him in the face and her in the back with pistols with suppressors. Then they're inside to do the rest of their bloody work."

"We're thinking they're out of here in an hour, tops," I said. "They probably walked right out the front gate."

"Carrying that coco mat," Mahoney said.

"Arrogant bastards," Loughlin said. He looked at me. "You might be right, you know, Alex."

"What's that?"

"About going to see Marco Alejandro. I know Judge Sands."

"The sentencing judge?"

"We go way back to Boston," Loughlin said. "He worked in the Suffolk County DA's office back in the day. I don't like to use that kind of influence normally, but once he sees the pictures of the kids, he just might let you into that supermax a little early."

CHAPTER

28

Northwest of Laramie, Wyoming

MATTHEW BUTLER WAS SWEATING LIKE a stuck pig, hidden in some bushes, baking in the sun, but sitting resolutely behind a Swarovski BTX spotting scope with dual eyepieces and a 115-millimeter objective lens. He had the six-thousand-dollar scope aimed across the lush green field in front of him, beyond the low, dry sage flat to the first rise and the first timber.

The wooded hillside was a thousand yards off. But when Butler looked through the BTX's twin eyepieces, which gave him thirty-five-power magnification as well as stereoscopic vision, the first timber appeared to be a hundred yards away.

Butler could clearly see magpies flitting about and squabbling. And he could make out every branch, every twig, and every grass stalk waving in the hot afternoon breeze around the bighorn sheep ram that lay on the hill just inside the timberline.

He knew the ram. He'd named it Kong because of the mass of its horns. Kong was as big as they came in Wyoming, real record-book material, and a remarkable animal to see in the wild.

Butler had been watching the ram come and go on the ranch for the past two years. He and his men had tried to monitor and protect the rare wild sheep as much as was possible. But around three o'clock that morning, Vincente woke Butler up at the ranch house and said he'd gotten up for a piss and heard what he thought was a low-caliber rifle shot outside the bathroom window. They'd come down and used the infrared scopes to find the dying bighorn out there on the rise.

It had been gut-shot. They'd dispatched the animal and left him there.

Vincente checked the game camera they'd had installed in the trees beyond the gate and east boundary fence of the Circle M Ranch. Sure enough, around two a.m. a small, beat-up motor home without license plates had come by the camera.

Thirty-five minutes later, the same vehicle went by again, moving in the opposite direction. In both photographs, they could see two men, one much older than the other, in the cab of the motor home. In the photo of them leaving, the old guy had his head thrown back and was laughing.

That picture had so enraged Butler, he had climbed in the makeshift blind at five thirty a.m. and waited. He'd been there seven and a half hours. With the temperature north of ninety.

But Butler and his team were stubborn hunters. They would wait until dark and all night to catch the poachers who'd shot the ram, likely in their headlights or with a thermal scope, which enraged Butler even more.

He was not against hunting, not in the least. But he despised poachers who'd shoot an animal at night, defenseless. And they hadn't even killed it outright, just left it to suffer.

The irony that he had often hunted people at night with such devices was not lost on Butler. But then again, the people he hunted were by no means defenseless.

"Cap?" Vincente said in Butler's earpiece. His voice sounded crackly from the sweat.

"Here."

"It's showtime. We see the motor home. Arkansas plates on it now. Just turned into the campground."

There was a Wyoming state campground on a nice trout stream a half a mile from the ranch gate. Of course that's where they'd be.

"Let me know when they start walking our way."

"Roger that."

Vincente's alert came a half an hour later, at three in the afternoon, almost twelve hours after the poachers had put a bullet through the ram's belly.

"They just crossed the road, climbed the ridge in camo and face paint," he said. "They're probably forty minutes from that ram."

Butler triggered his mike, said, "Purdy, crawl that motor home."

"On it," she said.

Twenty minutes later, his burglar said, "Got in the rig and you were right. They've got false compartments and three big bloody sheep skulls and horns in them. And there's a custom twenty-two bolt-action rifle in here with a thermal scope that must cost five grand."

"Identification?"

"On both our crackers. Dudley Bob Hole, age fifty-two, of Stuttgart, Arkansas. Jim Bob Hole, twenty-four, looks like he still lives at home with dear old pops."

"Heartwarming," Butler said. "Anything else?"

"GPS tracker under the back left bumper."

Butler did not like that. "Law enforcement?"

"Can't tell."

"Where are you?"

"In the motor home with the engine on and the AC blowing."

"Hide the tracker somewhere there in the campground where you can find it and drive the rig up to the barn. Put the chemicals and the rest of it inside and hold your position until my call."

"Roger."

"JP, let's get up there and in position opposite Cortland and Big DD."

"On my way," Vincente said.

Ten minutes later, Vincente drove up the ranch road in a green Honda Pioneer 1000 side-by-side utility vehicle.

"We got them now, *jefe,*" Vincente said as Butler climbed in. "Smooth hunting from here on out."

Butler nodded. But he was thinking about that tracking device and who might have put it there and how he could use it to his advantage.

CHAPTER

29

THE SIDE-BY-SIDE WAS fitted with an aftermarket exhaust that made it almost dead silent as Vincente drove the inner ranch roads toward that dead sheep in a roundabout way so as not to alert the poachers.

As they drove, Butler enjoyed the breeze after all those hours in the sun. He drank a Gatorade and called for updates.

"Nothing yet," Big DD said. "I expect they're pausing out there to my south somewhere, taking a look for the ram with their own optics."

"Ten-four," Butler said. "Purdy?"

"At the barn," she said. "Chemicals loaded. Waiting on your call, boss."

Vincente pulled the Honda to a stop in the shade of a grove of western pines. They got out and stayed in the shadows as they snuck toward the tree line and the edge of the rise where it fell away to the sage flat and the ag field.

Before they reached it, Butler's radio crackled. Cortland said, "Vultures on the bait, Cap. Knives and saws at work."

Butler had hoped to be there when they tried to cut the head off Kong. But he was a practical man and Cortland and Big DD were highly skilled.

"Take them," he said. "We'll be right along."

Butler and Vincente ran laterally across the hill through the timber toward the shouting voices. By the time they broke free of the trees, Big DD and Cortland had the poachers on their knees to either side of Kong, hands behind their heads, cowering before the two AR rifles with sound suppressors a foot from their faces.

Two pistols, two butcher knives, and a bloody folding saw lay behind Cortland.

The stench from the rotting ram came and went on the shifting breeze.

"We're good, boss," Big DD called.

Dudley Bob Hole, the older poacher, looked fifty going on seventy and wore a filthy, bloodstained camo jumpsuit and a filthier ball cap with the logo of a turkey-call company on it. He watched as Butler and Vincente approached and stayed quiet. He'd been down this road before.

His kid, Jim Bob, had shaggy brown hair, acne scars under his face paint, a scraggly red beard, and a camo kerchief tied around his head.

"There's no need to be pointing those guns at us, man," Jim Bob complained in a twangy accent. "We just found that ram lying there."

"True?" Butler said to the older man.

"Out for a hike, stumbled on him," Dudley Bob said in a cigarette-hoarse voice. "Seemed a waste to leave him there for the coyotes."

"Fibber," Butler said. "One of you guys shot him last night with a custom twenty-two fitted with a thermal scope that must have cost you five grand, Dudley Bob."

The older Hole's jaw sagged.

"Hey, man," his son said. "You the law?"

"Of a kind, Jim Bob," Butler said.

"What the hell does that mean?" the old man said, squinting at them all suspiciously now. "And how'd you know our names? Show me a badge or identification, and you better have had a warrant if you went inside our rig."

"We didn't need a warrant," Butler said. "The door was open and it smelled like something was burning. Probably your rocket-scientist son's fault."

"You idiot," Dudley Bob said.

Jim Bob got a sour look on his face. "Nah, Pa, I locked her tight."

His father glared at Butler. "I still haven't seen a badge. I want to see a goddamn badge or we are getting up and walking out of here."

"We found three bighorn sheep heads in there," Butler said.

"That's it," Dudley Bob said and started to get to his feet.

Big DD took two strides and kicked him in the solar plexus with a steel-toed boot. The older man dropped like a stone and writhed.

"Pa!" his son cried and started to go to him.

"Don't move or you'll get the same," Big DD said.

Jim Bob seemed torn, looking from his father to Big

DD and finally to Butler. "Whoever you are, we want a lawyer, man. Call a cop, a sheriff. Whoever's justice around these parts."

"We were thinking of some Old West justice instead," Butler said. He triggered his microphone. "Purds, drive the motor home up to the north ranch road. They'll be done and we'll be down in twenty minutes or so."

"What do you mean, 'They'll be done'?" the younger Hole said, anxiety rising.

Butler said, "That ram? Kong? He might as well have been cattle to us. And you know what they do to cattle rustlers out west, don't you?"

Jim Bob's scraggly chin retreated as if he were trying to hide his throat. Then he laughed nervously. "Nah," he said. "You're just messing with us."

"I'm going to sue your ass," his father croaked, getting up on one elbow.

"No, you're not," Vincente said. "You won't be around to do any suing or any poaching ever again."

"People know where we are, man," the younger Hole said.

"No, they don't."

"Yes, they do," Dudley Bob said. "Tracking us by GPS from back home."

"Really?" Butler said. "I'm actually happy to hear that. And you'll be unhappy to know that we've loaded the volatile components used to cook methamphetamine in your camper, including ether, methanol, and anhydrous ammonia. No one will question the explosion or the fireball that took your lives and burned your bodies to cinders."

"Wait!" the kid cried. "No!"

"Kill them," Butler said. "I've got more important things to take care of."

He walked away, immune to the Holes' pleas for mercy. Two suppressed shots thudded and a pair of humanity's least desirable elements simply ceased to exist.

CHAPTER

30

Washington, DC

AT A QUARTER TO SIX John Sampson parked his car at home and walked to pick up Willow in the church parking lot. He got there a little early so he could check the street for any sign of Hayden Brooker.

But Sampson saw no one who even vaguely resembled the former Delta Force operator. Soon, the buses arrived.

The second his young daughter came off the bus, the sense of threat Sampson had been feeling all day eased. Maybe he'd been mistaken.

He grinned as he scooped up Willow, who looked both happy and exhausted.

"Did you bring the car, Daddy?" she asked.

"Nope."

She made a dramatic face. "I can't take another step."

"Need a ride up top?"

"Yes, please!"

Sampson lifted her higher and turned her so she could sit on his broad shoulders, which delighted her no end. Willow giggled and waved to her friends as they left the church.

He again scanned the area by the tree where Brooker had been earlier in the day, but he saw only harried moms and dads bringing their kids to waiting cars. He turned toward home as Willow did a data dump of her day, describing every game she'd played, all the times she'd gone swimming in the lake, and the glorious hot dogs they'd cooked on sticks over a fire.

Sampson relished every second of it and put his girl down on their front porch feeling as if he'd lived the day himself. Jannie Cross opened the door. Willow ran in and hugged her favorite babysitter, who told Sampson she'd brought over some mac and cheese and the rabbit leftovers from the night before and she was heating it up for dinner.

"Perfect," he said.

"Do you have to work late?" she asked.

"Couple of hours? I want to be back to tuck her in."

"That helps. I've got a big workout in the morning."

"See you soon, Daddy, I'm hungry," Willow said and tugged on Jannie's hand.

"Nice to be needed," she said smiling, and she shut the door.

Sampson felt as if nothing in the world could go wrong as he bopped down the stoop stairs and along the walk, heading for his car in the drive. Then he glanced across his street and spotted the silhouette of a man among the shadows thrown by a big maple. He was big and broad enough...

When the man took a step into the slanting light, Sampson

had no doubt who it was, even after a decade and a half. Master Sergeant Psycho himself.

Brooker raised both palms, held them at shoulder height. Sampson walked by the car and across the street.

When he'd gotten feet from the man, he stopped. "Master Sergeant Brooker."

Brooker laughed hoarsely at that; he sounded as if he was a smoker or was getting over a cold. "No one's called me that in years."

In his forties now, Brooker appeared no less fit than Sampson remembered, still with the height and build of a pro basketball guard. Indeed, the way he kept his palms raised, his knees slightly flexed, and his balance forward over his black sneakers suggested a guard playing defense. Or an assassin expecting trouble.

"Heard you're a big-time homicide detective now," Brooker said.

"And I heard you're a killer for the CIA."

He laughed even harder than before, which started a ragged coughing fit. When it ended, he laughed again. "Sorry, no one's called me that in years either. And it was never true, by the way. I went private security is all."

"Good for you," Sampson said, though he did not like mercenaries in general. "Why are you here, Brooker? Outside my house? Outside my church this morning?"

"Hey, man, I'm sorry about that. I honestly didn't think you'd hear me out if I called."

"Hear you out about what?"

"Making amends," Brooker said, sounding quieter and more unsure of himself. "I, uh, got sober last year, John. AA. And this is step eight. Well, nine. Step eight, you write a list of everyone you ever harmed when you were under the influence. Nine is facing the people you harmed and making amends."

"Okay?"

"I seem to recollect harming you," he said and coughed again. "One drunken night in Kandahar."

"You broke my jaw," Sampson said.

"And you covered for me, said you fell on patrol," Brooker said, lowering his hands. "I want to say I appreciated that and you in no way deserved a broken jaw. And I apologize. Seriously, I'm a different man now, someone who...ah, it doesn't matter. I'd like to shake your hand and take that memory with me as I continue my search for inner peace. But if not, I totally understand."

He took two steps forward, reached out his right hand, and held Sampson's gaze with a sincere gaze of his own.

"Fine," Sampson said, moving toward Brooker. "I don't begrudge anyone trying to find inner peace."

"Appreciate that, John," he said, a slight catch in his voice. "I really do."

Sampson reached for the former commando's hand. He heard a soft click just before Brooker gripped his hand tight and came up with a knife blade in his left hand.

He yanked Sampson forward, shoved the knife tip against his throat. "I hate to say this, what with you being a recent widower and your little girl waiting for you, but I bring you sad tidings of your imminent death, John Sampson," Brooker said. "From M."

CHAPTER

31

SEEING BROOKER'S EYES UP CLOSE like this—cold, ruthless, amoral—triggered the intensive training deep in Sampson's brain.

He no longer cared about the knife at his neck or the fact that the spook of his nightmares held it or that said spook claimed to have brought sad tidings from M. The only thing that mattered to Sampson now was that Brooker had been sent to kill him, and if he did, Willow would become an orphan.

That was not going to happen. He was not going to let that happen.

He heard a calm voice in his head say, *Weapon?*

Sampson's service gun was in the house; his backup was at his ankle.

Hand, he thought instantly. He trusted that thought.

Pick a target, the voice said.

Lower ribs, liver, he thought. And again trusted that thought. *Strike.*

Brooker smiled at the same instant Sampson used his superior size to yank out of the assassin's grip. Brooker was thrown off balance and twisted to his left.

Sampson felt the tip of Brooker's knife skitter and cut skin along the side of his neck; he pivoted on the balls of his feet and drove his left fist hard into Brooker's side about ten inches above his hip with his full weight behind it. He heard and felt the assassin's rib snap.

With a deep grunt, the killer staggered sideways across the sidewalk toward the lawn. He dropped into an odd crouch, his head and torso bent, guarding his broken rib and potential liver laceration.

Brooker was injured, no doubt, but still not down.

Weapon? the calm voice said again.

Sampson reached to get the small nine-millimeter Ruger he kept in his ankle holster just as Brooker attacked, exploding from his protective crouch and slashing the air with the knife. Sampson jumped back, the blade just missing him.

He landed on his heels, off balance, and almost went down. Brooker saw it and charged forward with the blade tip leading.

Left forearm.

Throat.

Sampson did something then that the assassin did not expect. Instead of trying to stay away from the blade or grabbing the man's wrist, he ignored the knife, found his balance, and stepped forward with his entire weight, holding his bent right arm at chin height.

He felt the stab like a gut punch at the same time the ulnar bone of his forearm smashed hard into Brooker's throat, almost crushing his larynx; they crashed off the sidewalk and onto a neighbor's lawn. Sampson felt the wind go out of him on impact. He knew the knife was in him and that he'd been wounded badly.

Brooker struggled beneath him. Sampson pushed himself up and off the knife and straddled Brooker's hips.

Though wild-eyed and gasping for air, Brooker stabbed Sampson in the thigh. Sampson howled with pain but heard that calm voice in his head again.

Weapon? Target?

He knew both answers and trusted them.

Sampson raised both fists as one and hammered them down on Brooker's solar plexus, just below the center of his rib cage. Brooker doubled up in pain but did not let go of the knife. He yanked it from Sampson's thigh and pulled back to stab him once more. Sampson smashed his right fist into Brooker's solar plexus and his left into his broken rib, again and again, and then he put his hands around the man's throat and finished crushing his larynx.

Brooker began to suffocate. His hand let go of the knife finally and his eyes lost all their ruthlessness before he lay still.

"John!" Jannie screamed. Sampson, dazed, looked back at his house and saw Alex's daughter running at him with Willow, hysterical, behind her.

Sampson started to hyperventilate and shake from the shock of being stabbed twice and all the adrenaline from the fight.

"Call 911," he gasped at Jannie before keeling over next to the man M had sent to kill him.

32

Paris

BREE STEELED HERSELF AS SHE walked toward the lion's den— a glass-faced high-rise in La Défense, France's big financial and business district, some three kilometers west of Paris's official border.

For the occasion, she wore a black pantsuit, a black silk blouse, low black pumps, and the single strand of Tahitian pearls around her neck.

Glancing at her reflection as she went to the building's main entrance, Bree told herself she certainly looked the part of a woman on the edge of business respectability. But she was about to deal with Philippe Abelmar, self-made billionaire, a man sophisticated in the ways of both business and finance.

Being married to Alex and being friends with Ned Mahoney, Bree knew a lot about shell corporations and how they were structured and interlocked. Still, as she entered the lobby and crossed to the security desk, she feared being unable to prove her capabilities, despite Marianne Le Tour's assurances earlier in the morning that her cover in Saint Martin was well documented and rock solid.

After inspecting her Saint Martin's passport, the guards made a copy and told her that she was expected and that a Monsieur L'Argent would be down to escort her to her meetings. Then they put her bag through a scanner, which made her glad that she had left the pistol in the hotel room's safe.

"Madame St. Lucie?" a man called after she'd gone through a metal detector.

It was the same big, muscular guy from Le Canard, the one who enjoyed sopping up garlic butter with the fresh bread, only now he was wearing a five-thousand-dollar suit and moving toward her with total confidence.

"We never had the pleasure of meeting properly," he said, making a half bow. "I am Luc L'Argent, personal security director to Monsieur Abelmar."

Bree smiled. "*Enchanté*. It's nice to meet properly."

"Very much so," he said and gestured toward the elevator. "I understand you are from Saint Martin and here talking with clients."

"Potential clients," she said.

They boarded the elevator. He pushed the button for the forty-ninth floor. "Monsieur Abelmar says you are in the shell-company business."

"We help people organize them and put them together with local banks," she said as they began to rise. "The

Caribbean is an attractive place for people with money. Not far from the U.S. and, of course, beautiful."

"It is that."

The elevator doors opened, and they emerged into the lobby of the French offices of the Pegasus Group. He led her inside and showed her the layout of the facility, including the currency and futures trading desks.

Then he offered her coffee, which she accepted and drank in a lounge area. Afterward, L'Argent took her to meet with three people who questioned her about her service and its merits and weaknesses.

Bree did her best to answer questions about the shell-company operation and how it might benefit Pegasus France in general and Philippe Abelmar in particular. She also did her best to walk the line between earnest and coy, legal and illegal, focusing mostly on the regions' shared language and therefore ease of doing business in Saint Martin.

After the third talk, she was taken back to the lounge area, where she sat for almost an hour before Valentina, Abelmar's young personal assistant, appeared.

"Congratulations," she said and shook Bree's hand. "Everyone is very impressed. Philippe wanted to take you to lunch but he has been called away at the last minute. Can you meet us for dinner tonight at Le Canard? Eight thirty? He has a proposal that he thinks you will find intriguing."

Bree tilted her head and gave Valentina her sincerest smile. "How could I say no to an invitation like that?"

CHAPTER

33

Fremont County, Colorado

THE ALCATRAZ OF THE ROCKIES squats in desolate high-desert country well outside the dusty town of Florence. Were it not for the pale, bulbous water tower, seen from a distance, the parapets and the upper floors of the supermax penitentiary could easily be mistaken for the low rocky bluffs and wind-carved spires that naturally jut up out of the dry, barren landscape in the area.

But the closer you get, the more you appreciate the scale and strength of the penitentiary, which features a series of massive bunkers half buried in the ground. A wall stout enough to take a tank round or two surrounds the bunkers and is topped by giant, tight-rolled spools of razor and concertina wire.

Above the wire, at the corners of the penitentiary wall, are towers with turrets and narrow, horizontal bulletproof windows that give the guards a 360-degree view of their world.

I looked all around, taking it in, as I passed through the main gate and then several hydraulic doors of steel and bulletproof glass. I showed my identification again and again as I went through one security system after another. But the entire time, most of my thoughts and prayers were with the best friend I've ever known.

Jannie had called me hysterical the previous night as I waited for a flight from LAX to Denver. Across the street from John's house, a man had stabbed Sampson twice before John was able to kill him with his bare hands.

Sampson had passed out and was rushed to GWU Hospital, where they did emergency surgery on his abdomen. The last I heard before entering the supermax was that he was in stable but serious condition in the ICU. Willow was at our home under the care of Nana Mama, Jannie, and Ali.

Please keep that good man alive, I prayed as I went through another series of steel and bulletproof-glass hydraulic gates.

On the other side, I was met in a small octagonal room by the warden. Ainsley Perrin was a small, thin woman in her fifties with faded freckles and lank red hair that kept falling in her eyes. At first, she reminded me of Pippi Longstocking, one of Jannie's favorite characters, but once Warden Perrin opened her mouth, she was all command and business.

"Dr. Cross," she said, shaking my hand. "Your reputation precedes you, but I must let you know, I disagree with Judge Sands's decision to alter part of Alejandro's sentencing guidelines. I think he should have done the full year of silence."

"He's done almost fifty weeks," I said. "And he may have

information vital to us as we investigate his cartel's role in the murders of two federal law enforcement agents and the murder of an innocent family the day before yesterday."

"Is interviewing Marco now rather than two weeks from now really going to change things?" Warden Perrin asked.

"I'm hoping it will prevent more bloodshed and more innocent lives lost," I said. "Judge Sands agrees."

"His decree is my command." She sighed. "How long do you need?"

"An hour?"

"I can give you that," she said. "But you will be separated by three inches of bulletproof glass and you will wear full stab armor. Oh, and I cannot make him talk to you if he doesn't want to."

"All we can do is try."

After putting me in green stab armor, which covered my torso and groin, she led me through a door and along a windowless hallway as she described the cartel leader's life since being sent to the Florence supermax.

For most of the past year, Marco Alejandro had been kept on a strict schedule. He was awakened at six a.m. by a bell and fed at seven, noon, and six in the evening. Guards passed him his meals through a slot in the door, and the guards were rotated weekly and forbidden to talk to him.

"Has he tried to talk to them?"

"He tried repeatedly at first," Perrin said. "Less after six months. Almost no attempts the past eight weeks other than discussions with the prison doctor and nurse during two recent trips to the prison clinic when he had kidney stones. He's evidently prone to them and has high uric acid in his blood, which means he's probably going to suffer from gout at some point. That's the difficulty of facilities like mine these days, Dr. Cross."

"What's that?"

"Florence is the end of the line for these prisoners, whether they understand it or not. The worst of the worst are sent here for life or to await execution. They will never leave."

She stopped by the sort of steel, hatch-shaped door with a wheel you might expect on a submarine and said, "This is a problem, because the worst criminals tend to mistreat themselves and age poorly. As a result, we have a growing geriatric prison population with increasing medical challenges that we, as a system, have an extremely difficult time addressing."

"I imagine so," I said.

Warden Perrin put her hand on the wheel. "Are you ready to face the devil himself, Dr. Cross? I guarantee you, he's not what you'd expect."

"I have no expectations. And there's no time like the present."

"One hour," the warden said. She threw the wheel and pushed open the hatch door for me.

CHAPTER

34

I DUCKED THROUGH THE DOORWAY and stood up in a five-by-five-foot space. A wooden chair bolted into the concrete floor faced a counter and a three-inch-thick pane of bulletproof glass two feet wide and three feet high midway up the far wall.

LED lights poking from the concrete ceiling lit the room. A small, remote-controlled camera glowed in the upper left corner.

The identically furnished room on the opposite side of the bulletproof glass was empty. The warden shut the hatch door behind me. The wheel spun the lock shut. I wondered what I'd gotten myself into.

From everything I'd read about Marco Alejandro, I knew I was dealing with a ruthless drug lord who was also a brilliant, multilingual, self-educated man who presented himself as a philosopher-king to his cartel members.

Alejandro was an alpha–alpha male who'd read, thought, connived, and murdered his way out of poverty in rural Mexico and eventually came to hold immense power as the leader of an ultra-violent, ultra-successful cartel.

Instead of sitting down to wait, I stood behind the chair and pulled myself up to my full six foot two inches to try to get a psychological edge over Alejandro, who was barely five six and, according to rumors, had had a chip on his shoulder about his height his entire life.

I didn't have to wait long to see if it was true. The big hatch door in the other room opened and three guards in helmets, visors, and full stab gear escorted Marco Alejandro inside.

Alejandro, dressed in a blue prison jumpsuit and rubber slippers, wore a restraint system the warden had shown me as I'd donned the stab suit. Keyless, digitally controlled, electromagnetic handcuffs kept Alejandro's wrists pinned to an electromagnetic belt at his waist, and around his ankles were electromagnetic cuffs connected by a length of twelve-thousand-pound-test airline cable that could be shortened with the touch of a button.

With close-cropped salt-and-pepper hair, forty-nine-year-old Alejandro was built like a gymnast—big chest, shoulders thrown back like a matador, head up, present and alert as he moved to the chair. He studied me with interest even when the guards forced him into the chair, which had an electro-magnetic plate that pinned the belt to the back. The cables retracted, giving him two inches of play between his feet.

Only then did the guards leave us alone. Only then did I come around, sit in the chair opposite him, and flip the single switch on the counter.

"Can you hear me, Señor Alejandro?"

He smiled, revealing a gold upper-left incisor and an otherwise perfect set of bright white teeth. When he spoke, it was with the barest of accents in near-perfect English. "You're only the third voice I have heard in almost a year. Who are you?"

"My name is Alex Cross," I said. "I'm a psychologist and investigative consultant to the FBI."

"Who gave you permission to talk to me before the year was gone?"

"Judge Sands."

"Judge Sands?" he said, sounding surprised. "Señor Cross, you must be a powerful and persuasive man to get that judge to change his mind."

"A number of murders, including two U.S. law enforcement agents, convinced him that my talking to you sooner might help."

Alejandro thought about that. "Why don't I have a lawyer present?"

"Because I'm not here to accuse you of anything," I said. "I'm here because there is an escalating war going on in the outside world."

"War? Where?"

"Continental United States so far," I said.

His eyes widened. "Is this true? On U.S. soil?"

I nodded. "On one side of the war is an as-yet-unidentified group that is kidnapping U.S. law enforcement agents, torturing them, getting them to confess to their corrupt ties to your cartel, and executing them. And on the other side of this war is your cartel, which, in response to one of those confessions, slaughtered the dead agent's family. Three kids. Two grandparents. The wife tortured before having her throat slit."

Alejandro took his eyes off me for the first time. "I am sorry to hear this."

"You didn't know?"

The drug lord's gaze returned to me, his expression direct, amused. "What don't you understand about a year of silence, no communication whatsoever?"

"You no longer run the cartel?"

"How could I? No, Señor Cross, I have passed my time talking to myself, wondering how life brought me to this solitude, confined to a small white room with no contact, nothing but me and the walls."

"And God."

He snorted. "The white man in the sky has not made an appearance yet. What do you want from me?"

"Your perspective," I said. "Your opinion. You know, like an athlete who retires and begins a whole new lucrative career as a commentator."

"You mean you want a snitch?"

"I want someone who can help me understand the situation enough to halt the needless killing before it develops into a full-scale war with a lot of innocent bystanders murdered in the process."

He snorted again. "You do know that you can never stop that kind of violence, Señor Cross. I've spent my whole life in it. Never once stopped. Oh, maybe a week here, a week there. But violence, fighting for what's yours, building an empire, becoming a king—that is the natural course of life. How are you going to stop life from doing its violent thing?"

35

I THOUGHT CAREFULLY ABOUT WHAT the cartel leader had just said before replying. "You have children?"

Alejandro smiled, but it was bittersweet. "Two sons, two daughters. I have not heard from them in nearly two years."

"You want your sons and daughters in the family business?"

"You'd have to make my wife my second dead wife for that to happen."

"I didn't ask if it was possible. I asked you if that was something you actively want for them, for their lives. To end up like this. I mean, like you."

His face clouded. "Screw you, Señor Cross. I'm done answering you."

"You just did answer me, Señor Alejandro," I said.

"Yeah? What'd I say?"

"The fact you got angry suggests you love your sons and

daughters and want better lives for them than the life that awaits you—no possibility of parole from that white room, where all you get to keep is silence, the memories of the good times, and the regrets."

Alejandro looked away, then shrugged. "Sure, I don't wish this life for them. Not to end up here or dead in the desert somewhere."

"No one wants that for their kids," I agreed. "Your younger daughter, Estella. How old?"

"Five."

"Two of the victims in the slaughter I described were twin girls, five years old, just like your daughter."

He tasted something sour and sensed something worse. "For real?"

"For real. And I'd like to figure out a way to stop that from happening again."

"Your problem."

"I actually see it another way. Who are the next likely targets in a retribution war? If this group killing federal agents because of their ties to your cartel want to make a statement, whose families do you think they'll go after, Marco?"

For the first time, I really got to him. Alejandro struggled and then said, "I'm not helping you take down the cartel, even if it isn't mine anymore."

"That's not what I'm asking. I just want to understand who could be behind this group killing federal agents. Any ideas? A rival cartel? DEA agents gone rogue? An old enemy of yours? If you think about it, helping me in this way only helps the cartel."

Alejandro sat there, head bobbing slightly. "But what's in it for me?"

"I am authorized to offer you access to written material, a satellite-radio receiver, and an hour a day in an exercise room."

He thought about that. "I need better food once a week and visitation rights."

"Depending on how cooperative you are, I'll see what I can do."

Alejandro nodded. "Those other things—they start today?"

"As soon as we're done here. I mean, if you can actually tell me who is at war with your cartel."

"Oh, yes, I know exactly who is doing this. They killed five of my best men a few years ago and let me know it. Texted me pictures of three of them with bullet holes in their heads. Up close. Personal."

"Who are they?"

"Real names?" Alejandro said and laughed. "I don't know if they have those. But, depending on the day, they call themselves Maestro or M."

CHAPTER

36

Paris

BREE ENTERED CANARD DE FLAQUE at eight thirty p.m. on the dot, still wearing her business attire but now back to carrying the pistol in her purse. Henri smiled and said, "It appears you make powerful friends easily, Madame St. Lucie."

"It's never happened before, Henri," she said.

"Somehow I doubt this. But come, he is waiting for you."

As she followed him toward the booth where it appeared Philippe Abelmar took most of his evening meals, she glanced over at the bar and saw Valentina sitting with Luc L'Argent, who raised his drink to her as she passed. Valentina smiled and gave her a slight wave.

Bree wanted to figure out a way to get the personal assistant alone and warn her of what might await her in the coming days if her boss held to his pattern of nurturing young female aides for six months and then debasing them and blackmailing them for the next six months.

The billionaire wore another blue blazer and crisp white shirt. He rose to meet Bree, smiled as he made a slight bow, and gestured her into the booth, where flutes of champagne awaited.

Abelmar picked up his champagne glass and raised it to her. "You appear to be a rare find, Madame St. Lucie."

Bree picked up her flute and clicked it against his. "Is that so?"

"It's rare to meet someone by chance who has skills and contacts that I and my company and contacts lack. Which is why we find you intriguing."

Before she could reply, the waitress appeared. "Shall I tell you our specials?"

Abelmar said, "I'll be having the duck."

"And I am going to have the veal dish that Carole the bartender raves about."

"The veal?" Abelmar said, surprised.

"The duck three nights in a row?"

"I have done it too many times to count."

She laughed. "I'm going to stick with the veal just the same."

The waitress nodded and left them.

The billionaire said, "May I ask you a few hypothetical questions?"

"If I can give you hypothetical answers," she said and took a sip of champagne.

"I'd prefer practical answers, if you don't mind."

"I'll try," Bree said and set the drink aside.

Abelmar asked her several hypothetical questions

regarding the establishment of shell companies and bank accounts in Saint Martin. Then he asked if it would be possible to set this up as a network throughout the Caribbean that was overseen and managed from Saint Martin.

"Of course it's possible," Bree said. "But will you excuse me one moment before I explain?"

"Bien sûr," he said.

Bree took her purse and went to the ladies' room. In a stall, she turned on her phone's voice-activated recording app and slipped the phone into the purse's outside pocket, zipper open, microphone facing up. From the first hypothetical question on, she had suspected Abelmar was looking to move money out of France to avoid taxes. Or to move the hundreds of millions of dollars he was suspected of siphoning out of Pegasus. In either case, she wanted to get him talking particulars if she could.

Having Abelmar actively discussing questionable financial activities would likely be enough for the Pegasus board to make its decision regarding the billionaire's continued involvement in the company he'd founded. And if she got lucky, she might get enough to turn over to Marianne Le Tour's contacts inside French law enforcement.

When Bree returned to Abelmar's booth, their entrées were being served. She slid into the booth after the waitress left, noticed the bottle of burgundy he'd ordered and smelled the veal in thin mushroom sauce with leeks.

"Does it look good?" he asked.

"I have no doubt it will be excellent," she said. "But I'm having trouble not gazing at your duck with longing."

"I understand completely. As I always say, it's an addiction."

They ate. The veal *was* excellent, though not as extraordinary as the duck. The amazing wine was from a Grand Cru vineyard in southern France that Abelmar told her he'd recently purchased.

Bree took small bites of her food and smaller sips of the amazing wine while trying to steer the conversation back to Saint Martin. But the billionaire was unable to stop talking about the vineyard and how he was considering moving to the estate for part of the year, although he'd need to figure out what to do with his yacht in Nice.

She wanted to say, *Problems of the mega-rich,* but she held her tongue.

Finally, after they'd finished dessert and were sipping espresso, Abelmar said, "We—Pegasus—are looking to increase our involvement with a group of wealthy investors from Mexico and Central and South America. These people need a way to diversify and protect their portfolios by spreading out not only what they invest in but the locations where their wealth is held. Does this make sense?"

"Perfect sense," she said. "So you'd be moving money into these accounts to do what, exactly? Invest in real estate or businesses in the Caribbean?"

"Among other things, yes," he said. "They are looking to do this all over the world, as a matter of fact. And, frankly, they were not looking at the Caribbean because their advisers warned them of the threat of climate change to any investment there. But you know, meeting you, I am now thinking we should move money there precisely because no one else will."

Bree nodded. "Sounds smart to me. People from the States and Europe are still going to want a warm-weather vacation during the winter for the foreseeable future."

"Exactly," Abelmar said. "Shall we continue this discussion at my apartment? It's just up the street. Walkable."

37

ABELMAR'S APARTMENT. THE PLACE WITH the secret rooms where unspeakable things had allegedly been done to a stream of young women over the past fifteen years.

Bree smiled but said, "Well, I do very much wish to continue this discussion, Monsieur Abelmar. However, I am not in the habit of accompanying powerful men to their homes late at night."

"Oh," he said. "No. Nothing like that. Luc and Valentina will be there as well. It's just more comfortable to relax there and continue our discussion."

Bree could potentially search for the secret rooms. And maybe she'd get a moment to talk to Valentina. "In that case, of course," she said, throwing all the warmth and sincerity at the billionaire that she could muster.

"Wonderful," he said and then paused. "You are up to this sort of work, yes? The needs and objectives I've described?"

"The firm I work for was made for this," she said.

"Du Champs and Vickers. We did some research. They're very, very discreet."

"*Secretive* describes us better."

"*Secretive* it is, then," Abelmar said. "Shall we?"

Bree got up from the table a bit confused. She'd thought for sure that Abelmar was looking to hide his own money or the embezzled money, and here he was, motivated by the needs of other wealthy clients. Or so he claimed.

"Please," the billionaire said, gesturing for Bree to lead the way.

With Abelmar behind her, she felt slightly uneasy. He was a monster. There was not an iota of doubt in her mind about that. The stories the women told had had too many similarities. The secret rooms. The assaults. The videotaping. The despicable demeaning and blackmailing of the young women afterward.

Yet he had been a perfect gentleman the entire night; charming, even. It didn't jibe at all with what she'd read in the horrific sealed files.

By the time Valentina and Abelmar's chief of security had come from the bar to join them, Bree had resolved her inner conflict by remembering that monsters could be wealthy, and they could also be charming when they needed to be.

Luc L'Argent led them out of the bistro. On the sidewalk, Abelmar said, "It is only a short walk up the street. Ten minutes."

"I can do that," Bree said.

"Fantastic," the billionaire said and went ahead to walk with L'Argent, leaving Bree alone with his personal assistant.

Before Bree could say anything, her cell phone rang. She looked at the number and saw it was Alex. They hadn't spoken since the day before yesterday. "Sorry, it's my brother," she said in English to Valentina. "I have to take this. I'll tell him I'll call him back later."

"Take your time," the Australian said, getting out her own phone and walking on.

Bree slowed her pace to answer. "Alex?"

"You finally picked up," Alex said.

"It's been crazy. Where are you?" Bree asked, watching Valentina walking a few yards ahead of her on the sidewalk and Abelmar and L'Argent another fifteen yards ahead of Valentina. The two men paused at an intersection and talked intently.

"Denver airport," Alex said. "Heading for home and Sampson. Did you hear?"

His question barely registered. Just as she was about to ask Alex if she could call him back, Bree heard a thud, and the front window of a shop on the corner shattered. The billionaire and his security chief were two steps out into the intersection.

In one motion, L'Argent drew his weapon and spun around to protect his boss. Before he could, a second suppressed shot blew a chunk of the security chief's head off.

He crumpled in the street. Valentina screamed. Stooped over, terrified, and sprayed with L'Argent's blood and brains, Abelmar ran back toward Bree and dove behind a small parked Citroën. One of its windows erupted. Valentina screamed again.

Bree ducked behind another small car, dropping her phone and hearing it clatter on the sidewalk as she clawed in her purse for the pistol. "Valentina!" Bree shouted. "Get down! Now!"

CHAPTER

38

Denver

I'D BEEN SITTING IN A cowboy-themed restaurant at Denver International Airport with an hour to kill until my flight home, still trying to wrap my head around everything Marco Alejandro had told me, when I dialed Bree's phone in Paris.

"Alex?" Bree said, answering for the first time in two days.

"You finally picked up," I said.

"It's been crazy," she said. "Where are you?"

"Denver airport. Heading for home and Sampson. Did you hear?" There was a noise like glass shattering; Bree grunted with surprise. "Bree?"

A woman screamed. There was another shattering sound, and the woman screamed again. I heard scuffling, then a clatter.

"Valentina!" Bree shouted. "Get down! Now!"

I could hear the slapping of shoes coming closer to the phone and a woman saying hysterically, "Luc's dead. He's really dead!"

"Bree!" I said, loud enough that the other patrons in the restaurant looked over at me. I didn't care. "Bree! Talk to me!"

An automatic weapon opened fire with a quick burst that clanked off metal. As the bullets pinged, the woman screeched with fear.

A gun went off closer to the phone, two rounds. I jumped up, digging in my pocket for cash.

"Call the police, Valentina!" I heard Bree shout. "I can't find my phone."

I threw two twenties on the table, grabbed my carry-on, and left the restaurant.

There was another burst of automatic gunfire, and the woman went insane. "Philippe!" she screamed. "No! Don't!"

I heard another burst of weapon fire, longer this time, and more pistol shots. "Bree?" I shouted.

"Valentina!" Bree called. I heard scuffling and more shots going off very close to the phone. And then the line went dead.

"Bree!" I shouted, not caring that other travelers in the hall were staring at me.

A female police officer walked up to me. "Sir? You'll have to lower your voice or—"

"I'm Dr. Alex Cross and I've been in law enforcement for twenty years, Officer Finch," I said, my voice trembling as I read her nameplate. "Working homicide in DC and now consulting for the FBI. That was my wife, a former police chief, on the phone. She's in the middle of a firefight in Paris with automatic weapons."

"No lie?"

"No lie," I said, trying to call Bree back, though I was shaking so badly, I could barely hold the phone.

"How can I help, Dr. Cross?" Officer Finch asked. "Anything."

I handed her the phone and said, "Can you hit Redial for me?"

The police officer took it, punched Redial, and gave it back to me.

After two rings, it went to voice mail. "Bree, it's Alex, call me as soon as you can." I hung up, feeling breathless and more frightened than I had in a long time. I hit Redial again, but nothing happened. I tried a third time, with the same result.

Knowing I was no use to anyone in this state, I forced myself to breathe deep and slow so I could make a decision based on logic rather than impulse.

"Is there anything else I can do?" Finch asked. "Someone I can call?"

I looked beyond her at the big electronic display showing flight departure and arrival times. A United Airlines flight to Paris was leaving from the international concourse in twenty-seven minutes.

"Dr. Cross?"

I pointed at the board. "Call the gate for the Paris flight. Tell them I have my passport and credit cards and I need any seat on that plane. It's an emergency."

Then I turned and took off like my life—and Bree's—depended on it.

CHAPTER

39

Paris

BREE WAS DOWN ON HER knees behind a small Peugeot with her pistol out. Abelmar's assistant was forward and to her right, still standing on the sidewalk. Valentina had been frozen in place and screaming since the billionaire's security chief was shot, but when Bree shouted for her, she finally ducked, ran to Bree, and crouched beside her.

"Luc's dead. He's really dead!" the young woman cried.

An automatic weapon opened fire from a rooftop on the opposite side of the street. Bree saw the muzzle flashes and heard the bullets smack the sides of the cars near Abelmar. She jumped up and aimed at where the flashes had come from, shot off two rounds, and ducked back down.

After a moment, Bree rose to peek through the windows of the Peugeot that shielded them. "Call the police, Valentina! I can't find my phone."

Valentina was hysterical, screeching with fear. The machine gun opened up again, raking the car Abelmar was crouched behind. The second the shooting stopped, the billionaire started to rise.

"Philippe!" Valentina shouted. "No! Don't!"

Abelmar took off toward them in a low charge. Bree rose up and fired twice more at the rooftop to cover him but the shots did not stop the automatic weapon from ripping the night in a sustained burst that caught the tycoon, riddled him with bullets, and cut him down. He crashed to the sidewalk.

Valentina ran to her fallen boss.

"Valentina!" Bree shouted. She emptied her pistol at the rooftop. When the action jammed open, she ducked down and sprinted to Valentina, who was draped across Abelmar, weeping and moaning. From one look, Bree could tell that Abelmar was dead.

Bree grabbed his personal assistant by the arm and dragged her away a split second before the machine gun opened fire yet again. Bullets pinged off the cars and chewed up the concrete sidewalk as the long, raking burst swept at them from behind.

CHAPTER

40

I ARRIVED AT THE PARIS gate a sweaty mess. Officer Finch had alerted the United representative at the counter, who told me they had a seat in business class available. It cost me a small fortune, even with the miles I threw at it from my frequent-flier account, but I was glad I'd done it when I settled into my window seat and got ready for takeoff.

There was a delay in departure due to a sensor malfunctioning, which allowed me to continue to dial Bree's number in Paris. After three more strikeouts, I called the Washington office of Bluestone Group and got Elena Martin on the phone.

When I told her what had happened on my call with Bree, Martin said she knew nothing about a firefight in Paris but she'd find out immediately and get back to me either by phone before we took off or by text if we'd left the ground.

I hung up and confirmed with the flight attendant that the plane had Wi-Fi.

"Something to drink?" he asked.

"How long's the flight?"

"Eleven and a half hours."

I told him I'd take a beer, and I started trying Bree again. Nothing. Ten minutes later, the pilot came on and told us the sensor issue had been resolved and we'd been cleared to button up the doors and leave for Paris.

I was about to put my phone on airplane mode until takeoff when it rang. Elena Martin.

"I can confirm a firefight in Paris in the seventeenth arrondissement," she said. "The entire area has been cordoned off and is under the control of French anti-terror police. As of now, they are not telling us anything more."

"Do we know if Bree's in there? If she's alive?"

"I'm sorry, Dr. Cross, I cannot confirm anything else. But I have Marianne Le Tour, chief of our Paris office, en route to the scene. We should know more soon."

Over the loudspeaker, the flight attendant told us to turn our phones off before we pulled back from the gate.

"Text me the second you hear anything," I said.

"Absolutely. And our thoughts and prayers are with you and Bree, Dr. Cross."

I thanked her, hung up, and switched the phone to airplane mode. The flight attendant who came to take my empty beer glass said the Wi-Fi for texting and internet would come on above thirty thousand feet.

We took off and my mind started to play tricks on me. It shifted to the oldest part of the brain, the limbic system, the reptilian place where fear and worry and terrible images and impossible questions dwell and fester.

Bree's dead, the lizard brain said. *You have to prepare yourself for it, Alex. You've been down this road before. Your first wife was taken from you without warning or mercy, a beautiful mommy out for a stroll with your young children, cut down in a senseless drive-by shooting. You don't think that kind of thing happens in Paris?*

I kept trying to counter the argument as we climbed steeply northeast away from Denver. Bree was one of the most competent and well-trained law enforcement officers I'd ever known. For a year before becoming a detective and meeting me, she'd been on the city SWAT team and knew how to handle herself in dangerous scenarios involving weapons.

But we're talking automatic weapons. What did Bree say she had with her? A small nine-millimeter? You heard several bursts of machine-gun fire, at least one of them sustained. Those shots that sounded closer could have been Bree firing back. But a machine gun versus a pistol? The odds aren't good.

This battle in my head couldn't be won, so I abandoned my mind to it, closed my eyes, and went to my heart and my faith, praying for Bree's safety, reminding the Almighty what a good and decent person she was, how human and connected she was, even in her past role as chief of detectives, where she'd had to deal with all sorts of personalities, politics, and pressures. Bree was more than my wife, my partner, my best friend, and my equal in every sense—she was my love, my greatest gift from God.

Don't take a second one from me, Lord, I prayed. *Please don't let Bree—*

A loud ding interrupted my prayer. I opened my eyes as

the loudspeaker crackled. I anticipated the flight attendant again, but the pilot's voice came on.

"Well, folks, I've got some good news from the cockpit, some not-so-good news, and some bad news. Bad news: that sensor-light issue we had on the ground is back."

People began to groan all around me.

"But the good news is we are still on our way to Paris. The sensor has nothing to do with the way we fly. It's linked to our Wi-Fi system. So while we are still expecting to touch down at de Gaulle on schedule, I'm afraid you'll have to spend your time on this flight the old-fashioned way, without text or internet."

CHAPTER

Clichy, France

WITH THE SOUNDS OF SIRENS still wailing in the distance, Matthew Butler shifted in the front passenger seat of an old gray Mercedes work van with decals on the side advertising a twenty-four-hour emergency plumbing service that did not exist. The van was crossing a bridge over the Seine, heading northwest away from Paris.

"ETA seven minutes," Butler said over his shoulder to Big DD, Cortland, and Alison Purdy, all of whom sat in the rear wearing coveralls with embroidered logos featuring the same nonexistent plumbing firm. "Let's be smooth, now. It was ugly, but we did what we came to do, so let's slip out easy, head back to the ranch."

Vincente, who was driving, said, "Make like we were never here."

Big DD grumbled, "Oh, we were definitely here."

"Don't start," Cortland said.

"It was supposed to be surgical," Purdy sniffed. "Instead, we got civilian casualties, Cort, which means they'll be hunting for us twice as hard."

"I got the job done," Cortland said. "Mission accomplished."

Butler said, "We'll discuss the ad lib later, Cort. After we get clear."

Vincente turned north on the other side of the bridge and drove them to a light industrial area in the town of Gennevilliers. Butler got out at the gate and used a combination to unlock it. He locked it behind them after Vincente drove through.

They drove around the back of a long, high-roofed metal building and past a series of shut loading docks to one where the overhead door was just rising. A stout ramp was in place against the dock.

Vincente drove up the ramp and into a large, airy space that held a machine tool-and-die business. The door lowered behind them.

He parked in front of a short, burly guy in a welding smock. Graying hair, late forties, he had huge forearms and puffed on an unfiltered cigarette while squinting at them suspiciously.

Butler climbed out and noticed the oily smell in the air immediately. "Francois."

Francois ripped the cigarette from his lips, spat a bit of tobacco on the concrete floor, and said in a thick accent, "It is done?"

"It is done."

The Frenchman nodded. A smile came slowly to his lips and then he threw his head back and laughed with gusto, shaking his hands and the cigarette at the ceiling. After that, he came at Butler and bear-hugged him so hard, the rest of his team started chuckling.

"Thank you!" Francois said, beaming as he pulled back. He gestured to the others. "From the bottom of my heart, all of you, thank you."

"Our pleasure," Vincente said as he ripped off one of the decals from the right side of the van. "Anyone who would do something like that to a man's daughter deserves punishment."

Purdy ran her fingers through her close-cropped hair. "No matter how rich the son of a bitch is."

Francois looked at Butler, his eyes glistening. "There is nothing I can ever do to repay you for this."

Butler smiled. "You can take this van apart by morning."

Cortland set a long canvas duffel at the Frenchman's feet. "The guns are already broken down into parts. I'd say melt them quick."

Francois gazed at the duffel a few long moments, nodded, and threw his arms wide. "Yes, of course, all of it! And strip off your coveralls. I will burn them in the blast furnace for you. It will be as if you were never here."

"Just the way we like it," Vincente said.

Butler removed his coverall and dressed in the casual clothes he'd stored at the shop hours earlier. After that, he grabbed a black carry-on along with his passport, wallet, and cell phone. When he turned it on, it almost immediately pinged, alerting him to a text: Call Maestro.

He was about to do so when Francois came up to him.

"The Land Rover is waiting for you outside whenever you are ready."

"Thank you."

The burly Frenchman put his hand on his heart. "And if you happen to talk to M, tell him a grateful father sends his sincere regards."

CHAPTER

42

Washington, DC

IN THE INTENSIVE CARE UNIT at GWU Hospital, John Sampson groggily opened his eyes to see his young daughter, Willow, standing at his bedside grinning at him through tears of joy.

Overwhelming relief filled Sampson. He had been spared. He was still alive for his little girl.

Before he could say anything, a bolt of pain shot through his gut. He gritted his teeth and moaned but kept his smile alive for Willow until the agony passed. Then he shifted his right leg and felt another spasm of pain go through his thigh.

"Hi, baby," Sampson said in a croak when the spasm passed.

"Hi, Daddy," she said, still crying. "The doctor said don't move much."

"Just figured that out," he said, noticing that Nana Mama, Jannie, and Ali were also in the hospital room. "What day is it?"

Jannie said, "July first. You were stabbed last night, right around this time."

"Been out ever since," Nana Mama said. "You gave us a fright, John."

Willow said, "I have never been so scared in my life, Daddy."

Ali, who looked tired, said, "She wouldn't go to sleep last night because she didn't want to wake up an orphan."

"You kept trying to leave the room," Willow said.

"No, I didn't."

"Yes, you did."

Jannie said, "Anyways, Willow's been here all day, waiting."

Sampson's daughter took her eyes off Ali and said, "I wanted to be here when you woke up, Daddy. I wanted to be the first thing you saw."

John felt such exploding love, his head swam. It took several moments for him to say, "And you were, baby. Thank God, you were."

A big force of nature named Juanita Alvarez chugged through the open door behind them wearing hospital scrubs and a stethoscope around her neck.

"Too many people," the nurse said in a singsong voice. "Who let you all in here?"

Ali said, "You did."

"I must have been out of my mind," Juanita said, smiling as she went to the other side of Sampson's bed to check his IV lines and the monitors. "We thought you were going to sleep all week, Detective. The staff's been calling you 'patient RVW.'"

"RVW?"

"Rip van Winkle," she said and laughed. "That's pretty funny, you have to admit."

"How bad am I?" Sampson asked.

"You're pretty damn good, considering," Juanita said. "The knife wound to the thigh missed your femoral artery, and the one to your abdomen got only a little of one lobe of your liver. They had to remove a chunk, but luckily the liver grows back."

He was becoming more alert. "How long until I can leave?"

She shrugged. "A few days? They're going to want to see that you don't show signs of infection and that you're on your feet walking."

"Walking?" he said, anticipating the pain of that. "When?"

Juanita looked up at the clock on the wall. It was seven thirty in the evening. "I'd like to see you on your feet before midnight," she said. "But let's get you peeing on your own first."

"Why? Doesn't it work?" Willow said and broke into infectious giggles. Soon they were all laughing, even Sampson, although he tried not to and grimaced when he did.

"Glad I could provide comic relief," he said when the laughter died down.

Juanita said, "She is a funny little thing, isn't she?"

Sampson gazed at his daughter and smiled. "She is that. Got it from her mom. Where are you staying, baby?"

"At Uncle Alex and Aunt Bree's house," Willow said.

He frowned. "Where is Alex?"

"On his way to Paris," Ali said.

Nana Mama nodded. "He texted us that Bree was in trouble and he was taking a plane straight there from Denver."

"What kind of trouble?"

Jannie glanced at Nana Mama before saying, "There was some kind of terrorist attack in Paris. Bree was involved. That's all we know."

CHAPTER

43

Paris

THE LAST TWENTY MINUTES OF the flight were endless. I barely got an hour of sleep despite the reclining seat and I was feeling frayed as we made our approach to the city almost twelve hours later.

As we came in for a landing, I prayed for Bree, as I had on takeoff and a hundred times since. And I prayed for myself, asking for the strength to carry on should the worst-case scenario prevail. My stomach lurched when we touched down. My fingers trembled as I turned on my phone.

I expected a barrage of texts but got only one, from a number I did not recognize. It said: You'll thank me later—M.

Before I could digest that, my phone started to go haywire. The housing got hot, the screen flashed several times, and it shut down. I started it again and tried to call Elena Martin but I got an error tone and a recording in French. The same thing happened when I tried to call my home phone and Jannie's cell.

It was maddening, but I managed not to explode with frustration as we pulled up to the gate. I had my carry-on down the second the seat-belt sign dinged off and was fourth in line for the door.

When it opened at last, my entire focus was getting through to a Wi-Fi connection as soon as possible. But I had taken only one step beyond the plane door when a man said, "Dr. Cross?"

He was tall, black, and wore a full SWAT outfit. He was also carrying a submachine gun. So was the shorter woman beside him.

"Yes?" I said.

"Directorate for Internal Security," the big man said, opening a side door off the Jetway. "You will come with us, please."

There's no arguing with agents of the French organization dedicated to counterterrorism, so I went through the door and down the steep staircase. Two other French agents similarly clad and armed were waiting at the bottom.

When the tall agent reached the tarmac, he said, "Are you carrying a weapon?"

"No," I said.

"We must be sure. Turn around. Hands on the stair railings."

I did as he asked and spread my legs as well. He patted me down thoroughly and then used a metal-detecting wand.

"Passport," the female agent said when he was done. "And your phone, please."

I got both from the top pocket of my carry-on and handed them to her. "Can I ask what this is all about?"

"You can ask," she said. "But we cannot give you answers because we do not know them. We are here to transport you, nothing more."

The big agent's name tag read HEBERT; the female agent's read RIVIÈRE.

"Where are we going?" I asked as they led me toward a waiting black van.

"To a place with no name," Hebert said.

Rivière said, "Which is why we cannot let you see the route there."

I didn't like it but I climbed inside the van. "Please, can you at least tell me if my wife is alive? I believe she was caught in the middle of the terrorist attack in the seventeenth arrondissement last night."

"Again, Monsieur Cross," Hebert said as I took a seat by a blacked-out window facing black drapes separating us from the driver, "we do not know. In terror cases, this is how it works until authorities decide to talk."

The rear door shut. The van started moving.

"But the attack must have been reported on the radio," I said. "There must be basic publicly known facts you can share with me. Are there confirmed dead?"

Rivière looked at Hebert, who said, "There are multiple confirmed dead and wounded. Victims have not yet been identified."

Multiple confirmed dead… "What else?"

"The terrorists were on rooftops shooting down at people in the streets."

"Arrests?"

"None," Hebert said. "They managed to elude police and remain at large."

"No leads?"

"Not our job, sir. The investigation continues."

I had no idea where they were going or how long we drove. I was so tired, my chin dropped and I dozed deep and dark.

Rivière shook me awake. "We're here, Dr. Cross."

The van's door slid back. We were in an underground garage facing a set of bulletproof glass doors. Two armed agents stood between the van and the door as I stepped out. Rivière and Hebert stayed with the van when the doors slid closed.

The new agents walked behind me down a short hall to an elevator, which opened for us. I immediately caught a whiff of an unmistakable odor: the cleaning liquid used to scour morgues.

CHAPTER

44

I WOBBLED ON MY FEET and had to put my hand out on the wall of the elevator to keep from collapsing. Clearly, they were taking me to identify Bree's body.

As the elevator doors closed, I breathed in through my nose again and smelled that same vile odor I associate with autopsies. We rose. My stomach churned. I thought I was going to be violently ill in the small space.

Bree is dead. Why else bring me to a morgue?

The elevator stopped. The doors opened into a large, high-ceilinged space that bustled with a good fifty agents, most in plainclothes and carrying pistols in shoulder harnesses or hip holsters, working phones and making notes in French on huge whiteboards set up all around the room.

Here and there stood several large video screens. One showed a 3-D rendition of what I assumed was a Parisian street.

There was a bigger crowd standing around the farthest screen, which was showing an aerial view of that same street. We walked up to the back of the crowd, where a woman in her fifties turned, smiled, and shook my hand.

"Inspector Simone Marché with French counterterrorism, Dr. Cross," she whispered. "We know your work and welcome you."

I was about to say, *Can you please tell me if my wife's alive?* when I heard a weary but familiar voice speaking in French.

"Bree!" I shouted.

My wife stood in front of the screen next to a tall, willowy woman with steel-gray hair. Bree looked like she'd been through hell, but when she saw me, she grinned with relief. Agents moved aside as we walked to each other, both with tears in our eyes. We threw our arms around each other and people began to clap.

"Oh, Alex, you don't know how much I needed you here."

"And you don't know what it took me to get here."

She drew back from the embrace. "Thank you. For loving me enough to…" Bree couldn't go on and buried her head in my chest, weeping.

Inspector Marché came up and said, "She's been through a lot, and we haven't been easy on her."

The willowy woman walked up and introduced herself as Marianne Le Tour of Bluestone Group's Paris office.

"Can she leave now?" Le Tour asked Marché. "So she can get some sleep?"

"We should hold her," Marché said. "There is still the matter of the gun."

"She had a legitimate permit," Le Tour said. "And thank

God she had the gun, Inspector, or who knows if Valentina Ponce would still be alive."

"Allowing her to walk after she participated in a firefight in the streets of Paris is going to be a difficult thing for me to sell to my superiors."

"Can you tell me what happened?" I asked.

Marché hesitated and then said, "We believe one person, maybe more, got access to the basement of a building nearly two blocks from the shooting. All the buildings in the seventeenth are connected in one way or another. These people somehow knew the route. They got to the top of an apartment building near the restaurant Canard de Flaque and shot Philippe Abelmar's chief of security with a silenced weapon."

Bree nodded and said, "After that, they shifted to an automatic weapon to draw out Abelmar and kill him."

"Your wife is a very brave woman, Dr. Cross," Inspector Marché said. "She rescued Abelmar's young personal assistant while the bullets were still raining down."

Bree shook her head. "I thought for sure they were going to cut us in half, but they stopped shooting when the bullets were less than a foot away. Valentina and I weren't targets, I guess."

"They were professionals, no doubt," Marché said. "Which is why I suspect this is not terrorism but an assassination."

"Motive?" I said.

Marianne Le Tour said, "I've got one. Desmond Slattery, our financial expert, has been looking into the books of the Pegasus Group, especially the Paris operation. There appear to be ties to accounts in banks in Mexico that have been known to do business with the Alejandro cartel."

"Wait, what?" I said. "From here?"

"It fits, Alex," Bree said. "Abelmar was talking to me about setting up shell companies to move money to the Caribbean."

"This also fits," I said, reaching into my pocket for my cell phone. "Before I flew here, I was able to interview Marco Alejandro in prison in Colorado. He told me that the cartel itself has been under attack for years from a group of people known as Maestro or M."

I showed them the text I'd received when I landed. "I've been getting texts from this M for years and always assumed it was a single person. But Alejandro convinced me that Maestro is actually a group of people acting in concert under the command of a leader they call M."

"You think this Maestro group is behind the shooting in the seventeenth?" Marché said.

"I do. I also believe M or someone in Maestro stopped the shooter from cutting down Bree and Abelmar's personal assistant."

CHAPTER

45

Schiphol Airport, Amsterdam

MATTHEW BUTLER SAT IN THE KLM/Delta lounge, forced another espresso shot down his throat, and picked up his cell phone. He had not slept in nearly thirty hours but could not afford the luxury of closing his eyes and resting when there were so many tasks at hand.

He called a number in Luxembourg that transferred him through towers and stations around the world before he got an answer.

"Mmm?"

"Sorry not to have called earlier, M," Butler said. "I thought it wise to wait until we'd left France. The cartel's international financier is no more. Francois sends his regards and deepest thanks."

"I'm glad we could kill two birds with one stone. Cross's wife?"

"We didn't touch her. Though she almost got Cortland."

"We can expect a retaliation of some sort from the cartel. What is your ETA at the ranch?"

"Fifteen hours?"

There was a long pause. "Once you get there, lie low for a month. You're getting too hot."

The line went dead. Butler immediately punched in a second number.

"Circle M Ranch," a man said. "Dexter Mann speaking."

"It's Matt, Dex," Butler said. "How's the weather?"

"Gonna rain but we got in that first cut on the alfalfa yesterday, so we won't lose a thing there."

"You moving the herd up onto Forest Service?"

"I'm taking Wheeler and Sandy up in the morning to start."

"Sounds like we'll be around the ranch for a while. The next month, anyway."

"Well, we've a couple miles of fence down on the upper pasture."

"Fence work never ends."

"Never does," Mann said. "Safe travels, boss."

CHAPTER

46

Paris

INSPECTOR MARCHÉ FINALLY RELEASED BREE around noon. We went to her hotel and both of us collapsed into a long, dreamless sleep that left us a little befuddled when we woke around six that evening.

Elena Martin texted us both (Bree's phone had been found, and mine was working properly again) and offered to have her office arrange our flights home, which we gladly accepted. Next, we made a FaceTime call to Ali's phone. But my grandmother answered; she peered at the screen as if it were some crystal ball before smiling.

"You're both good!"

"I texted you and told you that, Nana."

"I know, but I had to see for myself."

Bree waved at her. "We are intact. All fingers and toes. Where are the kids?"

"Jannie's with Willow at the hospital. John may be able to leave the day after tomorrow."

"That's great news," I said. "Where's Ali?"

"Sleeping, the last time I looked."

"Okay, then. We're going to go. We're on a plane tomorrow morning and should be home by dinner."

Nana Mama smiled. "I promise you it will be a good one."

After we hung up, I told Bree, "I need to exercise. Do something to clear my head."

"We'll shower and go for a walk," Bree said. "We're in Paris and it's so beautiful at night, Alex. I want to show you."

Refreshed by our showers, we called Sampson's hospital room and got him on the phone. He'd had a solid sleep and needed fewer painkillers.

"Sounds like the trip to Montana is off for this year," I said.

"Not if I can help it," Sampson said. "The docs say I was lucky and should recover in five or six weeks or so. Still gives us enough time."

"Let's play it by ear. Did Master Sergeant Brooker say anything to you before he attacked you?"

"He said a lot of things, but when he was about to kill me, he said he'd been sent by M to do it."

We told him about M possibly being involved in Abelmar's murder and about how Marco Alejandro believed Maestro was a group of people led by M.

"Makes more sense," Sampson said. "I was beginning to think he was everywhere at once. But why kill me?"

I closed my eyes. "I don't know. And I don't know why they decided to save Bree in Paris. Or why they're fighting the cartel and us at the same time. I'm struggling to understand the agenda."

"So am I," Sampson said. He paused. "I gotta go. My doc just walked in."

"Get better."

"ASAP," he said and hung up.

Bree and I left the hotel around seven, with the air still warm, and the sun just setting. The light on the Seine was golden and we stopped often just to look around us at the sheer grandeur of the city.

Along the way, Bree brought me up to speed on all that had transpired in the few days she'd been in Paris, including how she'd been about to warn Abelmar's personal assistant that she was in danger just before the shooting started.

"Are you going to tell her?" I asked.

"I'm going to make sure the Pegasus board of directors tells her," Bree said. "What else did you and Marco Alejandro talk about?"

"He said Maestro has been sabotaging the cartel's business for nearly a decade. Disrupting shipments, bombing drug labs, assassinating high-ranking cartel members. He also blamed Maestro for hacks into cartel computers that wreaked havoc on their accounting and tracking systems."

"No idea who they are?"

I shook my head. "No names, but Alejandro had all sorts of theories. The most compelling had M as the strategist and director of a small army of mercenaries and former agents of U.S. law enforcement upset by corruption."

"What's the big motive?" Bree asked. "Maestro's? M's?"

"I can't figure that out," I said. "On the one hand, they're engaged in a private war with the cartel and corruption. On the other, M claims to have killed Billie Sampson and sent an assassin after John. M's been taunting us for years, sometimes helping us, sometimes interfering. What's the angle?"

"Maybe personal?" Bree suggested. "Maybe somewhere in the past, you offended M or thwarted Maestro or did something that stuck in their craws."

"I don't know."

We wandered by a restaurant that smelled incredible.

"I'm hungry all of a sudden," Bree said. "Part of me wanted to take you to Canard for the duck, but we're right here."

We went in and were lucky to find a table for two at the back. I ordered a bottle of champagne with dinner to celebrate life, and we vowed not to talk about crime the rest of the evening.

After we'd toasted and taken a sip of the champagne, Bree reached across the table and took my hand. "I want to tell you how touched I am, how wonderful I felt when I found out you'd jumped on a plane to Paris just because you thought I was in danger."

Gazing into her tear-filled eyes, I said, "There was no thought about it. The decision was just made and I had to go. My baby needed me."

"She did," Bree said. "She does."

"I admit I was scared on the flight over. Not being able to do anything for twelve hours—it makes a guy's mind play tricks on him."

"I've never known you to be scared of much, Alex. What were you afraid of?"

"A life without you."

"Aww," she said and reached up to stroke my cheek. "You don't have to be afraid of that ever."

"Some things are out of our control," I said, touching

the back of her hand. "But not my love for you. That is forever."

Bree smiled and flushed, and her eyes sparkled. "You are on fire tonight."

"It's Paris. And the champagne."

She laughed and sat back in delight. "Alex Cross turns romantic! Yet another reason to love this place. It's just magical what it does to people, isn't it?"

CHAPTER

47

Washington, DC

IN THE SIX WEEKS THAT followed our return from France, life became a lot less hectic. No other federal agents were killed by Maestro, and no innocent families were attacked by the Alejandro cartel.

Elena Martin had given Bree a hefty bonus and a week's vacation after her ordeal in Paris, both of which were unexpected and appreciated.

John Sampson's surgeons were impressed by his progress and released him from the hospital three days after his stabbing. He got up on his own and walked from the wheelchair to my car—a little hunched over and limping on the right leg, but he did it. He climbed into my front passenger seat dripping with sweat.

"That hurt?"

"You have no idea," he said through gritted teeth. "But

that's not stopping me from getting out of that hospital. People die in those places, you know."

"Yeah, I'd heard that," I said and drove him home.

At the end of July, my older boy, Damon, came home for two weeks after his stint as a camp counselor was done. He and I and Ali and Jannie played a lot of basketball before he headed back to Davidson, where he was to be a resident adviser in a freshman dorm.

Ali often seemed tired and cranky, which was unusual. Ordinarily, my youngest is upbeat and full of energy. Nana Mama had commented on the constant yawning and grumpiness as well, and I was thinking about taking him to his pediatrician.

After a month and a half of rehab, Sampson was walking three miles a day without the cane. He had recently returned to work when we both got a call from Ned Mahoney at a quarter to six on a Thursday morning.

"We've got another body with a confession," he said. "I want you both there."

"Where?" I asked.

"Congressional Country Club," Mahoney said.

Thirty minutes later, we pulled into the parking lot of the toniest golf club in the greater DC area. I got out and offered to help John, but he waved me off.

"I got this, Alex," Sampson said, though he looked stiff climbing from the car and he limped a little when we walked over to meet Ned.

"We've got a problem," Mahoney said. "Victim is DEA, and the DEA got here first."

"Where's 'here'?" I asked.

"Eighteenth hole."

There were five of them in DEA windbreakers when we came around the side of the country club and approached the eighteenth hole, where a body was propped up and lashed to the flagpole. Male, Hispanic, and slightly bigger than a horse jockey, he had been badly beaten and shot in the face.

One of the DEA agents, a woman in her forties with pale skin and brassy-red hair, noticed us and came our way with both hands up. "Whoever you are, back off."

"Supervising Special Agent Mahoney, FBI," Mahoney said. "This is our case."

"The hell it is," she said. "I am Special Agent in Charge Jill Hanson and the victim was one of our best."

"Be that as it may, Special Agent in Charge Hanson, the FBI has had control of this investigation since CIA officer Catherine Hingham's body was dumped with her confession almost two months ago."

"Be *that* as it may, Supervising Special Agent Mahoney," she said, "we are gathering our own evidence and will conduct our own internal investigation as well."

Mahoney was not happy. "I want the confession."

"What confession?"

"The one the groundskeeper saw," Ned said. "The one in the envelope."

"Oh," Hanson said. "No, we are keeping that until the allegations can be looked into by our internal investigations team."

"Are you looking for a federal injunction or something?"

"Bring it," she said, smiling. "In the meantime, the confession stays with us. Don't worry, it's been properly bagged and entered into our evidence logs."

"Can you at least identify the deceased?" I said.

"DEA Special Agent Eddie Hernandez," she said. "He was a superstar in Albuquerque who transferred here to work intelligence three months ago."

Sampson said, "Mr. Hernandez have a family?"

"Married. Two kids—a boy, ten, and a girl, seven."

"I advise you to move them, put them under witness protection," I said.

"Cartel won't go after them," Hanson said. "They've gotten the man they wanted."

"I don't think the cartel did this," Mahoney said.

"I do," she said. "This was payback for our taking down Marco Alejandro, pure and simple."

"Maybe you're trying to protect your department's hero," I said. "But his surviving family members are in danger."

Hanson said nothing.

Sampson said, "Do you really want to be responsible for two dead kids and their dead mom?"

The DEA supervising special agent's jaw tightened and then she stomped off, digging her cell phone from her pocket.

CHAPTER

48

MATTHEW BUTLER WORE AN EARPIECE and carried a microphone and a small video camera as he slipped among the satellite trucks and reporters already swarming the parking lot of the Congressional Country Club. In his pocket, he carried the ID of Harry Falk, a freelance radio reporter and internet blogger.

Butler's camera was on. He panned it beyond the yellow police tape, saw DEA, FBI, and other investigators moving about the scene.

"Were you clean?" the familiar voice said in his ear.

"Spotless in and out," Butler muttered into the mike.

"All cameras?"

"Everything on their network was neutralized."

"Your team?"

"On their way back to the ranch. I'll follow tomorrow. I'm guessing we can expect another retaliation?"

"And more civilian casualties. It's how they operate in Mexico—they use the deaths of innocents to sow terror."

Butler kept panning the camera around the scene. "We have another target?"

"Several domestically, but in anticipation of the cartel's counterattack, I think it's time we take it to their territory, let *their* families feel vulnerable, exposed. They'll start making mistakes and—stop. Go back left with the camera."

Butler did.

"Stop. Zoom in on the two big African-Americans talking to the short white guy in the suit."

Butler pressed the zoom button and brought the three men into tight view. "Who are they?" Butler asked.

"Big guy on the left is Dr. Alex Cross, an FBI consultant regarded as one of the best investigators in the country. Guy in the suit is Special Agent Ned Mahoney of the FBI, Cross's former partner and the Bureau's go-to in a crisis. Big guy on the right is John Sampson, Cross's best friend and a detective on DC's homicide team. Also a very tough man. You are seeing Sampson six weeks after he was stabbed by a pro who was trying to kill him and whom he killed instead."

"Impressive. Our pro?"

"The impostor's."

"Really?" Butler said. "What's his beef with Sampson?"

"We're dealing with a sick mind, so I can't tell you. But Cross, Sampson, and Mahoney make a formidable team and we should not underestimate them in any way. Let's start keeping tight tabs on all three of them."

"Geo-location?"

"Their phones, anyway. I want to know where those three are at all times."

CHAPTER

49

AFTER SEVERAL MOMENTS OF STRATEGIZING, Mahoney called his FBI superiors to work out clear jurisdiction on the case. Sampson and I returned to our car and drove to Falls Church, Virginia, where the late DEA Agent Eddie Hernandez had lived with his wife, Rosella, and their children, ten-year-old Eddie Jr. and seven-year-old Naomi.

The house was in an older neighborhood of split-level ranches and short driveways with basketball hoops mounted above many of the garage doors. I pulled over across the street from the Hernandez residence, where a painting crew was at work scraping and priming the exterior in blistering heat.

We'd no sooner arrived than a tan minivan pulled into the driveway and Rosella Hernandez exited the house with the children behind her, the kids dressed for day camp and carrying knapsacks. She kissed them both, got them into the van, and began talking animatedly with the driver, who appeared to be another mom.

"Jesus," Sampson said. "She doesn't know."

"What the hell is going on? The DEA swarms the scene but doesn't dispatch someone to inform the superstar's wife that her husband's dead?"

"It's not like we haven't had this terrible chore before," Sampson said, opening the car door as the minivan pulled away. Rosella waved to her children and turned to speak to one of the painters.

I steeled myself and then climbed out of the car and walked across the street.

"Mrs. Hernandez?" I said, holding up my credentials. "My name is Alex Cross. I'm an investigative consultant to the FBI. This is Detective John Sampson with DC Metro Police."

Her head cocked to one side. "Yes? How can I help you?"

"Is there somewhere we can talk?"

Twenty minutes later, we were all sitting in Rosella's kitchen, and her initial shock had turned to anguish. Her sobs shook her from head to toe. "Eddie said he was going to a training program for a few days. He said he'd be back for Naomi's birthday." She shook her head in bewilderment. "What am I going to tell her and little Eddie? It's going to break his heart. He idolizes his dad."

"Do you have family around here?"

"No," she said. "Everyone is back in New Mexico."

There was a loud knock at the front door. I offered to get it, and the DEA agent's widow nodded.

I could hear Sampson telling her about Billie as I walked down the hallway to the front screen door to find Supervising

Special Agent Jill Hanson standing there with two other DEA agents.

"What are you doing here?" Hanson demanded.

"What *you* should have been doing instead of tampering with our crime scene," I said. "Consoling a grieving widow."

"I'm going to have to ask you to leave, Dr. Cross."

"And I am going to have to refuse, Special Agent in Charge Hanson. Every action you've taken today stinks of cover-up."

"There's no cover-up," Hanson shot back. "We just want to talk to...oh, hello, Rosella. I'm so sorry for your loss."

I looked over my shoulder to see the new widow standing about ten feet behind me with Sampson at her back.

"Thank you, Jill," Rosella said coldly. "I'd have thought you'd be here sooner."

"It's been chaotic. May I come in and talk to you? Dr. Cross said he was just leaving."

"No, I didn't."

Hernandez's widow glanced at me and then back at Hanson. "You'll have to wait outside, Jill, until I'm done talking to Dr. Cross and Detective Sampson."

"I would like to hear what you have to say to them as well," Hanson said.

"Not now," Rosella said, and she headed back to the kitchen. "Can you shut the door for me, Dr. Cross?"

"With pleasure," I said and slowly shut the door in the DEA agent's face.

50

ROSELLA HERNANDEZ LED US BACK into her kitchen. She trembled as she walked and had to put her hand on the wall several times. I thought it was due to her grief, but when she sat down, she looked hard as nails.

"Before I say a word, I want witness protection for me and for my children and my entire family back in New Mexico. And Eddie's too," she said. "I want the U.S. Marshals Service arranging for us to disappear. Tonight."

I said, "We don't have that authority, Mrs. Hernandez."

"Then call someone who does," she said and sat back, her arms crossed. "I know things."

I went into another room, called Mahoney, and explained the situation.

"She credible?"

"She hasn't said anything yet," I replied. "But she acts like she's holding aces."

"I'll call Justice and get it rolling. But Alex, I'm going to need something concrete to convince them to move her and the children into witness protection that fast."

"I'll call the second I have it."

After we hung up, I went back into the kitchen. Rosella looked at me. "Well?"

"We're getting DOJ approval before we talk to the U.S. Marshals office. But we need to hear something that justifies witness protection or no deal."

Rosella thought a few moments, then said, "The DEA? U.S. Customs? ICE? Border Patrol? Police in all border states? Riddled with corruption. All of them. Even FBI down there. You know what? It's understandable. There's so much money and so many reasons to take it."

"From the Alejandro cartel?"

"No doubt."

Rosella said she had been a New Mexico state trooper before she joined the DEA, and she'd met her husband shortly afterward. Eddie Hernandez was assigned to be her partner and trained her. Though they tried to keep their relationship professional, the attraction between them had been immediate and intense.

"I fell in love with Eddie the moment I met him," she said, shaking her head. "It's what made me blind to it all while I was at the agency. I didn't last long. I got pregnant and resigned so we could marry. By then I already suspected Eddie wasn't true blue but I ignored it. Until I couldn't."

"Extra cash around a lot?" Sampson asked.

Rosella looked in her lap and nodded. "Eddie said almost everyone working down near the border took some at some point. Especially if you had a family. See? That's one way they get you."

According to Rosella, the Alejandro cartel kept tabs on new agents and waited until they were in a financial squeeze before approaching them with a small bribe, something easy to take, easy to justify as a onetime deal. But the hook was set and they kept you on the line. "The money got bigger as you became a bigger fish," she said.

"Like Eddie coming here to work intelligence?" I asked.

She nodded again. "It gave the cartel a direct line into what the honest agents were doing and what those agents knew about the cartel's activities."

"But I thought Eddie was part of the team that put away Marco Alejandro," Sampson said.

"At a certain point, everyone on both sides of the border knew that Marco was going down. He'd gotten too big, too public. In the end, Eddie gave his allegiance to the cartel, not the man who founded it."

"Where's Eddie's money?" Sampson asked.

"Various security boxes around the country," she said. "And he changed a lot of it into cryptocurrencies. That's where it's all going these days, Eddie said. According to him, eventually cash will become irrelevant and governments will be unable to trace digital currency."

"Do you know the names of other corrupt agents?"

Rosella straightened in her chair. "I do, but I won't name them and I won't tell you how I know until we're safely in witness protection."

"But you will testify as to what you know?" Sampson said.

She hesitated before nodding. "If that's what it takes to protect my kids, yes."

"Is Special Agent Hanson on the take?" I asked.

"I don't think so," she said. "Eddie seemed leery of her. But better safe than sorry. I hate to sound paranoid, but you have to protect us if I'm going to blow this wide."

"We'll protect you from the cartel," I said.

"The cartel?" she said. "I'm more worried about whoever killed Eddie."

"You have suspicions?"

Rosella pursed her lips and closed her eyes for a moment before saying, "A couple of years ago, two DEA agents were shot to death in the desert outside Nogales, Arizona. Eddie said he believed it was a rogue law enforcement insider, probably DEA, who'd gone vigilante against agents on the take."

"Eddie knew who it was?" Sampson said.

"No, but the killer left a note on an index card on one of their bodies saying both agents were completely corrupt and deserved to die. Eddie said DEA covered the note up, but it was signed *Maestro*."

51

WE WAITED UNTIL NED MAHONEY arrived to talk with Rosella Hernandez while her demand for federal witness protection worked its way up the chain of command at the Department of Justice.

Mahoney also had orders from the U.S. Attorney General's office for DEA Special Agent in Charge Jill Hanson; she was directed to stand down, cooperate with the FBI, and immediately hand over all pertinent evidence. Including the confession.

Hanson was furious but did as she was told. Within minutes we had the evidence bag containing the bloodstained, unopened confession. We read it inside Rosella's house as she worked with two officers from the U.S. Marshals to pack in anticipation of a move.

Written in a shaky scrawl, the late Eddie Hernandez's

confession corroborated and gave details on what his wife had told us. The agent had been compromised his second year with DEA, taking a twenty-five-thousand-dollar bribe to look away when the Alejandros ran ten pounds of illegal fentanyl across the border. It was a test and Eddie passed.

By the time his wife-to-be joined the agency and came under his influence, Eddie was socking away nearly two hundred grand in cartel cash every year. But the Alejandros had bigger plans for him. They wanted Eddie to rise up the chain of command so they would have access to the best intelligence regarding threats to their empire. The cartel helped him along the way, sacrificing low-level soldiers and lieutenants in return for Eddie's increasing stature and influence inside the DEA.

With his transfer to Washington, the agent had expected to earn a million dollars a year for his services to the Alejandros. In the confession, Eddie listed his bank accounts, the location of his security boxes, and the information required to access his cryptocurrency stashes. He also named ten other agents on the take in New Mexico, Arizona, California, and Texas. Special Agent Hanson, his superior in Washington, was not among them and was clearly shaken when Mahoney invited her inside to read the confession.

"I vetted Eddie myself," Hanson said. "I told you, I thought he was a damned superhero."

"Someone else knew he wasn't," I said. "Any ideas who that might be?" Before she could reply, Mahoney's cell rang. He turned away and answered.

I said, "Mrs. Hernandez says there's a vigilante named Maestro killing corrupt agents in the Southwest."

Hanson nodded. "At least five we know of."

Mahoney lowered his phone. "We've got a break. Whoever hacked the security system at the Congressional Country Club didn't know about a battery-operated night-vision still-photo camera independent of the system and mounted overlooking the terrace. It caught one of the killers. They're sending over the picture now."

His phone dinged. He opened the attachment. The still showed a tall, rangy man in a white coverall crossing the terrace and headed toward the green where Hernandez's body had been found. The man's entire face was clearly visible.

"Facial-recognition software?" I asked.

"Quantico's already running it," Mahoney said. His phone dinged again. He looked at the screen in shock. "They've got him."

"Already?" Sampson said.

"Immediate hit, hundred percent accuracy," Mahoney said, scrolling down the new attachment. "Dale Cortland. Former U.S. Army Ranger. Private contractor in Afghanistan who…damn!"

"What?"

"Cortland was killed by a sniper outside Kandahar nearly five years ago."

CHAPTER

52

AROUND FOUR THAT AFTERNOON, THE DOJ approved the Hernandez family's move into the federal witness protection program. I had to take Nana Mama to a doctor's appointment and left the house as Sampson and Mahoney continued interviewing Rosella.

Special Agent Hanson was on the porch. I scanned the area, saw a few other agents I recognized from earlier in the day.

"No satellite news trucks," I said.

"We're keeping Eddie unidentified until Rosella and the kids are gone. Marshals will be here after dark."

"And they'll slip out and vanish."

"As if they never existed," Hanson said. "I'm sorry I got in your face this morning, Dr. Cross."

"Emotions run high when someone you trust dies like that."

"Makes me sick now, knowing he didn't deserve that trust. My trust."

"Until we meet again, Special Agent Hanson," I said and offered my hand.

She shook it. "Under better circumstances, I hope."

I left, walked down the street, and called an Uber. On the ride, I tried to wrap my mind around the clear photo of Dale Cortland outside the country club almost five years after a bullet from a .50-caliber gun had reportedly torn his head off in Afghanistan.

We'd heard rumors, of course, of deep, secret groups operating within the U.S. intelligence apparatus whose members were people like Cortland, soldiers whose deaths were staged so they could operate with impunity while the government denied their very existence. After all, the soldiers were dead. The official death certificates said so.

Was that what we were facing? A group of dead people with nothing to lose taking on the biggest drug cartel in the world?

I still had no answers to those questions when I got home and found Nana Mama dressed and waiting. We turned right around and got another Uber. On the ride, she said, "Ali's tickled pink about something and can't wait to tell you."

Before I could reply, my cell phone rang. Caller ID said it was DC Metro Police.

"This is Alex Cross," I said.

"This is Detective Wendy Sutter, Dr. Cross," she said. "Do you remember me?"

"How could I forget?" I said. "The Gabe Qualls case."

"That's right," she said. "I'm calling to tell you your son's been at it again."

Inwardly, I groaned. "Sticking his nose into another investigation of yours?"

"The arson case at Maury Elementary."

"I knew he was interested in that but—"

"Ali solved the case," she said and laughed. "I don't think you're going to be happy about how he did it, but there's no doubt. We've got an arrest warrant and are about to serve it. You should be proud of him."

"I am proud of him, always," I said, smiling. "What exactly did he do?"

"I think I'll let him tell you. I'm just giving you a heads-up that he did good."

I thanked her, hung up, and repeated the gist of the conversation to Nana Mama, who laughed and said, "I told you he was excited about something!"

Nana Mama and I returned home about an hour later. Her cardiologist visit had gone well, and I still had Detective Sutter's call on my mind, which made me eager to get inside.

Bree was in the kitchen, cooking duck, of all things, and even my grandmother thought it smelled delicious.

"How long until dinner?" I asked.

"Twenty minutes?" Bree said.

"Perfect," I said and went upstairs.

I found Ali's door ajar. I pushed it open to find my almost-eleven-year-old with his shirt off, on the floor, trying valiantly to do a push-up with trembling arms that just couldn't get him there.

Ali flopped on his belly, groaned, and looked at me. "This is hard."

"How many did you do?"

"Two," he said, sounding disgusted with himself.

"It'll come," I said as he got to his feet. "What's this I hear about you having something to do with finding the arsonist?"

Ali grinned. "Detective Sutter called you?"

"She wanted me to know that you did some impressive investigative work."

My youngest child beamed. "It gave me the best feeling ever, Dad. Better than school. Better than mountain biking or even climbing. That's why I'm doing push-ups."

"Okay?"

"I have to be strong if I'm going to be a detective," he explained.

"You want to be a detective?"

"Like you and Bree. Can I take, like, judo or karate or boxing lessons?"

I smiled. Ali had always been the most bookish of my children, the one who had shied away from sports of all kinds until he'd taken an interest in mountain biking and climbing walls the year before. Next came sports camp. And now he wanted to learn to fight.

"Whichever one you want," I said. "Learning to defend yourself is a good thing, but why don't you tell me how you identified the arsonist."

"Oh," Ali said. "I realized that the only elementary school in Southeast that had not been vandalized or burned was Amidon-Bowen."

"Okay?"

"So I did surveillance, like you do," he said. He looked down, scratching his arm. "I know I should have told you or Bree or Nana, but I snuck out of the house and went to the school three nights a week."

"What?"

"Dad, I hid myself near the dumpsters and watched until I saw him two nights ago, the guy with the camo mask sneaking around. I followed him home and told Detective Sutter. She says it's him and they're going to arrest him."

"I heard that," I said. "Who is he?"

Ali shrugged. "Some older kid, a teenager. Detective Sutter said he was expelled from school last year. How did you learn to box?"

I remained extremely unhappy that Ali had been sneaking out in the middle of the night but allowed the change of subject. "Friend of Nana's taught me and John to box," I said. "Charlie Elliott. He had a gym about two blocks from our house. It's not there anymore."

"Dad, I think I want to learn to box," he said. "And also how to grapple with suspects."

I almost laughed but I could see the seriousness in his eyes. Ali tended to jump from one interest or obsession to another every six weeks. But this felt different. It was the second time in the past year that he'd come up with vital information in a sensitive investigation. This felt like resolve, like he absolutely intended to follow in my and Bree's footsteps.

Part of me wanted to tell him about the harsh realities of the job, mention the men and women I'd known who couldn't handle the pace or the demands of a high-profile investigation, the ones who'd turned to booze or drugs or anything to dull their pain. But I didn't. "You really want to be an investigator?" I said.

"Maybe an FBI agent like you were," he said.

"I worked there because I received a PhD in criminal

behavior, and I published a research paper based on my interviews with violent criminals. The Bureau decided it needed someone with my skill set and recruited me."

"How did you learn to be a detective?"

"I was a homicide detective before I joined the FBI. Then I went through basic FBI training at Quantico just like any other agent. Then the agents in the behavioral unit trained me in the rest."

"The behavioral unit," Ali said. "They hunt serial killers."

"They do," I said. "Among other things."

"Did you like hunting serial killers?"

"I enjoyed the process of trying to predict their actions based on their prior actions. I was very good at it."

"That's profiling, right?"

"Part of profiling," I said. I happened to glance at the clock on his wall. "You'd better put your shirt on. It's almost time for dinner."

Ali grabbed his shirt. "Okay, Dad. And thanks for talking to me!"

"Anytime," I said, and stepped out of his room. *That kid will do special things with his life. He'll make us all proud, no matter what he decides to do. My God, he already has! At ten!*

I laughed and shook my head at how wonderful life could feel at times.

CHAPTER

53

DUSK WAS FALLING ON THE street where Rosella Hernandez and her family had lived for less than six months. Up and down the road, lights in other Craftsman bungalows were going on.

John Sampson could hear children playing tag and laughing when he and Ned Mahoney came out on the porch of the Hernandez home. The porch light was off. Special Agent Hanson was smoking a cigarette in the shadows.

"ETA?" Mahoney said.

"Two minutes," Hanson said. "They'll be gone in ten and everyone can go home except the sifters."

"Sifters?" Sampson said.

"Watch," she said. "The marshals come in two teams— one to move the family, one to stay behind and sift through everything that's left. Anything to do with Rosella, Little Eddie, and Naomi Hernandez will be destroyed. Their social media accounts will be erased, their hard drives seized. Even their Social Security numbers will get rubbed."

"Tonight?"

"Probably before midnight," she said. "Here they come."

Two black Mercedes-Benz Sprinter vans turned onto the street from the north and backed into the Hernandezes' driveway. One backed all the way into the garage.

A four-person crew in hazmat suits came out of that van and entered the house by the back door. Another four-person team, two men, two women, left the other van and walked up to the porch.

"Benjamin Taylor," the taller male said. "U.S. Marshals Service."

"They're inside and waiting," Mahoney said.

Taylor and his people went in. Sampson said, "I've got to get home to Willow."

"And I have reports to write," Mahoney said. He looked at Hanson. "Sorry we got off on the wrong foot."

"And I apologize for being me," the DEA agent said and laughed.

Mahoney and Sampson climbed down off the porch and headed to their vehicles parked at the far end of the block. A dark Ford pickup came around the corner and passed right by them as they walked beneath a streetlamp.

Though the windows of the pickup were tinted, Sampson could see the silhouette of the driver's head, which was turned to look right at them. Something about it bothered him.

He slowed and looked back in time to see hooded figures rising in the pickup's bed. Two of them were kneeling with shouldered automatic rifles.

Two of them were standing and holding weapons far more terrifying.

"No!" Sampson shouted, going for his service pistol.

The pickup slowed as it came abreast of the Hernandez house. The kneeling men's machine guns opened up, sending a hail of bullets at the front porch.

The two men standing fired their weapons in unison. The long tubes of the rocket-propelled-grenade launchers on their shoulders shot fire out the rear and death out the front.

One of the small missiles detonated against the front door of the Hernandez home. The second blew through a window and exploded inside.

Fire erupted and billowed in the suburban sky as Sampson and Mahoney ran at the pickup, shooting until one of the gunmen turned his automatic weapon on them.

They dove behind a hedge and scrambled deeper into the darkness while bullets chewed the ground. The second the burst stopped, they were back up and over the hedge, chasing the now retreating pickup and emptying their pistols in vain.

Only then did they pause to look at the Hernandez home, which was completely engulfed in flames. The porch was already gone.

There was no movement anywhere around the house.

"Oh my God," Mahoney said.

"They're all gone," Sampson said, dumbstruck. "Every one of them."

CHAPTER

54

SAMPSON WAS STILL FEELING THE shock of the previous evening when he entered the offices of the DC medical examiner the next morning.

"Lauren's waiting for you," the receptionist said. "You know the way, Detective."

Sampson did know the way and soon rapped on the door frame of DC assistant medical examiner Lauren Pickett.

Pickett looked up with a smile, but her smile turned to concern when she saw him. She jumped up and waved him in. "I just heard you were there last night."

He nodded soberly. "One of two surviving witnesses. Me and Mahoney."

"Jesus," she said. "Should you even be out and about? I mean, I'm so sorry I texted you. How are you feeling? We can do this another time, John."

"No, other than muscle pain in my belly and around the thigh wound, I feel good."

"Sit," she said. "Or not."

Sampson sat. "You said the autopsy is done?"

"It is," she said. "And Billie's body has been cremated, as you requested. I want you to know that we treated her with great dignity, John."

Sampson felt guilty he hadn't been with her coffin, that he'd been in the hospital when his late wife's body was exhumed, examined, and cremated. "Cause of death?"

"Cardiac arrest secondary to *Borrelia burgdorferi* infection," the medical examiner said. "Otherwise known as Lyme disease. The official cause of Billie's death will remain unchanged, John."

Sampson blinked and swallowed that statement, finding it familiar and more than a little bitter. His wife had died because of a hike in the woods and bacteria that had attacked her heart, Billie's greatest asset.

Pickett said, "You can delete that madman's text to you, John. He played no role in Billie's death. I have no idea why someone would say something so despicable."

Sampson said, "It was sadism, designed to inflict pain. But sadists like to prolong their torture."

"Meaning?"

"Why did he try to have me killed before Billie's body could be exhumed? Why not enjoy my pain for as long as possible?"

Pickett said, "Because he knew what the results of the autopsy would be?"

Sampson squinted, trying to see that angle. "Could be, but

I just feel like there has to be more at stake than that for him to send an assassin after me."

The assistant ME thought a moment. "Is it possible you were getting close to him? Close to cracking his identity?"

Sampson racked his brain, trying to think through the events leading up to M's text claiming responsibility for Billie's death and Master Sergeant Psycho's showing up at his house to knife him at M's behest.

He said, "Alex and I worked the Catherine Hingham case and M's connection to it before that text. But we felt like we were getting very little traction. After the text, Alex went to LA with Mahoney on the second murder-confession case, which left me pretty much out of the game until after the stabbing."

"Maybe you weren't out of the game in M's mind," Pickett said. "Maybe you had become a threat."

"Or maybe he just didn't want to play with me anymore," Sampson said. "I'd become something to discard and be done with. Like a chess piece taken off the board in a game of strategy only he understands."

CHAPTER

55

I LEFT MY HOUSE THE next morning wondering how long this war between the cartel and the vigilante group would go on before one side cried uncle. There was certainly no sign of a de-escalation, not the way Sampson had described the night before to me.

It was one thing for vigilantes to kidnap, torture, and kill a federal agent. It was another for the cartel to retaliate against his family with missiles and machine guns, killing a mom, two kids, eight U.S. Marshals officers, and four members of the DEA, including Special Agent Hanson.

And they'd done it within ten miles of Capitol Hill.

As I headed toward the corner where Ned Mahoney was supposed to pick me up for a meeting at the Justice Department, I decided that the cartel's act was beyond brazen. It was defiant and reckless and—

My phone buzzed in my hand.

Congratulations on your youngest's latest exploits, Dr. Cross. Ali is quite the chip off the old block. Well done. Applause from the cheap seats and all that.

On another note, you deserve to know that all is not as it seems when it comes to the letter M. In this case, you should know that there is an impostor posing as me. He is a madman—cruel, vindictive, cunning, brutal, and highly intelligent. He hired the man who stabbed Sampson. Focus your efforts on finding the impostor and leave us to ending the corruption and the Alejandro cartel. The Hernandez family will be avenged.—Maestro

Ned picked me up a few moments later, looking haggard.

"How are you, Ned?"

"Shell-shocked, to be honest," he said. "I mean, they care absolutely nothing about human life. And John and I were on that porch just a few minutes before. It makes you think, Alex. It really does."

I waited until we were almost to DOJ before reading him the text.

"Two Ms?" Mahoney said. "How does that happen?"

"I have no idea," I said. "But it's true, now that I think about it, that there have been two different kinds of messages from M over the years. One was always insulting, derisive, and bent on disrupting our efforts. The other showed us the way in multiple investigations."

"I'd have to see the messages sorted that way."

"Good idea. I think it can be done. I've saved every one of them."

Mahoney pulled into the parking lot below the Justice Department. "Two different criminals under the same name, one psychotic and one avenging."

"Or one psychotic and the other the leader of an organization operating under the name Maestro."

As we took the elevator up, I explained Marco Alejandro's theory that Maestro was a partnership or a team that had taken the law into its own hands.

"Which makes them murdering criminals in my book," Mahoney said as we got out. "No one's above the law, Alex. No one's allowed to claim justice for themselves."

"Agreed, a hundred percent," I said. "But let's use the idea of a team to filter the evidence we've gathered so far. See where it gets us."

"I've learned never to underestimate your instincts, Alex. If that's where your nose is leading you, have at it. But let's not mention this text or this idea until the evidence is stronger."

Upstairs, we met Sampson. He and Mahoney briefed a task force of high-ranking agents from every law enforcement branch under the DOJ umbrella. All of them were chosen because of their reputation for integrity, honesty, and grit in the field.

"This situation is appalling and we have to get it right," Mahoney said. "We have to look at the very real corruption that this vigilante force has exposed as being like a cancer that spreads from one organ to another. We have to cut the corruption out before it causes any further damage to U.S. law enforcement. That is also our path to finding these vigilantes and ending this war. We track down and verify every detail in those confessions and use them to figure out how the vigilantes knew who was corrupt."

I said, "What about the cartel? Don't we want to be fighting this on both fronts?"

"Absolutely," Mahoney said. "That attack last night will not go unanswered. The director is forming a second task force to track down whoever is responsible."

"With all due respect, Ned, we know who's responsible. Whoever took over the Alejandro cartel after Marco Alejandro was put in supermax."

"What do you want us to do, Alex? Go down to Mexico and ask them to stop?"

"That might be a starting point," I said.

"I'll take it under consideration," Mahoney said.

Sampson raised his hand. Ned acknowledged him.

"The vigilantes. Maestro. M. Their computing power and reach has to be massive," Sampson said. "Like, National Security Agency—massive."

Mahoney looked at him oddly. "Come again?"

Sampson said, "I have been thinking about M for as long as anyone. The way he—or they—are able to just text us, the way they know what's been happening in our lives. I read that book by Edward Snowden. I know what the NSA can do. Listen in on everything and everyone if they want. Download your data. Look back at you through your cameras. Mess with your computers. It's the most secretive agency in the world, and a connection to that organization would explain how M is able to contact us at will and without a trace and how he always seems three steps ahead of us."

Honoring Mahoney's wish that we not divulge the text I'd received earlier, I said, "It does make sense. Someone who works at the NSA or who has access to someone who works there."

Mahoney said, "We're talking a highly sensitive situation, then, above my pay grade. I'll have to seek guidance on that angle, John. The rest of you should start running down the bank accounts listed in the confessions. I want you to trace the money backward. I have a strong feeling that all roads eventually lead to Mexico."

My cell buzzed for the second time that morning. I looked at it, half expecting M to repeat exactly what had been said in our top-secret meeting.

It was from Bree: Call me. I may have found a way to identify Maestro.

CHAPTER

56

South of Oaxaca, Mexico

MATTHEW BUTLER SHIVERED A LITTLE as the sky lightened in the east. In a few hours, it would be one hundred and five degrees, but there'd been no cloud cover during the night, and currently the desert air swirled in the thirties.

Butler had not come prepared for it, but he was highly trained. He could shut off something like pain or cold at will.

He did so as he left the spot where he'd spent the night, leeward of a wall of dull red rock. He climbed the side of a ledge, and when he got to the top, he took the raw wind straight in the face.

Butler scooted forward in the low light to where the ledge became the farthest point of a pinnacle some four hundred vertical feet above a gravel state road that wound through the mountainous terrain. He settled into a wide crack in the side of the pinnacle facing almost due south, assembled his Swarovski BTX spotting scope, and took his long-range rifle from its case.

When he had it locked in and aimed down at a tight bend in the road, he triggered his jaw mike. "Everyone awake?"

"Sipping my espresso," Big DD said in Butler's earbud.

"Mocha latte here," J. P. Vincente said.

"Put caramel in mine," Alison Purdy said.

"None for me," Cortland said. "Caffeine gives me the shakes."

Butler smiled. "And now we wait."

Several minutes later, as light came on slowly, he began to be able to pick out other rock formations overlooking the road bend and the steep hillside on the opposite side where scrub gave way to groves of piñon pine.

"We've got them leaving the hacienda gate," M said in Butler's other earbud. "Three black Escalades."

"They've gone with three vehicles this morning," Butler said, relaying the word.

"Roger that," Vincente said. "Adjusting the plan."

"I'm with him," Purdy said.

"We are less than twelve minutes out."

Butler looked around at the highest point on the other side of the road, unable to make Cortland out. But the sniper was there. He'd been in place all night, lying prone beneath dun-colored camouflage, eager to prove his skills.

Cortland had been embarrassed that he'd missed the pervert Frenchman in Paris six weeks ago and had vowed it would never happen again. Butler believed him. Paris had been a rare error on Cortland's part. Butler expected his accuracy to be exceptional when the time came.

"Six minutes," M said and Cortland passed it on.

The sun was rising above the eastern horizon when M said, "Two minutes. Road is clear to you. Both directions."

"Rocks," Butler said.

Above the near side of that tight bend in the road, Butler saw a flash and heard a muffled, delayed thud as a slab of rock the size of a refrigerator broke off and fell, shattering debris across the road.

"Well done, DD," Butler said.

"Once a sapper, always a sapper," the big man said.

Butler got behind his rifle, dialing in his scope to the distance to the debris while calculating for the steep down-wardness of the shot. He looked south, saw headlights slashing the road.

"Eyes on," he said. "Cort, you're up."

"Watch 'em fall," he said. "Cartel swine."

The first Cadillac rounded the bend, the other two tight on its bumper. The driver saw the rocks and slammed on the brakes a little too late. He crashed into the rubble; his front wheels went up onto it with a screech before the vehicle stopped. The others hit in a bumper-to-bumper chain reaction.

"Perfect," Butler said. "Everyone, steady now. Wait for it."

He watched six men climb out of the first and last SUVs carrying automatic weapons. They looked nervous, sensing an ambush.

"Patience," Butler said.

A minute ticked by, then two. The six armed men let down their guard. Two went to the middle vehicle. The other four inspected the damage on the front one.

"Still clear," M said in his earbud.

Butler tracked the pair of men going to the middle vehicle. When the right rear window rolled down, he said, "Take them."

Cortland's first shot blew the top off the head of one of the four front guards. Butler's shot hit the guard standing by the open vehicle window, dropping him in his tracks.

The other cartel men were screaming now, ducking, trying to figure out where the shots were coming from.

Cortland's second, third, and fourth shots finished the rest of the guards on the debris pile. Butler tried to swing with the other man running away from the middle Escalade toward the one in the rear.

He could hear that SUV spinning its wheels, trying to go in reverse, but the bumpers were locked for a few moments before they freed. It didn't matter. Purdy drove a Ford pickup around the bend, blocking any retreat. Vincente stood in the pickup bed aiming an AR rifle over the top of the cab.

Vincente shot the last armed guard as he tried to get in the rear Escalade. Big DD barreled down the far hillside toward the middle vehicle, his own gun shouldered and ready for business.

Big DD's first shot blew out the middle Cadillac's driver's-side window and sprayed the passenger window with blood. Butler's second shot got the man who'd driven up on the debris.

Big DD swung his weapon at the rear passenger window of the middle rig, shouting, "You shoot, you die! You shoot, you die!" The big man wrenched open the rear door and stuck his rifle inside.

"Don't!" a man shouted in English. "No guns!"

"All of you, out. Now."

The first man to emerge from the middle Cadillac was dressed in a military uniform and held his hands high. The second man out was slim and elegant with black, slicked-back hair; he was wearing a business suit and dark glasses. The third man wore a plain white shirt, jeans, and a Miami Dolphins baseball cap.

"You will die for this," the suited man said in a thick accent.

"Not if you can help it," Big DD said.

Vincente ran to him. They turned the men around, zip-tied their wrists, put duct tape over their mouths, and hustled them to the pickup.

After Big DD restrained their ankles, Vincente got a tarp, covered the prisoners, and slapped twice on the hood of the pickup. Purdy threw the truck in reverse and began to back away from the carnage.

"Pull out, Cort," Butler said.

"Not yet" came the reply a split second before the driver in the third Escalade jumped out and tried to aim an AK-47 at the retreating pickup.

Cortland shot him through the side of his chest.

"Now I'm pulling out," Cortland said.

"Pickup in three hours for you, two for me," Butler said and ran in a crouch to his backpack, where he began dismantling his weapon and the spotting scope.

Three minutes later, he was heading northeast across a broken desert landscape toward his pickup spot some six miles away. The sun was barely above the horizon but he could already feel the inferno building.

CHAPTER

57

Boston

JOHN SAMPSON, NED MAHONEY, AND I drove north from Logan Airport the following morning. Forty minutes later we pulled into a campus of anonymous concrete-and-glass office buildings near the New Hampshire border.

The largest building on the campus sat toward the back and was shaded by towering spruce trees. We parked near the trees and got out, knowing we had ten minutes before our appointment.

"I was impressed with the memo and supporting information Bree got us," Mahoney said as we walked. "I still am. Damn impressive."

I smiled in agreement. Bree had taken an offhand comment by her boss at Bluestone Group and in a matter of hours had gathered enough information to warrant phone calls and an early flight north.

"We're still on something of a fishing trip," Sampson said, rubbing at his wounded side and still limping slightly as we reached the front door.

"But this is a good pond, I think," Mahoney said.

We entered and found ourselves in a tight lobby with steel walls on three sides and bulletproof glass on the fourth. Behind it sat a woman in her forties with the biceps of a professional arm wrestler. The nameplate on her blue polo shirt read RIGGS.

"Can I help you, gentlemen?" Riggs asked.

We held up our credentials. Mahoney said, "We have an appointment to see Steven Vance and Ryan Malcomb."

She smiled. "You are expected, gentlemen."

After asking to copy our credentials, which we passed through a tray, Riggs buzzed us into a larger reception with a stacked-granite weeping wall that gave the room a pleasant sound. Beside the wall hung a small, understated logo: PALADIN INC. superimposed over a faint number 12.

Bree had explained it to us in the summary of her research. In twelfth-century French literature, the paladins, or twelve peers, were said to be the elite protectors and agents of King Charlemagne, comparable to the Knights of the Round Table in the Arthurian legends.

Paladin Inc. had been launched five years before by Vance, a veteran Silicon Valley CEO, and Malcomb, a brilliant tech wizard who'd started and sold four companies before the age of forty. The focus of Vance and Malcomb's most recent venture involved data mining.

The company had corporate and U.S. government contracts based on ingenious algorithms written by Malcomb that allowed Paladin to scour and sift through monstrous amounts of data at an astonishingly fast pace. The system had yielded investigative targets of interest to various U.S. law enforcement agencies and private security operations like Bluestone Group, all of which increasingly looked to Paladin because of the company's unrivaled accuracy.

A door opened on the other side of the weeping wall. A short redheaded woman with a bowl haircut exited; she was wearing a baby-blue puffy jacket despite the August heat outside and looked like a cruise-ship passenger who'd just been told there was a norovirus outbreak onboard.

"I'm Sheila Farr, Paladin's legal counsel," she said stiffly. "Unfortunately, Mr. Malcomb's mother has had a bad fall in her Palo Alto home and he's on his way there. But Steve will see you now."

CHAPTER

58

Mexico City

LATER THAT MORNING IN THE Mexican capital, Matthew Butler went to the window on the empty fourth floor of a building at the corner of Calle de Venustiano and José María Pino Suárez. With latex gloves on, he moved the window shade just enough to see diagonally across the intersection to the Mexican National Supreme Court of Justice.

"Highest law in the land," Butler said.

"Traffic?" M said in his ear.

"No less than any Tuesday when it's already blistering hot out at seven a.m."

"Timing has to be perfect for the statement to have impact."

"It does," Butler said. "We good?"

"You are go."

"Roll," Butler said into his jawbone microphone.

"Rolling," Vincente said. "Forty seconds out."

Purdy said, "Walking at my target."

"Squared up on mine," Cortland said.

Butler took his eyes off the street and looked over two windows to the profile of his sniper. Cortland held a powerful, accurate, multi-shot air gun attached to a small compressor. He had the barrel and the first two inches of his telescopic sight aimed through slits he'd cut in the blind.

"Thirty seconds, taking a right onto José María Pino Suárez," Vincente said. "Twenty-five seconds."

"Got you," Butler said, seeing the top of the nondescript white cargo van with graffiti on the side coming down the street at him in the far lane along a line of inadequate green traffic barriers. "Twenty seconds. Take him, Cort. Take him, Purdy."

Butler heard Cortland's first shot; it sounded like the thud of a beefy paintball gun. The dart whistled across the intersection and struck a federal police officer in the side of his neck. He staggered two feet and dropped.

Cortland changed barrels on his gun. On the far sidewalk, Purdy walked toward the main entrance to the seat of high justice in Mexico, using her skills at being small and going unnoticed, raising a kerchief over her face, just waiting for the first scream.

It came from the far corner of the block.

Purdy slipped diagonally left toward the two armed guards at the entrance to the supreme court. Seeing them strain to look toward the sounds of shouting, she brought out her two small air pistols and shot both guards at close range; it was no more than three feet from her to the sides of their necks, where darts were now embedded.

"Jump to it," Butler said.

The men dropped in their tracks. Purdy stepped over them a nanosecond before the reinforced-steel bumper of Vincente's cargo van smashed through the inadequate barrier designed to protect the courthouse and skidded to a stop on the sidewalk a few feet beyond the entrance to the court.

The rear doors flew open. Wearing a black Day of the Dead mask, Big DD leaped out, dragging two corpses by the napes of their necks behind him.

He hauled them up the steps of the courthouse and left them sprawled there, returning to help Vincente with the third and largest of the corpses, the one in the uniform of the Mexican army. They dumped him in the middle.

Purdy unfurled a banner over the three bodies, then ran to the rear of the cargo van and jumped in. Vincente accelerated down the sidewalk, laying on the horn before swinging the bumper at another inadequate steel fence that broke on impact.

"Diversion," Butler said.

Cortland's air gun coughed twice, sending a smoke bomb and then the tear gas into the street crossing. Vincente drove through the intersection and out the other side, leaving a curtain of yellow smoke and people coughing behind them.

Butler went to Cortland, grabbed pieces of the air gun as he disassembled it, and put them in his knapsack.

"Get rid of that van, JP, and get to the landing strip," Butler said as he left. "We have a plane to catch and I can smell the Wyoming high country calling."

CHAPTER

59

Northeastern Massachusetts

I DON'T KNOW WHAT I was expecting but it wasn't the bitter cold that greeted us when we followed Paladin's legal counsel Sheila Farr into a narrow hallway. This was more than icy air-conditioning to combat summer heat. I could see my breath and shivered and shivered again.

"What's with the ice age?" Sampson asked.

"The supercomputers." Farr sniffed as she pulled the collar of her puffy coat higher. "There are fifteen stories of them underneath our feet and two stories of them above us. They generate so much heat that we have to keep them at these temperatures just to do what we do best."

"Which is what, exactly?" I asked.

Farr stopped at a door, looked at me, and smiled. "We're asked questions. We analyze data. We give answers." She opened the door and gestured inside. "Come in where it's warmer, let Steve tell you how it really works."

Ned went through first. Sampson and I had to duck our heads to get through into a large office with glass walls, floors, and ceilings, a block of glass suspended fifteen feet above and in front of a much larger workspace that teemed with activity. The bigger space was set up with clusters of desks and computers interspersed with screens hanging from ceilings.

The people down there ranged from the outwardly nerdy to the seriously buff, kind of like Steven Vance, who stood up from behind a plain wooden desk in the glass cube. The former Silicon Valley CEO was as tall as me but sported an extra twenty-five pounds of solid muscle under his black polo and jeans.

Vance wasn't tanned, but his skin sure seemed to glow. I honestly couldn't tell how old he was as he came around the desk grinning with bonhomie.

"Steve Vance," he said, shaking our hands and looking us each in the eye as he did. "Ryan sends his apologies. His seventy-five-year-old mother was up on a ladder, painting her kitchen ceiling, fell and broke her femur in several places."

"Ouch," Sampson said.

I said, "Please tell him we send him our regards and best wishes for his mother's recovery."

"I'll do that," Vance said, gesturing us to chairs. "Water? Coffee? Tea?"

"Tea sounds good," Mahoney said.

"I'll call for it, Steve," his attorney said as she took off her puffy jacket.

"How can Paladin help you?" Vance said.

"We're working on a case," Mahoney began.

"The cartel and the corrupt agents," Vance said, drumming his fingers on his thighs. "I understand we've been helping you on that one already."

That wasn't the answer we'd been expecting and we all sat forward.

"Run that by us again, sir," Ned said.

"We have several ongoing contracts with the U.S. government, including the FBI, Special Agent Mahoney. Ryan told me after your call yesterday that we had had a request from your director just last week, asking us to look for links between the dead agents."

That was news to us.

Mahoney said, "And?"

"Just the obvious ones so far," Vance said. "Agency interactions. A few overlapping assignments. But they were all seemingly corrupted by the cartel and then murdered by a…rogue vigilante force, I guess you'd call it."

Sampson said, "You pick up any kind of chatter prior to the attacks?"

Vance nodded and looked to Farr, who had returned with a tray of drinks. She said, "We mined LA Basin cell phone data in the day prior to the attack on FBI Agent White's family in Pasadena. Looked at in retrospect, you can tell the Alejandros were gathering an army to retaliate."

"But nothing about the vigilante force?" Sampson asked.

"If they were communicating, they were doing it over some kind of localized supersecure network," Vance said. "We've picked up nothing on them so far."

Sampson said, "Can you tell us how you look?"

Paladin's CEO said, "Again, we use the supercomputers to sift through whatever the government authorizes us to sift through: cell phone data, computer data, internet traffic patterns, GPS location data, video, audio. Sometimes we have a specific target. More often than not, we're looking for possible targets."

I said, "You work for the NSA as well?"

Vance laughed. "Wouldn't that be the holy grail for us? No, for the most part the NSA does its own work of broadly monitoring the nation's communication lines in real time. We're more focused on the past. We're given a load of data after the fact and we sift through it until we find what our clients are looking for."

I said, "What else do you know about the cartel? Is this vigilante force correct? Have the Alejandros corrupted every law enforcement group operating in the southwestern United States?"

Vance said, "Well, that's for others to decide. We provide data and certain interpretations of it. After that, it's up to others to—"

Ding!

The sharp alert came from the CEO's laptop on his desk.

"Sorry," he said, frowning as he got up and crossed to it. Vance moved his mouse and studied the screen before looking up at us. "Three bodies were just dumped on the steps of the Mexican supreme court in broad daylight—a Mexican general, an unidentified American, and Marco Alejandro's cousin Enrique. They've got confessions pinned to their shirts and were covered in a banner that said 'Death to traitors. Death to the Alejandro cartel.'"

CHAPTER

60

MAHONEY GOT TO HIS FEET. "That's our case. What else do you have in that database of yours?"

Vance said, "About the three dead men?"

"And about the Alejandro cartel," I said. "Who's running it now? And who's got such a beef with the cartel they'd be willing to pull a homicidal stunt like this?"

Vance said, "I can't tell you any of that because I honestly don't know. We have not been given the green light to do that kind of precision sift yet."

"But you can do it."

"We can try."

"I'll get the FBI director to authorize your precision sift," Mahoney said. "And we'll want a bunch of other questions answered while you're at it."

"Such as?"

Sampson said, "Who is M? Who or what is Maestro? What's the common denominator that points to one person or one group of people? Why has Maestro declared war on the cartel? Where does M get all his information? And how does he manage to keep track of people? It's as if he has access to real-time NSA-level data."

Vance frowned. "I'd have to see the data you're relying on to support that, Detective. But I agree it sounds as if this Maestro or M must have an edge."

I said, "And a small army, including someone who supposedly died in Afghanistan five years ago."

The CEO sat back. "For real?"

"Perfect biometric match for a dead man," Mahoney said, nodding.

"Where do you want us to start?" Vance said. "You need to imagine the data that might yield what you are looking for and get it for us."

"Start with the most recent attack on the Hernandez family," I said. "Find the cell phones that organized the attack."

Vance squinted. "They probably used burners. But if we get the right data, we could look for communications going to Mexico from the greater DC area. And with the right permissions, we can look at all security feeds within ten miles of the attack site."

Mahoney said, "We'll get that authorization to you ASAP."

Vance smiled as he shook our hands. "Whatever you need, gentlemen. Paladin is here to help in any way we can."

Out in the parking lot, Mahoney read a brief from Washington. "They want us all on the next flight to Mexico City," he said.

Sampson cleared his throat.

I said, "Nana Mama, Bree, and Jannie will be glad to take care of Willow."

He struggled but said, "Mexico City, then."

"You two take the direct flight from Boston," I said. "I'm going to need to make a detour first."

61

Fremont County, Colorado

SHORTLY AFTER NINE P.M. THAT day, Warden Ainsley Perrin led me deep into the Alcatraz of the Rockies, and soon we were once again outside the room where I'd spoken with Alejandro.

"The judge gave you thirty minutes," Perrin said, opening the door.

"I'll use every second of it, starting at hello," I said and entered the small room. I felt creeped out again at the sound of the door shutting and locking behind me.

Alejandro seemed puzzled to see me when he entered the booth on the other side of the bulletproof glass, but then he shrugged and sat down to be electromagnetically fused to the chair.

When the prison guards left, the former cartel boss said, "Didn't think I'd ever see you again, Dr. Cross."

"I was kind of feeling the same way," I said, holding

up my palms. "But life has a way of playing boomerang with you."

"An hour in sunlight," he said. "Whatever it is you're after, I want sixty minutes in real sunlight once a week. An hour once a week or I'm sitting tight."

"I can't promise it," I said.

"Then get the promise."

"I don't have time and neither does your family or your cartel."

Alejandro narrowed his eyes. "What's happened?"

I told him about the attacks and counterattacks that had taken place since we'd last spoken, shortly before my emergency flight to Paris.

"Maestro made his latest move this morning," I said and described the bodies dumped on the steps of the Mexican supreme court.

"Who were they?" he asked.

"A not-yet-identified Caucasian male in his forties." Alejandro's brows raised slightly. "General Raoul Guerra, of the—"

"Guerra!" Marco said, surprised, but then he sat back. "And the third?"

"I'm sorry, Marco," I said. "It was your cousin Enrique."

Alejandro's shock was complete. Tears came to his eyes. "No, not Enrique. He was supposed to be out of it. Straight man for our straight businesses. Ah, Jesus."

"The three of them—Enrique, Guerra, and the dead white guy—supposedly signed confessions," I said. "I'm on my way to Mexico City tonight to read them."

"And what, you just decided to drop in and hit me with this?" he said, blinking back the tears. "What the hell is this?"

"It's much more than a courtesy visit, and I give you my deepest and sincerest condolences. I know you and your cousin were very close."

"Damn straight we were close," Alejandro shot back. "As kids. But he was never meant for the rough stuff, you know. He had brains. Book smarts."

"I'm sorry."

He stared at his lap a moment before lifting his head and asking, "So what else?"

"It's clear that Maestro means to destroy your cartel whatever the collateral damage," I said. "I think there will be more deaths in your immediate family in the very near future."

Marco hardened. "You know this how?"

"Maestro sent me a text, saying he plans to stamp out your cartel by stamping out your bloodlines," I said. "Including your wife and your children. No mercy."

Alejandro chewed on that a moment. "So why are you here?"

"To try to stop needless bloodshed. But to do that, I need your help."

"What help is that?" he asked suspiciously.

"A foolproof way to contact the current leaders of your cartel when I'm on the ground in Mexico City sometime early tomorrow morning."

He squinted at me. "Why?"

"To warn them of what's coming and ask them to stop the retaliations in the United States in the meantime."

Alejandro laughed scornfully. "Why would they do that? An eye for an eye still rules south of the border, hombre."

"I say they'll do it for their own self-interest. With all due respect, your cartel has proven its ruthlessness, but M has more than cruelty in his corner. We believe he may have access to the NSA, the kind of people who can listen in on your phones, the ones who know exactly where you are at all times."

"That's some movie nonsense."

"Believe it," I said. "Or don't believe it, but act as if it's true, because it is. Maestro is going to start picking off your family—your wife, your kids. Give me a name, Marco. Give me a number so I can warn them."

The former cartel leader gazed at me for a good thirty seconds before he said, "One hour in the sunshine."

CHAPTER

62

Mexico City

THE FOLLOWING MORNING, I WAS up drinking strong coffee after sleeping for an hour on the plane and getting another two hours of fitful drowsing in my hotel room. Ned Mahoney and John Sampson had arrived here long before me but they looked barely more rested than I did when they came down for breakfast in the little café off the lobby.

"Last night the Federales were flat-out refusing to let us read the confessions, especially General Guerra's," Mahoney said. "I was up until three a.m. putting diplomatic pressure on them and woke up to find that a government liaison is coming to take us to see the bodies and the confessions in half an hour."

"Just enough time to eat," Sampson said.

"I'm not going," I said.

"You are technically under my authority, Alex, and I flew you in so you could be there," Mahoney said.

"I know you did, Ned," I said. "But you can easily take pictures of the victims and the confessions and text them to me here while I try to contact the cartel using the system Marco described to me last night."

"I don't like that idea," Sampson said. "Not alone."

"I'm not doing this alone. I won't leave the hotel until you both come back. Marco was adamant about that. No moving around once contact is made."

"Which means they'll come to you," Mahoney said.

"This is evidently a long, drawn-out process," I said. "How much time can it take you to look at the bodies and get copies of the confessions?"

"There are people who don't want us here. Who knows how long they could drag this out or what new ways they could find to interfere?" Sampson said.

"Point taken," I replied. "But, look, I have my phone on me. You can track me."

"Not good enough," Mahoney said. "I've got a GPS transmitter the size of a quarter upstairs. You cut a slit in the inside of your belt and slip it in there."

"I can do that."

I installed the GPS transmitter in my belt and waited until they'd eaten and left to meet their Mexican law enforcement liaison before I started the process of contacting the leaders of the deadliest drug cartel in the Western Hemisphere. The first step was texting three words to a phone number Marco Alejandro had recited from memory.

"*Madre de Dios,*" I muttered as I thumbed in those words.

Ten minutes after I'd hit Send, I got another phone number in response. I texted that number another four words in Spanish that translated to "Pray for us sinners."

I received a third phone number about twenty minutes later.

My stomach fluttered as I thumbed in what was supposed to be the final response, this one in English: My name is Dr. Alex Cross. I work as a consultant to the FBI. I saw and spoke to Marco Alejandro last night in Colorado. He sends his regards and asks you to please see me on an urgent matter. Now and at the hour of our death. Amen.

I finished the text with the last lines of the Hail Mary prayer on Alejandro's specific order. Without the lines, whoever was on the other end of that text would evidently not believe what I'd written.

They believed it. I'd no sooner sent the text and ordered another cup of coffee than my cell buzzed with an incoming message.

Be out in front of your hotel in twenty minutes. No weapons. No recording devices of any kind. You may bring your phone but it will be placed in a lead-lined bag for the duration of your journey.

My journey? I felt uneasy. How far would they be taking me?

I tried to call Ned and John but they didn't answer. I texted them to call me. The message seemed to go through, but I noticed it wasn't marked as delivered.

It still had not been delivered after I paid for breakfast, so I tried again out in front of the hotel, facing a busy street with cafés, high-end stores, and other hotels. The doorman asked if I needed a taxi and I told him in my rudimentary Spanish that I was waiting for a ride.

It took several attempts before he understood, and he gestured that I should wait to one side of the doors. I walked over and sat on a small bench and got anxious at the idea that my words to the cartel leaders might be mistranslated and therefore misunderstood. Then again, Marco Alejandro spoke perfect English.

A ruggedly built man who looked like he had Indian blood in him sat on the bench next to me and sipped from the coffee cup he carried.

"Dr. Cross," he said in thickly accented English, his eyes dancing over me, his expression amused. "You understand the rules, yes?"

"Yes."

"Your phone, please."

I didn't like it but handed him my phone. He put it in a thick pouch.

"Here is our ride, then," he said. "You will climb in the back."

He got up, carrying my phone, walked to a white Chevy Tahoe with dark windows, and opened the front passenger door. He paused to watch me open the rear door, then nodded and climbed in.

I followed suit, was unsurprised to see a second man sitting in the seat beside mine and another even bigger man behind me.

"Hands on your thighs, Señor Cross," the one beside me said after I'd shut the door and the SUV had pulled away from the curb.

I did as he requested and sat passively as he patted me down. He was thorough but found nothing more than my wallet, FBI credentials, and passport.

"He's clean," he said.

A hood came down over my head from behind. I tensed up.

The man beside me said, "No need to panic. We're putting headphones on you as well. I hope you like mariachi music."

CHAPTER

63

JOHN SAMPSON FOLLOWED NED MAHONEY and Captain Eduardo Rodriguez, their Mexican liaison, down the old green-tiled halls of the central morgue in Mexico City. The place reeked of disinfectant and they saw several autopsies under way in the small operatories they passed.

Captain Rodriguez stopped at a set of double doors. "I must warn you, cell phones don't work in here. Something about the X-ray machine and natural magnetic lines beneath this building. I always turn my phone off because it goes crazy trying to find a signal and the battery gets shot."

Sampson and Mahoney thumbed off their phones and put them in their pockets before following Rodriguez into a huge cold-storage locker where bodies awaiting autopsy were kept in individual chilled drawers.

Rodriguez went directly to the three drawers on the bottom, opened the first one, slid the corpse out, and drew back the sheet to reveal the face of a handsome guy who looked to have been in his late thirties when he was shot with a small-caliber bullet that entered between his eyes.

"Enrique Alejandro," Rodriguez said. "Tortured before they did him the favor."

He drew the sheet all the way down. He'd been burned repeatedly across his torso and his groin. "The coroner says they used a soldering gun on him with different size tips."

Rodriguez covered Marco Alejandro's cousin, slid his body back inside the cold drawer, and opened the one next to it. The corpse was Latino, fit, early fifties, by Sampson's guess. He too had been burned repeatedly with a soldering gun.

"General Guerra," Rodriguez said. "His involvement is especially tragic and hypocritical. He had a son who died of a drug overdose and he always said his son's death was what drove him to fight the narco-traffickers."

Mahoney said, "His confession says otherwise?"

"You will read it for yourself when we are done here."

"Give us the highlights," Sampson said.

Rodriguez hesitated but then said, "The general was under the influence of the cartel long before his son overdosed. The tragedy of his son's death gave Guerra cover to act as if he were fighting the Alejandros while working on the cartel's behalf at the highest levels of the Mexican government."

"And door number three?" Mahoney said after Rodriguez pushed the general's body back in its locker.

He opened the third locker, pulled out the corpse, and drew back the sheet on a buff man in his mid-forties, blond hair slicked back, shot between the eyes.

"We have an ID on him?" Mahoney asked.

"I have not yet read his confession," Rodriguez said. "So I personally do not know who he is."

"I think I do," Sampson said, coming closer. "Yeah, that's him. He showed up on the scene when Catherine Hingham was found, said he was her boss and tried to claim her body as part of a CIA investigation."

"Name?"

Sampson thought about that, remembered how condescending the man had been, how it had annoyed him. "Weaver. Dean Weaver. I'm sure this is him."

"One way to find out," Mahoney said. "Let's go read those confessions."

Captain Rodriguez got a slightly pained expression on his face as he pushed the CIA officer's body back into its drawer. "This will be in a few hours, señors."

"A few hours?" Mahoney said. "No, that is not happening."

"Special Agent Mahoney," Rodriguez said firmly. "The confessions are still being processed in our forensics lab. You will be able to examine them once that process is completed, which will be only a few hours."

They left the cold storage area and walked back down the hallway. Sampson felt his phone buzz with a text, saw it was from Alex asking him to call.

Mahoney said, "Can you at least get us pictures of the confessions in the meantime? So we know what we are dealing with?"

"I'll see what I can do," Rodriguez said and pulled out his phone.

Sampson called Alex. It went straight to voice mail, which was not part of the plan. At the prompt, he said, "Calling you back, Alex. We were in some kind of cellular black hole. Tag, you're it."

He hung up. Mahoney said, "He said he'd answer immediately if we called."

"He did say that," Sampson said, feeling the first drip of worry as he looked at his phone. "C'mon, Alex. Where are you when you're supposed to be sitting in that café waiting for us to reach out?"

CHAPTER

64

WE WERE IN STOP-AND-GO traffic for what seemed like hours. Despite the mariachi music and wanting to stay alert to my surroundings, I kept dozing off until the Tahoe suddenly lurched to a stop and I heard men speaking in Spanish.

They removed my earphones. A gate of some kind opened. I heard the hinges squeak and the grind of the lower rail of it against uneven soil.

We crunched up a long gravel drive and finally came to a stop. The front doors of the car opened and closed before mine opened.

The same young man who'd met me outside my hotel said, "Step out slow, Dr. Cross."

I felt a hand under my elbow and climbed out, smelling flowers. The air was cooler, which suggested we were higher in altitude than the city. A dog barked in the distance. Then a cock crowed.

"Stand still, legs wide, arms wide," someone said.

I assumed the position and heard the familiar sound of a security wand running over my arms and chest. As he went lower, I thought for sure that the GPS transmitter in my belt was going to trigger an alert.

It certainly caused a higher-pitch response the two times he went over the area but to my relief, the wand's wielder went on after patting down my lower back.

"He's good," the man said, stepping away.

We began walking. The surface beneath my feet soon changed. We were crossing slightly uneven brickwork or tile. The air was more perfumed here. A heavy chair moved. Someone took me by the shoulders, pivoted me, and sat me down on a hard wooden chair.

"Wrists on the chair arms."

I complied and felt zip ties come around and snug me to the chair. Only then did I wonder which of Marco Alejandro's possible replacements would be across from me when the hood was lifted.

The night before, the former cartel leader had given me three possibilities: his younger brother Juan Alejandro; his brother-in-law Claudio Fortunato; and Salvatore Menendez, who had been Marco's right hand from the time they were young men.

Marco felt his brother was too young and too hotheaded to act with the discipline and strategy the cartel required, and his brother-in-law lacked the vision and the skills to manifest that vision. Alejandro had predicted his friend Menendez would be in charge.

When the hood was finally removed, I was surprised to see none of those three men. I blinked at the sunlight, realizing I was on a terrace with trellises of blooming purple flowers overhead and sitting at a low stone table across from one of the most beautiful women I'd ever seen.

Her long hair was jet-black, drawn back, and braided to show more of her face, which featured high cheekbones, flawless pale skin, ruby lips, and large, roasted-almond-colored eyes, which flashed all over me. In her late forties, by my guess, she wore a starched white blouse, collar open, riding jeans, and tooled-leather boots.

She said, "I can't decide whether you are a brave man or a fool, Dr. Cross."

"I've been called both, if that helps."

Her lips curled ever so slightly toward a smile and she relaxed a little. I had no idea who she was until she spoke again.

"How is my brother these days?" she asked.

Marco's twin sister, Emmanuella. She was married to Claudio Fortunato but she's not wearing a wedding ring now. I said, "Given the conditions he's being held in, I'd say your brother is doing well. I'm a licensed psychologist and he seemed mentally healthy to me."

Emmanuella Alejandro scowled. "I don't believe it. Marco in a small cage, no contact, nothing for a year? My brother becomes a crazed man, a broken man."

"He was humbled," I allowed. "And he has spent the past year reflecting on his life. But in no way would I characterize him as broken."

"Who are you to him?"

"I'm the guy who ended his year of silence. I spoke with

him, got him books, a radio, one hour of exercise a day, and one hour a week of sunlight."

Alejandro's sister blinked and her features softened. "Marco sees the sun, then."

"Once a week now. I had to pull a lot of strings to get it done."

"He gave you the phone number?"

"And the contact method. He wanted me to talk to you."

Emmanuella laughed scornfully. "No, he wanted you to talk to Claudio or Salvatore or Juan. Am I right? Marco never in a million years thought it would be me, did he?"

I shook my head. "I guess he underestimated you."

"He always has. But in just one year, Claudio has become my ex-husband, Salvatore has unfortunately died, and my reckless younger brother has sampled too many of our products."

"There was no one else to lead, so you stepped in."

Not boastful but matter-of-fact, Emmanuella said, "Men tried. Salvatore among them. They all failed."

"Underestimated again."

"Yes. Now, why did Marco send you to talk with the cartel's new leader?"

"To warn you," I said. "Maestro intends to destroy the cartel and your family, Emmanuella. M intends to kill you all, rub out your bloodlines completely."

"Not if I kill him and his men first," she said coldly.

"You know who they are?"

"I am close to knowing. They made a mistake when they challenged us on our ground."

"What mistake was that?"

Emmanuella said nothing for a moment. "Who do you think M is, Dr. Cross?"

"Your brother thinks M is the leader of Maestro, a group dedicated to exposing corruption and ending your family business once and for all."

"They will fail, whoever they are," she said dismissively. "We are an infinitely funded business. Even if Maestro manages to kill every last one of us, there's too much money to be had feeding the cravings of addicted Americans. Another cartel will rise."

I let that slide. "How are Marco's children? His wife?"

"Louisa is taken care of. So are his kids."

"Two boys, thirteen and nine. Two girls, fourteen and five. You have children?"

"Three girls. Eleven, nine, and eight. Why do you ask?"

"Because they're in Maestro's crosshairs too. Both your brother and I believe he wishes to break you, and your children will soon be targets."

CHAPTER

65

MY LAST WORDS ANGERED ALEJANDRO'S twin sister.

"Are you threatening my daughters, Dr. Cross? And Marco's children and wife? Because you are in no position to do so. Your life is in my hands here."

"I acknowledge that, and I am not threatening you," I said. "I'm just stating facts that your brother wanted you to know. If M and Maestro have the chance, they will try to kill you, Louisa, and every one of the children the same way they killed General Guerra and your cousin."

"What would Marco have us do?" she said, flinging her hands out. "Give up? Take no action?"

I took a deep breath and said, "No. Just not the kind of action you have been taking. Stop retaliating against the families of the corrupt agents Maestro exposed and killed. What benefit is there in that strategy?"

Emmanuella looked at me as if the answer were obvious. "It tells others on your side of the border wall not to talk. They know the consequences if they do."

"But why not focus on M?"

"Believe me, I have not taken my eye off Maestro, not in the least."

"And you're close to identifying him? Because of something he did here in Mexico? On your home turf?"

"Why would I tell you this, Dr. Cross?"

"Because the enemy of my enemy is my ally."

"Not in this case," Emmanuella replied evenly. "In this case, the enemy of my enemy is also my enemy. If there were not dead U.S. agents involved, maybe you could be an ally. But there are dead U.S. agents involved, dead agents who were of great benefit to my business, so you are my enemy, Dr. Cross."

I sighed. "Again, I don't see it that way. Do I want corruption exposed? Yes. Do I think it's right for vigilantes like Maestro to declare themselves police, judge, jury, and hangmen? Absolutely not. That's why I'm here. And that's why I will continue to hunt M and not investigate your cartel. It's frankly not my job."

"Helping you hunt M is frankly not *my* job."

"But you'll reconsider retaliating against the families?"

She turned cold again. "I'm sorry I cannot be of more help to you, Dr. Cross. But our visit together is at an end."

The hood came down over my head. My wrists were cut free and a strong arm supported my elbow. As I was led away, I said, "Thank you for your time."

"You're welcome," Emmanuella Alejandro said.

CHAPTER

66

THE NEW LEADER OF THE Alejandro cartel watched Cross until he was placed in the back seat of the Tahoe. As the SUV drove away, she turned to Raphael Durango, the rugged-looking man who'd brought the American here from the city.

Emmanuella trusted him implicitly. Durango was strong, smart, well trained, bullheaded, and completely loyal to her. Even though her skin was pale and his was the deep, dark red of the Sierra Madre, he was also her half brother.

Her father had been a miner in the mountains and fell in love with one of the Tarahumara Indian women there. Durango had grown up running around and climbing in the steep mountains before joining the Mexican army, where he was part of an elite fighting unit similar to the U.S. Army Rangers for more than a decade.

After he was discharged, their father died and Durango had come to claim his inheritance. Marco had seen their half brother's value right away and made Durango Emmanuella's bodyguard. Since Marco's imprisonment, Durango had become her trusted confidant as well.

"Cross is sharp," Durango said. "He may find Maestro before we do."

"Unless he's allied with M and supportive of having us destroyed."

"Is that possible?"

"Why not, Raphael? Cross is a man of law and order. In any case, we are close to finding this pig M. I feel it in my bones. We need to learn who helped Maestro here in Mexico. Or at least figure out how they got in and out of Mexico City."

Durango poured himself some water. "Just so you know, when we used the wand on Cross, we found a GPS transmitter in his belt, low back."

"What?" she snapped. "Someone else knows he was here?"

Durango shook his head. "Calm down. The new Tahoe has an electronic jammer, and so does this entire hacienda. No one knows he was here. But now we know where he's going and we will for as long as he wears that belt."

"How's that?"

"We got the transmitter's frequency off the wand readout. It won't take much to have it send his location to us."

"That could be useful. Especially if my instincts are correct and Cross is aligned with M, wanting to see us destroyed and using his ability to go inside that penitentiary to bring Marco unwittingly to his side."

"Why didn't we kill him, then?" Durango asked.

Emmanuella's cell phone rang before her fury could build.

She looked at the caller ID, gritted her teeth, and answered sharply, "Yes, Claudio?"

"I think I've got them," her ex-husband said. "Four men, one woman, all American. Left on a chartered jet from a private field in Cuernavaca yesterday afternoon at two, destination Denver."

Claudio had a reputation for impulsiveness, jumping to conclusions based on emotion rather than fact, so she said, "What makes you think it's them?"

"I slipped five grand to the woman running the counter at the jet service. The charter was covered by one of the passengers. His name is Matthew Butler. I have copies of his passport and those of the people traveling with him."

"But what makes you think it's them, Claudio?" she repeated impatiently.

"I'm getting to that, Emmanuella," he grumbled. "I had her look to see if Butler had chartered other jets recently through the same leasing network. He had. Four times in the past six weeks. And here's why I think it's them. The dates and the destinations line up with most of Maestro's victims. Catherine Hingham, the CIA agent found in Washington. FBI agent Mason White in LA. DEA agent Eddie Hernandez, again in Washington. And now the three dead yesterday."

Emmanuella thought about that, then said, "Well done. I mean that, Claudio. But I need to know more. I need to know everything about this Matthew Butler and the people who were with him."

CHAPTER

67

Washington, DC

TWO DAYS LATER, IN THE early evening, Mahoney, Sampson, and I landed at Dulles International, feeling tired but happy that the cartel had not retaliated against the family of Dean Weaver, the CIA officer killed and left at the courthouse entrance in Mexico City, before they could be put into the witness protection program.

At home, after I'd hugged everyone and gotten the latest family news, Nana Mama told me she'd saved me dinner before saying she was feeling tired and went upstairs to read. Jannie and Ali were out in the front room binge-watching the latest season of *Ozark*. Bree stayed with me in the kitchen and drank a beer while I ate an excellent meat loaf and told her what I could about the dead CIA officer's confession.

Weaver wrote that he had recruited Catherine Hingham into the network of U.S. law enforcement agents corrupted by the cartel. He named two others at the CIA as coconspir-ators and described his relationship with General Guerra and Enrique Alejandro.

Weaver said he and Guerra had been meeting for years, figuring out ways to subvert efforts by non-corrupt U.S. agents to halt the flow of narcotics north. Like the other victims of Maestro, Weaver began his relationship with the cartel when he took a small bribe during a time of financial distress.

"What about the other two confessions you read?" Bree asked. "The general's and Alejandro's cousin?"

"Both were written in Spanish but Captain Rodriguez translated them for us," I said. "Guerra was corrupt from year one and rose in the ranks as the cartel grew. It was a mutually beneficial thing. He had tens of millions of dollars in accounts in South America. In return, the Alejandros got protection and influence.

"Enrique got involved because Marco was sent to prison and Emmanuella needed him to step in. He had been active in the cartel less than a year when Maestro tortured and killed him."

Bree said, "Marco's sister has no idea who M is?"

"Actually, the opposite," I said, taking a sip of beer. "She told me she believed she was close to identifying him. She said he'd made a mistake coming onto the cartel's home turf."

"You believe her?"

"I have no reason not to believe her."

"Will she tell you if she identifies him?"

I thought about that and shook my head. "I doubt it. If she told us and we got to Maestro first, we'd probably figure out everyone corrupted by her money. No, I think

Emmanuella will use every ruthless means at her disposal to try to wipe out M and his men before we can get anywhere near them."

Bree got me some ice cream to go with the blueberry pie my grandmother had baked that afternoon. "What about Paladin?" she asked, setting it before me.

"They're sifting huge quantities of data for us."

"According to my boss, they're incredibly good at it."

"Well," I said, yawning and getting up to rinse off my dishes, "if so, we should have a better idea of where to focus our efforts in a day or two. Mahoney got the FBI director to request Paladin sifts on the Alejandros and on Maestro and M, a deep dive including the dark web."

She finished her beer. "What was she like? Emmanuella?"

"Cold, beautiful, ruthless. But also very shrewd."

"How so?"

"I have a GPS transmitter in my belt, but Mahoney couldn't track me because she had jamming devices operating all around her. Once I got in their car, it was as if I didn't exist."

"Well, I'm grateful to say you do exist," Bree said, coming into my arms and kissing me. "I feel like going to bed early."

"Do you, now?" I said and kissed her deeply.

CHAPTER

68

Northwest of Laramie, Wyoming

ON THE CIRCLE M RANCH, near the mouth of a canyon that ran back into forest and wilderness, Matthew Butler sat on the porch railing of his log cabin drinking a cold beer. It was a warm evening with a bluebird sky.

The ranch grass was high and green, ready for a second cut. Horses were cantering about their pastures. Some of the ranch employees' children were playing tag in the late-day sun while their parents drank beer and ate barbecue at picnic tables.

Down by the corral, several young teenage boys and girls were milling about, looking awkward. It was so perfect, Butler almost didn't answer his phone when it rang.

He finally did. "Butler here. Scrambled line?"

"Scrambled," M said. "Did you know Cross had a meeting

with Emmanuella Alejandro the day after you left Mexico City?"

"How would I know that if I left the day before?"

"Well, he did. Vanished from our digital surveillance for the better part of four hours. Emmanuella's evidently using signal jammers everywhere she goes now."

Butler said, "Tricky lady. Who told you?"

"We still have people where it counts. Based on what I heard, we must consider Cross compromised now. Why else go to see the leader of a cartel alone? Why go to a woman like Emmanuella alone? To get his piece of the pie, that's why."

This was the most heated Butler had heard his employer in a long time. "What do you want us to do?"

M breathed long and slow and then said, "I can't believe I'm saying this, but take Cross next. Get him to confess. Take Sampson too. I used to admire them as men of integrity and principle. But I have no doubt they've been bought now. They're in it up to their eyeballs. Justice shall be served."

Butler wasn't seeing the situation entirely that way, but he said, "Timetable?"

"Sooner than later. I do not wish to be distracted by them anymore."

"We'll let you know when we're ready to move," Butler said and hung up.

He got himself another beer, sipped it, felt the sweet chill on his tongue and down his throat. The sun was sinking. The laughter of the ranch folk got louder the more beer they consumed.

He and his inner circle had been together so long, it was almost as if they sensed something was afoot. Big DD

Dawkins emerged from the shadows with the three others trailing him.

They came up onto the porch, all of them carrying beers. Vincente offered one to Butler, who showed him the one he already had.

"What are you thinking?" Butler asked.

"We need some downtime," Dale Cortland said. "The past few assignments have been too close together. We're going to make a mistake if we keep up this pace."

He fell silent.

"That it?" Butler asked.

Alison Purdy cleared her throat and said, "I won't be involved in killing kids."

"We don't do that, remember?" he shot back. "That's the cartel's specialty."

"I'm saying if it comes to that, I won't go there."

"Heard loud and clear," Butler said, his eyes roaming over his other men. They did seem drained. "Four days' rest, all of you. Then we go east again. M has given us another assignment."

Big DD groaned, as did Cortland and Purdy.

Vincente was shaking his head when the shooting started.

CHAPTER

69

FROM HIGH UP THE FLANKS of the hillsides that cradled the ranch yard, the attack came in waves of automatic-weapon fire, sniper shots, and rocket-propelled grenades. One pickup truck and then another exploded, sending fireballs into the sky.

By the time Butler and his team sprinted for their weapons, four of the ranch hands had been hit. Two of their wives died in their tracks.

Butler knew in his gut that the cartel had found them. He ran out of his cabin with an AR-15 and struggled to put on his earbud and jaw mike. He saw two of the young teens, a boy and a girl, hit from behind as they tried to flee the corral.

He went berserk, shouldering his rifle and racing toward

the teens, who were weeping and trying to crawl in the dirt. "If you can hear me, I need help pronto," Butler said into his mike.

Cortland and Big DD raced toward him, firing their weapons toward the flashes and bursts of flame on the hillsides.

Butler dragged the teens to cover and told them help was coming. Then he jumped up and ran again, barking, "Spread out! Hunt them in pairs! Talk to each other. No friendly fire!"

"Roger that," Purdy said. "Moving with JP."

"Hearing you both loud and clear," Vincente said. "On your right flank, *jefe*."

The sun had set. Dusk was deepening. But Butler could still make out his men peeling out to the sides of the cove. He began watching the tracer bullets, figured there were eight shooters, maybe more, firing down at them. He raised his own gun, sighted on an area the tracers were coming from, and opened fire, sending a burst of bullets three hundred yards up the hill.

He heard a man roar in pain and saw the tracers stop. "One down," he said.

"Roger that," Cortland said. "And many more to come. I'm going thermal."

That's how Butler figured this would unfold now. The average cartel thug against his Special Ops veterans? The Alejandros might be able to sneak in and surprise attack, killing women and children. But now? In a fair fight? They didn't stand a chance.

There were only eight, after all, maybe ten men above—

The firing suddenly intensified, became a barrage, with eight rocket grenades coming at the ranch from four different angles, rifles and machine guns rattling from far more than ten positions.

"They sent an army at us," Butler barked. "We're going to be overrun. Retreat to the canyon. Repeat, retreat to the canyon."

He could see the silhouettes of cartel men streaming off the hillsides, firing their weapons in short bursts. Cortland stood his ground, picking them off one by one, while Big DD retreated to a large piñon pine. This was how a controlled retreat worked, one man covering the other as they made their way safely to the rear.

Purdy and Vincente rushed by Butler, who turned to cover their exit, spraying bullets at the men coming down his side of the cove.

"Got your six, Cort," Big DD said.

"Same here, go, Cort," Butler said, glancing to his right to see his sniper spin around and race away from his position in a zigzag toward that big piñon pine.

Big DD opened up to cover him. So did Vincente and Purdy.

Butler saw several cartel men drop before one of their shots connected. In mid-sprint, Cortland staggered, pitched forward, and sprawled in the dirt ten feet shy of the tree trunk where Dawkins was crouched.

Big DD saw the sniper go down, leaped out into the line of fire, grabbed Cortland, and dragged him to safety.

Feeling like a wave of cartel men was about to crash on him, Butler ran toward the canyon as he heard Big DD say, "Cort's gone. Heading your way."

"We've got the canyon mouth covered," Purdy said. "We're high left and right."

Butler sprinted past his cabin and up a slight incline, not caring a whit for everything that was being left behind, focused only on the black maw of the canyon ahead of him and on reaching its safety before a cartel bullet could strike him down.

He heard feet pounding over the sound of guns and picked up Dawkins coming hard to his left. Bullets slapped off tree trunks to their right and left. They pinged off the rock ledges at either side of the canyon mouth.

Butler and Big DD vanished into the blackness of the narrow canyon. But when they turned around, they could see a mob of cartel men coming up the incline behind the cabins and moving through the trees.

Butler found a boulder, got behind it, reloaded, and aimed at the killers rapidly approaching. "Give them hell, now," Butler said. "Make them pay before we get out of here."

All four of them opened fire at once.

CHAPTER

70

I HAD NEVER BEEN TO Laramie, Wyoming, much less in a state police helicopter flying fifty miles northwest toward the ten-thousand-acre Circle M Ranch. We arrived around noon mountain time, landing in a hayfield below barns, loafing sheds, and cabins set in a large oval of gently rising ground surrounded by pine trees and steep, rocky hillsides.

It was hot. Thunderclouds rumbled to the west as Mahoney, Sampson, and I hustled out from under the chopper blades toward flashing blue lights atop two Wyoming State Police cruisers that blocked the gravel road into the ranch yard.

"We know who this place belongs to yet?" I asked.

"Some Brazilian company that owns big working cattle ranches all over the world."

Sampson looked around, awestruck. "I don't think I have

ever been to a prettier place for a massacre. Or a mass murder, for that matter."

"Forty-plus dead?" Mahoney said. "I'd say that's a massacre in anyone's book."

But when we were given protective booties and gloves and led onto the scene by FBI agents out of Cheyenne, Mahoney was grim.

"Looks more like a battlefield," he said as he scanned the lower yard, seeing bodies baking in the sun—four adults around a picnic table to our right, a couple of teenagers who'd died in each other's arms to our left, and three younger kids apparently shot in the back as they'd tried to flee.

On the side of the barn behind those children, someone had spray-painted *Death to Maestro! Long live the cartel!*

Vultures and crows circled above nine other bodies strewn on the hillsides. Through binoculars we could see that most of them were heavily tattooed, Hispanic, and armed with war weapons: machine guns and grenade launchers.

Behind a huge pine tree about halfway up the gentle rise, the body of a tall, gaunt man in his forties lay beside a scoped rifle.

I went over, skirting the dark pool of dried blood where he'd fallen and the ribbons of it where he'd been dragged behind the tree. Two steps more and I saw his face and the gun, which was no hunting rifle.

"It's the same guy we caught on that camera at the country club," I said. "Dale Cortland. The sniper who died in Afghanistan five years ago."

The state troopers and FBI agents on the scene had told us that most of the dead were up behind the cabins, near a canyon mouth about twenty yards wide. We walked up there and found twenty-seven Hispanic men sprawled dead, with hundreds of brass rifle casings lying in the pine duff around them.

"The Alejandros didn't kill all of M's men," I said. "A group of survivors defended the canyon, shooting anyone who tried to come at them until the surviving cartel gunmen gave up."

Mahoney said, "Jesus, how many men did Emmanuella send after them?"

"Fifty? Sixty?"

Sampson walked into the mouth of the canyon, studying the dirt, then sniffing the air. "Smells like a grenade or two went off in here," he called.

Mahoney and I followed him into the canyon, smelling the acrid odor of a blasted place, seeing debris thrown against the wall and the charred spots where the explosives had gone off in addition to dozens of empty bullet casings on the ground.

Sampson, ahead of us, crouched and said, "I've got blood here. Looks like one of M's men was hit."

"Back out, John," Mahoney said. "I want a dog in here and the chopper above the canyon before we go any farther."

CHAPTER

71

WE WAITED FOR A POLICE dog to arrive and for the FBI helicopter to get in the air.

My cell phone buzzed in my pocket. It said Paladin on the caller ID.

"Alex Cross," I said.

"It's Steve Vance, Dr. Cross," the data-mining company's CEO said. "We've found definitive links from three different attacks by the cartel going back to a small town named Santa Madera. It's in the mountains about fifty miles east of Mexico City."

Fifty miles, I thought. *Sounds like the car ride I took to see Emmanuella.* "What about here?"

"Where's 'here'?"

"Southern Wyoming," I said. "There was a fight here between the cartel and Maestro. More than forty dead."

"Forty?" Vance said, shocked. "My God. Can you get us authorization to mine cell phone data in that vicinity?"

"Special Agent Mahoney will get it for you ASAP."

By the time Ned had made the call, a German shepherd named Maximus was on-site and the FBI helicopter was lifting off with a spotter aboard. From Google Earth, we'd been able to study Fell's Creek Canyon, which was narrow at the mouth but broadened and steepened deeper into the drainage.

"We going all the way to the back?" I asked as we entered the canyon for the second time that day, now carrying AR rifles we'd gotten from the Cheyenne FBI agents.

"Six miles," Mahoney said. "And we've got the chopper to bring us out."

Maximus got on the blood scent fast but his handler, Sergeant Arthur Brayton, kept him on a tight rein, especially when we approached the creek bed for the first time.

"You'll want to check for tracks there in the wet stuff," Sergeant Brayton said. "See how many folks we're dealing with."

Mahoney and I went forward and counted four different sets of human tracks. Three sets were made by large waffle-soled boots of varying sizes, one close to Sampson's size 13. The fourth set was smaller, with a running shoe sole, and the wearer had been limping badly. There were blood specks to the right side of the right shoe.

"Too heavy for a kid, too light for a man," Brayton said. "It's a woman and she's hit in the meat of her right leg somewhere."

The wound continued to throw blood, though it became sparser the deeper we went into the canyon. Brayton's ability to read tracks combined with Maximus's fine nose had us moving fast but alert in case we pushed them out.

"Anything upstairs?" Mahoney called into his radio.

"You're running quite a few elk and deer ahead of you," the FBI pilot replied.

We covered the first three miles in under an hour. Brayton had us slow while the helicopter flew off to refuel. He didn't want to push them up and over the head of the drainage before we could spot them.

The helicopter returned when we reached mile four. The sky was darkening. Thunder boomed to our west. The pilot made a run up the canyon and saw no activity.

"If they're still in here, they're right up ahead of us," Brayton said. "We get close, I'll let Max take over."

The wind picked up. The helicopter flew back to the pasture below the ranch to ride out the storm.

Tensions were high when we reached the last mile, where the trail passed through dense, dark timber before climbing into an alpine bowl. We could see the rock walls of the upper bowl ahead of us as lightning began to crack and flash.

"More blood here," Sergeant Brayton said, pointing to a thick splash on a rock. "I say they've got her in a tourniquet and probably have a coagulant patch on the wound."

"Fresh?"

He touched the blood. "Sticky. Hours ago. But she's hit hard. As long as Max can stay on the scent, we will find her."

We moved closer to the alpine bowl, scanning the steep mountain flanks that soared above it, looking for people climbing out. A quarter of a mile from the open ground, we passed through thick groves of low spruce, like Christmas trees, the kind of place Brayton said a wounded creature might hole up. We all had our AR guns at port arms, ready in case we got in a firefight.

I admit I suffered a few moments of incredible anxiety easing through the last hundred yards of Christmas trees, sure that M's men were going to spring up and mow us down as they'd done to so many of the cartel gunmen behind us.

Fifty yards from the edge where the trees met rocky alpine terrain, there was a tremendous crash to our right. We all spun toward it, guns shouldered, hearing more crashes, the dog barking wildly.

There was a flash of brown ahead of us. A cow elk and her calf broke from the timber with a clatter and snapped branches as they bolted out of sight.

"I almost had a heart attack there," Mahoney said.

"I almost soiled myself there," Sampson said.

My temples were pounding with my racing heart. But I laughed as I lowered the gun. Out in the bowl itself, we found another splash of fresher blood on a game trail that led toward a notch high in the cliffs above us.

"That's midmorning," Brayton said, staring up the steep path that led to the notch. "She's tough, I'll give you that."

Lightning flashed again. The bolt hit the ridge to our right. The rain came in a deluge that swept toward us like a dark curtain.

"That's it," Sergeant Brayton said, turning Maximus around. "Not even Mr. Nose Wizard could follow a track in these conditions."

The rain hit us and we were soaked before we reached the Christmas trees.

"The chopper can't come for us in this kind of weather," Mahoney said. "We'll have to hike back."

"Better we jog back, stay warm," Sergeant Brayton said. "This is classic hypothermia weather."

"What's back up that trail?" I asked. "I mean, over that ridge?"

"Eight miles of wilderness and misery before you hit a web of logging roads."

CHAPTER

72

MATTHEW BUTLER, BIG DAVID DAWKINS, and J. P. Vincente ignored the rain, the lightning, and the thunder, totally absorbed in working on their burglar's right thigh. They had Alison Purdy on her back below a tarp they'd rigged between several saplings to keep her and the wound dry.

Her pant leg was slit open. She had a piece of stick wrapped in a bandanna in her mouth, and she bit into it and screamed every time they probed the wound.

"Think I feel it," Dawkins said. "But I'm going to have to go deeper, Alison."

"Gimme more oxy," she said, panting. "Everything in my bugout kit."

Months before, as a precaution in case they ever had to escape the ranch on foot, Butler had insisted they stash packs filled with survival gear, medical supplies, ammunition, and new identity documents a mile up the canyon, off the trail in an old bear den.

They'd reached the den within an hour of the cartel's retreat and began tending to Purdy's wound, from a shard of grenade shrapnel within inches of her femoral artery. They put her in a tourniquet, doused the wound with antibiotic gels, and used blood-coagulant patches to stanch the flow until they could get her to a doctor.

With the three men rotating as Purdy's assist, they'd climbed steadily out of Fell's Creek Canyon and down into the far drainage. Even with the help of three men, Purdy had a hard time; she'd been weakened by the ordeal. Butler realized they were going to have to remove the shrapnel if they were to make it the last five miles to an old Toyota Land Cruiser he'd left covered with logging slash in the early spring.

Big DD groped in Purdy's kit and found the painkillers.

"How many?" she asked.

"Six," he said.

"Gimme all of them," she said.

"Negative," Dawkins said. "You'll stop breathing. You get three now and three when we're done."

Purdy didn't like it but nodded and held out her palm for the pills, which she threw in her mouth and washed down with water. "I wish this was vodka."

"I bet you do," Butler said.

They waited twenty minutes, until the rain began to subside, before trying again, using surgical tools to retract the wound and probe deeper with forceps. Even with the added painkiller, Purdy was weeping and biting down hard on the stick in her mouth.

Butler felt the tip of the forceps click against something. "Hold her, now," he said to Vincente, who held Purdy down by her shoulders. "This is going to hurt."

He spread the forceps, drove them deeper, and grabbed the shrapnel as Purdy writhed and screamed bloody murder.

"Hold her, I said!"

Big DD lay across her torso as Butler drew out a thin, jagged blade of metal about an inch long. To his relief, there was no pumping artery blood flooding the wound. "Got it," he said. "Alison, I just need to sew you up now."

Purdy was drenched in sweat and disoriented when Vincente and Dawkins got off her. Butler doused the wound again with saline and antibiotics, cleaned the forceps with alcohol, then used them to grip a fishhook needle that he used to sew the gash shut. As he was bandaging the wound, he heard thunder booming to their west.

"We've got more storms coming," he said.

"Ride it out here?" Vincente asked.

"Negative—we definitely heard that helicopter before the first storm hit. Someone's looking for us, so we go fast and hard under cover of the rain. And there's a bigger med kit in the rig. I can give her IV antibiotics and morphine, get her comfortable."

"You'll have to carry me," Purdy said. "No way I can take another step."

"I'll carry you, Alison," Big DD said. "No problemo."

"We all will," Vincente said, taking down the tarp. He sawed two of the saplings and lashed the tarp between them. Ten minutes later, as the rain and wind picked up again, they lifted Purdy into the makeshift litter and set off.

73

THUNDERSTORM AFTER THUNDERSTORM WITH VIOLENT lightning and driving rain battered south-central Wyoming that afternoon. It was nearly six before we exited the canyon behind the Circle M Ranch. We were all soaked, shivering, and hungry.

The army of federal, state, and local law enforcement personnel had removed most of the bodies, but a swarm of crime scene techs were still at work, searching every building and seizing evidence, as the last storm petered out.

Even Maximus seemed happy when we climbed up the porch of one of the cabins that agents said was unoccupied and heated. We crammed in there and kept warm while they found dry clothes for us all.

While we waited, Karl Paulson, the FBI supervising special agent in Cheyenne, filled us in on what had been found, learned, and done since we went into the canyon after Maestro's surviving men.

Due to the violence of the storms, the helicopter had stayed grounded, though the pilot planned to fly as soon as the weather cleared. In the meantime, Paulson had left it in the hands of the local county sheriff to set up roadblocks outside the matrix of logging roads beyond the wilderness area.

The Laramie morgue was overwhelmed by the number of corpses. A decision had been made to keep the sixteen bodies of the ranch hands and their families local for identification. The forty-two bodies of the cartel gunmen and the corpse of Dale Cortland were being sent to Denver in a refrigerated truck for autopsy.

"We have any idea who the four who made it out of here are?" Mahoney asked.

"Only that they occupied the three upper cabins," Paulson said, taking us out on the porch and pointing to them. "Two unidentified males lived in one on the left. Unidentified female in the center. Two more unidentified males on the right."

"You found nothing that says who they are? No documents? No computers?"

"If there were computers, they're gone, maybe taken by the cartel. Someone went through the cabins before us."

We wanted to see for ourselves. The cabins were spartan—simple twin beds, wood-burning stove, and gas lamps for light. Except for the clothes hanging on hooks and the basic toiletries in the bathrooms, there was literally nothing that said anything definitive about the occupants.

"It's going to be fingerprints and DNA from here forward," Sampson said.

"What about the ranch hands' homes?" I said. "And the ranch office? This is a big business. There have to be computers and records."

Agent Paulson nodded. "That's all there in the ranch manager's building down the road."

Mahoney said, "I want it all shipped to Quantico for analysis. And I want agents going to adjacent ranches. Find out what they know about the people who worked here and the Brazilian company that owns this place."

The rain finally stopped. We went up in the helicopter for the last hour of light.

The pilot took us over the wilderness area and did a loop above the logging terrain, where there was indeed a maze of two-track roads crisscrossing the mountains for as far as you could see. We spotted quite a few pickups next to skidders and filthy logging crews packing it up for the day but nothing suspicious before we banked southeast and headed back to Laramie for the night.

CHAPTER

74

THE THREE OF US HAD been up since three a.m. eastern. The flight, the lack of sleep, and the twelve-mile hike in the rain was catching up to us, but we needed to eat so we went to the chophouse across the street from our motel.

The food was good, and we ate ravenously. Sampson had talked to Willow, who was playing games on Jannie's phone and was up way past her bedtime. She was staying at our house, so I texted Bree and Jannie to make sure they got her to bed soon.

"Thanks," Sampson said. "She gets a little addicted to the phone."

"Story of their generation," Mahoney said, yawning.

"Oh," Sampson said, looking at his cell phone. He turned it to show me a photograph of a stunning mountain scene with granite peaks reaching toward a sapphire sky. "Taken two days ago in the Bob Marshall Wilderness by our packer. His wife wants to know if we're coming. We're running out of time for this year. It's almost the end of August."

"It is beautiful," I said, looking at the picture.

"Good for the soul." Sampson sighed and put his phone down. In the hurly-burly of the events of the past weeks, I'd forgotten how much he wanted to go on that trip, how much he needed to go on that trip to finally let go of Billie.

The thought must have crossed Mahoney's mind too. He chewed on the inside of his cheek and then said, "You know, John, as much as I value your contribution to this investigation—and yours, Alex—for the next week to ten days, it's going to be a whole lot of hurry-up-and-wait for the lab reports, DNA, and fingerprints to come back and for the computers to be analyzed."

Sampson's brow furrowed. "What are you saying, Ned?"

"I'm saying you're in Wyoming, for Christ's sake, which is a lot closer to Montana than the District of Columbia. You've got a window of opportunity. Why don't you rent a car, call your packer, and tell him you'll be ready to go the day after tomorrow or the day after that?"

"We don't have our gear with us," I said.

"But it's organized, correct?"

"Over-organized," Sampson said. "We've been packed for two months or more. It's all at Alex's house in dry bags."

"Have Bree express-ship them first thing tomorrow morning," Mahoney said. "You'll meet the gear wherever you're going."

"Bigfork, Montana," Sampson said, grinning at me. "What do you say? It's not the way we planned it, but when opportunity knocks, you've got to answer, right?"

The obsessive part of me wanted to come up with reasons we should stay close to the day-to-day grind of the investigation. But Mahoney was right. Unless the sheriff's dragnet picked up the four survivors of the massacre or something dramatic was found at the ranch in the morning, there really was no reason for us to stay and work this end of things.

"Let's do it," I said and clapped Sampson on the shoulder. "We leave in the morning. Montana-bound."

75

MATTHEW BUTLER AND HIS MEN had raced daylight and the cover of the thunderstorms that entire afternoon, rotating as they moved, one man resting while the other two carried the crude litter and the wounded Alison Purdy. The burglar was in and out of consciousness when they finally reached the clear-cut where Butler had hidden the old Land Cruiser, covered in tree limbs left behind by loggers.

It was past sunset, but Butler waited until almost full darkness before leaving the woods and moving to the slash pile. They laid Purdy to one side and pulled the limbs and branches off the rig until they had it freed.

Butler got the key from under the rear bumper, opened the door, and retrieved the medical kit while Vincente lowered the tailgate and dropped one of the back seats. They slid Purdy on the litter in with Big DD sitting beside her.

"Wait until we hit the deep forest up ahead and we'll turn on the lights enough to get an IV in her," Butler said and started the truck.

He held the night-vision monocular to his eye with his left hand and put the rig in low gear with his right. For the next fifteen minutes, the truck clawed and bounced across branches, stumps, and mounds of dirt until they reached a section of uncut trees.

Butler stopped and turned on the interior lights. "Go to work on her. I've got to make a call."

He reached under the front seat, retrieved a satellite phone, and got out. He walked into darkness while it warmed up and then made his call.

There was none of the normal, calm, calculated intellect when M answered. "Where the hell have you been? What in the hell happened down there? The chatter we picked up says—"

"Scrambled?"

"Yes, damn it, scrambled!"

"They came at us with a small army, M," Butler said. "Automatic weapons. RPGs. We lost everyone at the ranch. Even the kids. Cortland's gone too. Purdy's wounded but will live; we're getting an IV in her now. We took out most of the cartel's men before we bugged out."

There was silence on the line. Then: "How did they find you?"

"I was hoping you'd tell me. They came out of nowhere. We're lucky to be alive."

After another long pause, M said, "Cross. Or Mahoney. Or Sampson. The FBI. They must have found something that pointed to you, and Cross told Emmanuella Alejandro about it. Cross didn't want to be involved in the attack, but he wanted us defeated, so he told her."

At times, Butler could barely tolerate M's growing paranoia over Alex Cross.

"Or maybe there was a leak on your end," Butler offered.

"Don't you think I'd be in handcuffs if there were?" M roared. "It's Cross, I'm telling you. He's out there right now. Mahoney and Sampson too. In Wyoming. On the ranch! They're…they're after me!"

"At the moment, they are after the four of us," Butler snapped. "So why don't you help us figure out how to get out of here without getting caught."

M did not reply for several long moments and was much more composed when he did. "You're right, Butler. I apologize. We've got your GPS position and we have been monitoring law enforcement communications out there and know where the sheriff's roadblocks were as of one hour ago."

"They going thermal once the weather clears?" Butler asked, fearing a helicopter with a thermal-imaging system picking up the Land Cruiser.

"Not that we've heard, but it is the logical next step," M said. "Start driving as soon as Purdy is stable. We'll get you out of there long before they put a bird back in the sky."

"Roger that."

"And when you get free, Butler, I have decided that we are going to finish Cross. Then we're going back to Mexico to pay a visit to Emmanuella herself to end this."

"The Maestro leaves his podium?"

"I've waited a long time for a face-to-face, Butler. I want that murdering bitch to know who destroyed her and the cartel her brother built."

76

RAPHAEL DURANGO AND FIVE OF his remaining men were holed up in a motor home parked deep in Bureau of Land Management property some forty miles east-northeast of Laramie. They'd been there since before dawn, sleeping, eating, and talking their way through the battle, as warriors do.

Durango's instincts told him to move on at dark, to head east and then south toward Denver, New Mexico, and the border. But before that, he had to face his half sister.

He gave his men a bottle of tequila and ordered them outside before starting the motor home and booting up the satellite internet base station. When he had a solid feed on his laptop, he routed it through a VPN to give himself partial anonymity and then routed it through a second VPN to assure an untraceable connection.

Durango made the sign of the cross, opened Skype, and called Emmanuella.

Her face soon appeared. Her eyes flashed when she saw him.

"I was worried," she said in Spanish. "I've heard many, many dead. Is this true? Did you wipe them out?"

Durango knew not to sugarcoat anything, not with his half sister. "No."

"Did you get M?"

"Maybe," he said. "We shot at least twenty people there. Men, women, kids. You said to kill everyone."

Emmanuella swallowed hard. "It was the only way. What about this Butler?"

He shook his head. "He and three others, two men, one woman. They were professionals, ex-military, they had to be. They retreated into the mouth of a canyon, took positions where we couldn't hit them. They had the advantage."

"Advantage?" she cried angrily. "I sent you with an army and every weapon we could buy!"

"And they killed more than forty of our men before I pulled back."

Emmanuella blinked. "Forty?"

"And wounded six more, who probably won't make it," he said.

The cartel leader went stone-faced for several moments. "What happened to Butler and the other three?"

"Escaped deeper into that canyon behind the ranch," Durango said.

"I wanted them dead. I still do."

He finally lost his cool. "I know what you want, sister, but how in God's name am I supposed to do that? How am I supposed to find them with the FBI crawling all over the area?"

"I thought you were some great manhunter, Raphael. Great Indian tracker. Special Forces animal. You tell me how to—"

Emmanuella stopped her rant abruptly, frowning. Her eyes ran left and froze there, as if she were puzzling out some odd thought or hearing a distant voice become clearer. Then she said, "Wait a second." Emmanuella began typing on her laptop. She hit Return and sat back. "He's there! I knew he'd be there."

"Who?"

"Cross," she said, almost smiling as she returned her attention to her brother. "He's still wearing that belt with the GPS transmitter. It says he's in Laramie. Wait, there's a history function."

She typed, hit Return, and covered her mouth as she moved her head closer to the screen. "He was all over that ranch and that canyon today."

"Makes sense."

"That's true. But it doesn't change things. If I'm right and Cross is a secret ally of Maestro, he will meet up with Butler and his men very soon. You only have to follow Cross until it happens."

"You don't think we should come back to Mexico and let things cool down around here?"

Her smile vanished. "No, Raphael, I want you to finish this. Follow Cross wherever he goes. Sooner or later, you'll find Butler. And if I'm right, you'll also find M."

CHAPTER

77

Swan River Valley, Montana

THREE MORNINGS LATER, SAMPSON AND I were up early and wolfing down a hearty breakfast at a lodge overlooking beautiful Holland Lake in the remote Flathead National Forest. Above the thick pine-and-spruce canopy, towering peaks rose, forming the western boundary of the Bob Marshall Wilderness.

I don't think I'd ever seen Sampson so excited.

"I feel great," he said as he buttered his toast. "Slept like a log."

"I did too," I said and sipped coffee. "All the fresh air."

"And the eight-hundred-mile drive."

"Woke up a little stiff from that."

"You're going to get stiffer."

"Yeah, I don't think I've ever ridden a horse for more than an hour before."

We were done eating by seven. Five minutes later, we were outside with all our gear and calling home one last time.

"Be careful out there," Bree said.

"Don't get eaten by a grizzly," Ali said.

"I'll try not to," I said. "I love you all and we'll talk in six days."

I was about to shut off my cell phone for the duration of the trip when it rang. Paladin showed up on the ID.

I really didn't want to, but I answered. "Cross."

"Steven Vance here, Dr. Cross," the CEO said, sounding excited. "We found something we believe you are going to be interested in."

Sampson was making *We have to leave* motions and I nodded. "Steve, can you tell me this quick? I'm actually in Montana about to go on a trip into the wilderness for the next six days."

"Love Montana," Vance said. "Lucky you. I'll keep it brief. We did find chatter and traffic between southern Wyoming and that same small town in Mexico on the day before the attack. We also picked up a satellite-phone signal from the wilderness beyond that ranch. A satellite phone positioned in central Manitoba answered."

"Manitoba?"

"Near the town of Herb Lake."

"Do you know what was said? How long it lasted?"

"Seven minutes, but we have no idea what was said," Vance said.

"Can you relay this information to Special Agent Mahoney?"

"Of course. Enjoy your trip."

"What's up?" Sampson said, sounding defensive when I hung up. "There's no way we're pulling out of this now."

"No way," I said. "That was Vance. He says the night after the attack, there was a sat-phone call from the wilderness beyond Fell's Creek Canyon to an obscure town in Manitoba."

"M is in Manitoba?" John asked incredulously.

"Kind of my reaction," I said as a white dually pickup pulled up.

Our outfitter and horse packer, Lance Bauer, was a lean, long-legged man in his fifties who chewed Red Man and laughed at just about anything. He climbed out and helped us load our gear in the pickup bed while Pork Chop, his Australian shepherd, bounced all around.

"Nice binocs," Bauer said, gesturing to the brand-new Leica binoculars hanging on hunting harnesses we both wore.

Sampson said, "We heard there's a lot to see in there."

"Well, that's the truth," Bauer said.

He drove us up to the Holland Lake trailhead. When we got there, Bauer's wife, Lucy, and a hired man were loading the last of the pack mules, six in all.

We'd met the Bauers the afternoon before, shortly after we arrived at the lodge to find our gear waiting. Bree had shipped it all out express. After getting our instructions, the Bauers had taken the dry bags away to be weighed, balanced, and packed. We were just making it in as the last trip of the season.

When we got out of the pickup that morning, Lucy Bauer, a tough woman with a magnetic smile, introduced us to our horses for the twenty-nine-mile ride ahead of us.

"John, since you're the biggest, you'll be riding Queenie," Lucy said, patting the quivering flanks of a big chestnut mare. "She's a doll, a Tennessee Walker, and an absolute dream to ride in the mountains."

"She's done this ride before?"

"Fifteen to twenty times a year since she turned three, and that was fifteen years ago," she said, stroking the horse's nose. "Queenie could walk most of these trails blindfolded. Couldn't you, doll?"

Lucy smiled at me and gestured at a stocky, bluish-black horse with a jet-black mane that was smaller than Queenie. "Dr. Cross, you'll ride Toby. He's part Morgan horse, which means he's strong as an ox, has a heart that won't quit, and can walk forever and a day. He's twelve and been with us since he turned three."

"Hey, Toby," I said, holding out a lump of sugar I'd pilfered from the lodge.

The horse sniffed it and nibbled it off my palm.

"You've made a friend forever," Lucy said.

Her husband walked up holding two scabbards. "Where are your weapons?"

"We've got our service pistols," I said.

"Calibers?"

"Mine's forty-five," Sampson said.

"Not good enough," Bauer said.

"Forty caliber," I said.

"Definitely not good enough," he said.

"For what?" I asked.

"Grizzlies," Bauer said. "You're about to spend the next six days in some of the densest concentrations of *Ursus horribilis* in the lower forty-eight states. You need to be prepared, carry bear spray and enough gun. Your service weapons aren't enough."

Though I sobered at the thought, Sampson's smile could not have been bigger. "What're the chances we'll see one?"

Bauer shrugged. "They're all over the place up there, but this time of year it depends on the heat. If we'd been up on Gordon Pass at dawn we'd have had a good chance to see one through binoculars somewhere. But we'll be crossing it around two."

"In the heat of the day."

"Correct," Bauer said, handing us the scabbards. "We'll lend you two of our camp guns. I'd appreciate them coming back in one piece."

"Absolutely," John said.

Bauer went to his pickup and retrieved an Ithaca ten-gauge pump-action shotgun and a Ruger guide rifle with a low-power telescopic sight on it.

"It's chambered in three-seventy-five Ruger," he said, handing the rifle and a box of ammunition to John. "Shoots three-hundred-grain Alaskan bullets."

"What's the law on shooting a grizzly?" I asked.

"Gotta be self-defense," he said, giving me the shotgun. "That means he's inside thirty yards and coming at you hard and fast. First shot's buckshot. Next four are slugs."

"We have to wait until they're that close?" I said.

He nodded. "We'll give you bear gas too, which is what you want to use first. But if that doesn't work and you have to shoot one, preserve the site as if it were one of your crime scenes, because U.S. Fish and Wildlife Service will be investigating. To them a grizzly death falls under Napoleonic law."

"Meaning?"

"You're presumed guilty of murdering the bear until proven innocent."

CHAPTER

78

RAPHAEL DURANGO SLIPPED INTO THE trees at the far end of the parking lot at the Holland Lake trailhead in time to see Lucy Bauer kiss her husband, who then climbed on his horse and whistled for his dog.

"C'mon, Pork Chop," Bauer called. "Lead the way."

The Australian shepherd bounded up the trail with Bauer following, a lead rope wrapped around his pommel and attached to the mule behind him, which was tugging the lead ropes of the five other mules strung out to the rear. John Sampson was on a great big horse behind the mules with Alex Cross and a wrangler riding at the back.

Durango adjusted the Miami Dolphins ballcap on his head, left the trees, and walked up to Lucy Bauer. He smiled as he gestured toward the disappearing pack train.

"We don't see that kind of thing where I'm from," he said. "Wild West, yes?"

Lucy smiled. "It's wild up where they're going, that's for sure."

"Where are they going?"

"Over Gordon Pass into the Bob Marshall Wilderness, about twenty-nine miles," she said. "Tomorrow the clients will get on a raft and begin a long float on the South Fork of the Flathead River."

"That's sounds fantastic," he said.

"It is. Would you like a brochure, Mr...."

"Martinez," he said. "Pablo Martinez. And yes, please."

Lucy got one from the cab of her husband's pickup and gave it to him. "You need your own clothes, rain gear, sleeping bags, and clothes in dry bags. We provide the tents and the rafts and pack you in along with all the food you'll need, and we help pull you out at the other end."

"How long does it take to float the river?"

"This time of year it's five days; with the ride in, it's six," she said. "Earlier in the season, when the water's higher, you can do a faster float, four days, five in total."

"But they go for six days," he said. "Is there a map that shows the route?"

"A little one on the back cover," she said, turning over the brochure. "First night, after the ride in, you're up here on Grand Prairie at the confluence with Gordon Creek. Second night, you're on the river, and most folks camp here and then here near Big Salmon Lake the third night. Unless of course you're interested in a shorter trip, then you'd ride in and start from Big Salmon and float for just three days to the takeout."

Durango did the math in his head and realized he had a chance to get ahead of Cross and Sampson. But did he need to? Couldn't he just wait until they came off the river? Then again, Emmanuella had said to follow them wherever they went.

He said, "You do this? Pack people into this Big Salmon Lake?"

"We do, and we're taking reservations for next summer."

"I could not arrange this for me and my friends to go later today? Or tomorrow?"

"Today? Tomorrow?" she said. "No. That was our last trip in for summer rafting. And next week we get real busy with all the bow hunters going in after elk."

"Money is no object," Durango said. "And who knows when we will be back this way again."

"Like I said—"

"Double the normal cost? Triple?"

Lucy thought about it. "I suppose I could get my nephew to take you in first thing tomorrow morning. We'd have to get more of our stock and the rafts and supplies trucked down from Bigfork. Triple our normal fee? You're sure?"

"Positive," he said, grinning. "For me and five friends."

"Six of you?" she said. "Are you all staying at the lodge, Mr. Martinez?"

"No," he said. "In a motor home at the campground. Part of our big summer of exploration and adventure."

Lucy said, "I'd need the money wired to our accounts today."

"Not a problem," Durango said. "My friends will be so excited. It will be the trip of a lifetime."

CHAPTER

79

LATER THAT AFTERNOON, BUTLER PULLED into the Holland Lake trailhead, left Big DD and Vincente in the old Land Cruiser, and got out to make a call on the sat phone.

"Scrambled," M said. "You're finally there, I see."

"Just arrived."

"You should have used a different vehicle rather than that junker," he said, irritated. "Now we're too far behind them to do much good today."

"We're behind because we had to make sure Purdy was squared away."

"Mmm."

"You're still tracking their phones, I assume?"

"No," he said. "They're far out of service now, but we know exactly where they're going and why. It's all they blabbed about in their car. Again, if you hadn't used that blasted shitbox of a truck, we'd already be rid of them."

Butler ignored the dig, said, "We're here now, M, and they're six days from coming out of that wilderness. What do you want us to do? Wait?"

"Wait? No, I want you to go in after them. I want them eliminated ASAP."

"We don't have horses or rafts or any of the right equipment for this."

"You don't need any of it," M snapped. "We've already been in contact with a helicopter service about ninety minutes north of you. They're expecting you later this afternoon. I assume your pilot's licenses are up to date?"

"The fake ones," Butler said. "What kind of bird?"

"Bell Jet Ranger," he said.

"Weather?"

"On and off thunderstorms," he said. "Nothing you haven't faced before."

"And how exactly are we supposed to find them?"

"Follow the river. You're bound to spot them sooner or later. Let me know when you've got the helicopter down there and ready to go."

Butler thought renting a helicopter was a little over the top, and he didn't fully understand M's obsession with Alex Cross, but there was no arguing with the man once he had his mind set on something. "Your money," Butler said.

"One more thing," M said. "Our computers managed to pick up pieces of a conversation we believe happened between Emmanuella Alejandro and her half brother sometime in the last couple of days. We didn't get all of it because they were using multiple VPNs."

Butler's eyebrows rose. "You mean Raphael Durango? The Mexican Special Forces operator?"

"The same," M said. "We believe he led the raid on the ranch."

"Makes a lot of sense," Butler said, going stony. "Where is the son of a bitch?"

"Again, we only got fragments, but we believe Emmanuella told him to follow Cross wherever he goes. She believes we are somehow allied with the FBI and that Cross and Sampson are going to rendezvous with us somewhere in Montana."

"How did she get that idea?"

"No clue."

Butler thought about that. "You think Durango is here and going into the wilderness after them?"

"Would you cross Emmanuella Alejandro?"

"Any day of the week," he said. "And twice on Sunday."

"You're not her half brother," M said. "I want you to fly in there looking for Cross, Sampson, *and* Durango and whoever else is with him. And when you locate them, I want them all dead, never to be found. Is that clear?"

"As the big Montana sky," Butler said and ended the call.

CHAPTER

80

POUND FOR POUND, I'D HAVE to say that my horse, Toby, was the toughest animal I'd ever encountered. I am not as big as Sampson, but I tip the scales at two fifteen on a good day. That's a lot of pounds to carry on a long, steep, switchbacked ride to a place like Gordon Pass.

But Toby never broke stride, not once. Neither did John's horse. Queenie seemed to float up the trail, her gait so smooth that even with his recent injuries, John wasn't complaining about being saddlesore at all.

I, however, was getting my rump pounded and my inner thighs chafed. By the time we reached the head of the pass, around three that afternoon, and got down out of the saddle for a rest, I had blisters. While I hobbled around trying to get the blood to return to my legs, Sampson was photographing the dramatic alpine views to our east, all forest, high meadows, and crags.

"Makes you feel small, doesn't it?" John said, taking a panoramic shot.

"Like a gnat," I said.

"Puts things in perspective," he said, then called to Bauer, "Is that all the Bob Marshall ahead of us, Lance?"

"The thick of the Bob right there," Bauer said. "All right, let's saddle back up."

"What, already?" I said.

"We need to get to camp in time to eat, inflate the raft, and organize your gear before dark," Bauer said, climbing back on his horse and whistling to his dog.

I groaned as I got back on Toby. "I feel like my butt's been spanked with fifteen cricket bats."

Sampson looked at me. "You've been spanked by fifteen cricket bats before?"

"First time," I said and winced as I settled into the saddle again.

Bauer called back, "You can sit in the river when we get there, Dr. Cross. I guarantee it's cold enough to take the saddle ache away."

We rode another five hours that afternoon, following Gordon Creek down its long drainage, an experience I endured by focusing on the breathtaking scenery and the idea of an ice-cold river ahead rather than on my aching glutes and thighs. When we finally reached the point where Gordon Creek met the South Fork of the Flathead, we saw three wall tents in the aspens.

It was almost eight. We'd been in the saddle for eleven and a half hours. I immediately got off Toby, tied him to an aspen tree, and waddled toward the bank, where I took off my hiking boots and pants, put on my Chaco sandals, waded out into the cold river, and sat down in frigid water up to my rib cage.

"Oh, that feels good," I said, moaning. "Oh my God, that feels good."

Sampson took several pictures of me sitting out there holding a tin cup containing a couple shots of Jack Daniel's, which frankly did wonders. When I finally climbed out, my legs were comfortably numb.

Bauer smiled at me and said, "Where's your lover?"

I looked at him, puzzled. "Uh, Washington, DC?"

"No," the outfitter said. "Your weapon. The shotgun."

"It's still with our gear."

"I want that shotgun and your bear gas where you can reach them at all times."

"You're kidding."

"Do I look like I'm kidding, Dr. Cross?"

"Message heard loud and clear."

After dressing, I went and found the scabbard with the shotgun and carried the ten-gauge around with me with the bear gas in a holster on my hip. Sampson had his rifle less than five feet away as we helped Bauer pump up our raft and load the things we would not use that night.

We had twenty minutes of good light left when we finished. There were fish jumping in the river. John got out a fly rod.

"I didn't know you fly-fished," I said.

"I haven't yet," he said. "But I read a book and watched some YouTube videos. And look where we are. It would almost be a crime if I didn't at least try."

With Bauer's help, John got the reel and rod rigged correctly and followed the outfitter's instructions on how to cast. Sampson's attempts were more like thrashing the water, but he was as happy as I'd ever seen him when he quit and we went up near the fire where Harden, the hired hand, was grilling steaks.

"Everything you imagined?" I asked John.

Sampson grinned. "And then some. Totally cut off. No cell phones. No satellite phones. Just us and nature, Alex. And you know what? I will never forget that ride in here as long as I live."

"I have a feeling you'll never forget this entire trip as long as you live."

81

WE HEARD A BULL ELK bugle at dawn, an otherworldly sound that seemed to float through the trees and across the sky only to be joined by the howling of wolves in the distance. While I got a cup of coffee, Sampson went back down by the river to try his hand at casting again.

Ten minutes later, as I chatted with Bauer and his wrangler, who were already packing for their long ride back out, John returned with his line hopelessly tangled.

"How am I supposed to fix this?" he asked.

"Cut the leader off above that rat's nest," Bauer said. "Put a new leader on and a new fly, and you'll be good to go. Oh, and count on this happening at least four or five times before you get the hang of it."

"People actually get the hang of it?"

"They do, and the South Fork's a great river for beginners.

The fish are not selective at all. Just get a fly on the water with the leader upstream and they'll smash it. In the meantime, you should finish breakfast and get the rest of your stuff into your dry bags. I want to be rolling west in an hour after watching you safely start downriver."

Bauer and the wrangler were riding out, with Pork Chop in front, an hour and ten minutes later. We were already on our raft, floating downstream through an area known as Grand Prairie with Sampson on the oars and me up front looking for boulders. We traveled along a single channel through a long, broad sage flat with scattered spruce and aspen groves. To either side of the river, mountains towered and loomed.

The sun at that altitude was intense even early in the day. It beat down on us, hotter and hotter as an hour went by and then two. We reached an area where the river broke up into multiple channels that braided back and forth across one another. In several of those places, the water was too low, so we had to get out and drag the raft.

Thankfully, these events were all short-lived, and by midmorning we were both relaxing into the rhythm of floating through God's country, seeing bald eagles, a herd of mule deer, and a black bear sow and her cubs running across a far hillside.

I took over the oars around ten thirty and soon got the hang of using them to pivot and angle the raft so it rode the deepest water. Sampson was up front, taking it all in with a bittersweet smile.

"Gorgeous spot," I said.

He looked back at me. "Only thing missing is Billie."

"Who says she's missing?"

John thought about that and then nodded. "Yeah, I guess that's the point."

"You said you were bringing some of her ashes."

"And I did," he said. "I just wish she could have seen this, Alex. She would have loved it. The scenery. The animals. The silence."

"It is incredible. I haven't heard anything but the river for the past three hours."

"I'm hoping to hear nothing but the river for the next five days," Sampson said. "It's hypnotic. Good for the head and the soul."

"I feel you, brother."

Around noon, we stopped on a sandbar for lunch and looked at our position on Sampson's phone. He'd bought an app from a company called OnX that allowed us to download a satellite map of the entire river between Gordon Creek and the takeout. It looked like we had only a two-hour float to where the broad sage flat ended and the river wound into a long, narrow canyon with swifter water.

"See Burnt Creek, about mile seven? Above the canyon?" Sampson said, pointing to it. "Bauer said the fishing's always good where a creek meets a river. He showed me pictures of the area. It's beautiful, a fitting place for Billie's ashes."

"Then that's as far as we'll go today."

We packed up and got back on the river, with me at the oars in no hurry whatsoever. Just happy to be alive.

"I appreciate you being here, Alex," Sampson said after a long silence.

"I would not have it any other way, my friend. What do you think of bringing Ali and Willow out here in a few years?"

He looked over his shoulder at me and nodded. "I'd like that. I think the kids would like that too."

"I'm sure Ali would be going out of his mind right about now," I said and laughed.

"Especially if you had to take another butt soak in the river."

"Hey, you can't show those pictures to anyone."

"Really?" Sampson said. "I was going to get one framed for Bree for Christmas."

CHAPTER

82

WE KEPT UP THE EASY banter between extended periods of quiet while we soaked up the new and remarkable surroundings. Two hours later, Sampson got pictures of a big bull moose crossing the river in front of us.

After negotiating a few small rapids, we pulled the raft over on the west side of the river opposite Burnt Creek and the long pool the outfitter said always held fish. We unloaded the raft, pulled it all the way up on the bank and into the trees, and tied it securely to an aspen trunk. Then we set up the dome tent near it and suspended a tarp over a spot we decided would be our kitchen.

It was close to three in the afternoon by the time we had the portable table and camp chairs up and had gathered enough dead branches for a fire later. Sampson got his fly rod, bear spray, and the rifle before going to the river.

I followed him. It was a spectacular spot. There were more sandbars downriver. The mountain opposite us had burned several years before but was now covered in tall green grass and knee-high fir trees.

Sampson set the rifle and fly rod down and stood there a long time, his hand to his brow.

"Looking for fish?" I asked.

"Trying to figure out how to let Billie go."

I felt a surge of pity go through me and stayed quiet. After a few minutes, he picked up his fly rod, left the rifle, and started into the knee-deep back channel with his Teva sandals on.

"I think some of her should be right here in this river," he said. "She'll go first downstream, clearing the way for us the rest of the trip."

I smiled sadly as he waded the back channel to a long sandbar and crossed it to face the big pool where the creek met the river. After a few moments, he set down his rod, reached into his pocket, and retrieved Billie's ashes in a small purple velvet bag.

He held the bag to his chest, waded into the river a few feet, and looked skyward before he spread his late wife's ashes on the water. John stood there for the longest time watching as some of his love slipped downstream.

I got tears in my eyes as thunder rumbled to our west.

Sampson climbed out, got his fly rod, and walked north along the sandbar a good thirty yards. Figuring he needed time alone, I picked up the shotgun and went back to the kitchen to organize a gourmet meal of Mountain House freeze-dried chicken stew and vegetables.

Twenty minutes later, the thunder was closer. The wind

was picking up as well, and I was about to get my rain gear handy when I heard Sampson bellowing, "Alex! Alex! Come here! Fast!"

My first thought was *Bear! And he doesn't have the rifle!*

I grabbed the shotgun, raced to the river, and came out on the bank in time to see John running along the sandbar, his fly rod nearly bent in two.

"Alex!" he shouted. "I've got one! It's a monster!"

"What do you want me to do?"

"Bring a phone to take a picture in case I can land it!"

By the time I'd waded the back channel and run down the sandbar to him, Sampson was kneeling in the shallows by a cutthroat trout that was at least a foot long.

"It's huge!" I said.

"Told you." He grinned. "Now I'm going to scoop it up with my hands and you take the picture."

I set down the shotgun and dug out my phone. He lifted the fish with both hands and pushed it toward me as I snapped several pictures. Then he gently lowered the fish into the water with one hand, grabbed the fly with a pair of thin pliers, and twisted the hook free. He held the fish by its tail, moved it back and forth in the current several times, and let it go.

The fish lazed there a moment and then disappeared into the swifter water with a flick of its tail.

Sampson looked at me like he couldn't believe it. "I caught a big trout on a fly, Alex. How is that possible?"

"I think someone might have been helping you a little, John."

He smiled wistfully. "It is a beautiful place for her."

"It is," I said.

It was nearly four thirty. The thunder was getting even closer. I could see dark clouds cresting the mountain opposite us as we started back up the sandbar.

The sun vanished behind clouds. The wind gusted, threw grit in our eyes.

As we neared the back channel that separated us from the riverbank and our camp, we heard a faint buzzing noise far to the north.

Sampson said, "What's that?"

"No idea," I said, raising my binoculars from the chest harness and seeing nothing at first.

But as the buzz changed to a steady chop and thump, there was a flash in the air that I caught through the trees, the sun reflecting off a windshield that quickly became a helicopter flying low over the water as it arced around the bend three hundred yards north of us and flew south fast.

"What the hell? Helicopters aren't allowed in the wilderness," Sampson said.

"They can't land in the wilderness," I said just as a man leaned out the right rear door of the chopper with an AR rifle.

"Gun!" we both shouted and leaped into the back channel, going for the riverbank, cover, and our weapons.

The gunman opened up. Bursts of bullets from an automatic weapon skipped across the water and tore into the sandbar and the channel water right behind us.

CHAPTER

83

MATTHEW BUTLER HADN'T FLOWN A helicopter in more than three years and never a Bell Jet Ranger. He had hoped to pilot the chopper to Swan River Valley the evening before and then head upriver first thing in the morning.

But it had taken him longer than expected to become familiar with the Jet Ranger's sensitive controls. He'd finally flown the helicopter south at midday and landed in a clear-cut in the backcountry west of Condon, Montana, where he, Big DD, and Vincente set about removing the rear doors.

It was after three p.m. when they'd finally lifted off in search of Cross and Sampson. Big DD sat in the copilot's seat. Vincente was harnessed in the back, tethered to a hook set center high on the rear wall. He wore ski goggles and carried an AR rifle modified for full automatic.

Figuring Cross and Sampson were somewhere in the upper

river, Butler had flown in a more or less direct line to high above Big Salmon Lake. There, he'd dropped altitude, picked up the South Fork of the Flathead, and followed it upriver.

They'd crossed Murphy Flat, where the Flathead was joined by the White River and broke up into several braided channels. They saw a young couple in kayaks pulling small rafts of gear but neither Cross nor Sampson. Nor did they see them in the broad canyon upriver, where Butler was able to fly two hundred feet over the water. They saw no one in the first four miles.

By that point they'd been in the air almost an hour and forty-five minutes and their fuel gauge showed a little more than half a tank before reserve.

"We'll give it fifteen more minutes," Butler said as gusty winds began to buffet them.

"Here comes the storm," Big DD said.

"Ten more minutes, then," Butler said, following the river in a long, lazy S and working the stick to keep the helicopter steady in the relentless crosswind that made flying the unfamiliar craft a little dicey. Having the rear doors off did not help things.

Indeed, in the back seat, Vincente was getting pummeled by the wind and said into his mike, "Gotta be blowing thirty knots. What's the ceiling on wind for this bird?"

Before Butler could answer, Big DD said, "Got 'em both, crossing that sandbar."

Butler saw Cross and Sampson now, about three hundred yards ahead and approaching a back channel opposite Burnt Creek. He wasn't seeing the raft, but no matter. They were sitting ducks for a marksman like Vincente. This mission was all but over.

"Your game, JP," Butler said into his mike.

"Take a diagonal run to their right," Vincente said, moving to lean out the left side of the helicopter to get a clean shot at them.

Butler swung the chopper slightly off angle and accelerated toward Cross and Sampson, who were running into the back channel even before Vincente opened fire, bullets skipping off the river, the sandbar, closing on both men as they tried to scramble up the bank.

A fifty-mile-an-hour gust blasted the side of the helicopter. Vincente's shots went wide as he was thrown completely out the side of the chopper, where he dangled by his harness and tether.

Vincente was yelling something, but Butler paid no attention. Another gust hit, swinging the tail end of the bird so violently the rear rotor almost struck one of the pine trees on the west bank of the river.

The wind died down slightly. Butler got control of the helicopter and listened to Vincente curse in Spanish as Big DD leaned over, grabbed his tether, and pulled him back inside.

"Let's get the hell out of here," Vincente said. "I think I cracked a rib."

"Not until we're done," Butler said, taking the chopper in a loop upriver and then down, heading toward the last place he'd seen Cross and Sampson as they tried to crawl up the riverbank and get to the trees.

"Got their raft," Big DD said. "And their tent. In the woods, east bank."

"They have to be right there, JP," Butler said, swinging the helicopter broadside.

Vincente grunted as he slid across the back seat, got his foot out, and braced on the right step. Another gust hit, smaller than the earlier two but bearing the first wave of BB-size hail that broke over and around the bird.

Butler could barely see for a second before the wave passed and there was Cross, forty yards out, leaning out from behind a stout pine tree and aiming a shotgun.

"Kill him, JP!" Butler yelled a split second before Cross fired.

Buckshot spiderwebbed the windshield, door, and nose on Big DD's side, obscuring Butler's vision and striking Vincente's left arm and the side of his face.

Blood poured down his cheeks and forehead from five different wounds. But Vincente was a warrior. He wasn't down. He wasn't out of the fight.

"Swing starboard!" Vincente bellowed as he tried to aim his rifle at the tree where Cross had been hiding.

Butler hovered the helicopter, then angled it toward the bank, realizing his mistake in the next second. Back in the shadows of the trees and the peppering hail, Sampson was on one knee aiming a scoped hunting rifle at them.

It must have been one hell of a heavy gun because it left a hole the size of a dime going through the windshield, broke the sound barrier as it went by Butler's right earmuff, blew through the roof, and hit the rotor housing.

Butler felt the helicopter shudder and the stick turn dull but he did not lose control as he swung the bird away from the riverbank and flew downriver, hoping they weren't going to have to ditch the chopper in the middle of nowhere.

CHAPTER

84

"SHOOT THEM AGAIN, JOHN!" I shouted as Sampson ran forward in the pelting hail. He cleared the trees, went to one knee, and aimed downriver at the retreating helicopter, already vague in the hail, and fired again. But this time I didn't hear the tremendously satisfying sound of metal meeting a three-hundred-grain bullet fired from a .375 Ruger at less than sixty yards.

"Missed him that time," Sampson said as he got up, his forearm shielding his eyes from the wind and the hail. He came over to where I'd taken refuge on the leeward side of a big ponderosa pine.

My heart was still slamming in my chest. "Who the hell were they? The cartel? M's men?"

"Take your pick," Sampson said, panting with adrenaline

as he turned his back to the tree. "I want to know how they knew where we were."

I thought about that as the hail finally started to peter out. With it went the wind but not the dark clouds, which were now squatting on the mountaintop across the river from us.

"We forgot to take our batteries out of our phones on our ride up here," I said. "If M does have NSA-level access, he could have been listening."

The first drops of rain began to fall as Sampson said, "The cartel could have picked us up if they were monitoring law enforcement activity around the ranch site."

"Could have," I said, calm enough to take the shotgun and my camp chair under the tarp. "But a helicopter attack strikes me as more M's style than Emmanuella's."

Sampson followed me under the tarp as the sprinkles became light rain. "Whoever it was, if they can hire a helicopter, they aren't going to stop."

"You did some damage, John. I know I did too."

"They'll still come at us again," he said. "I think it's guaranteed before we reach the pullout. And I screwed us."

I frowned. "How's that?"

"I was the one who insisted on being cut off from everything, no sat phones, no SOS devices," Sampson said. "We should be calling Mahoney and getting an army of FBI agents swarming the area, looking for that helicopter. I mean, someone is going to report a chopper damaged by buckshot and a Ruger round, right?"

"You would think so. But don't be so hard on yourself about the satellite phone. I was as game for no contact as you were. Maybe even more so. It's been years since I've been truly cut off, and I was very much looking forward to it."

"Except here we are."

I nodded. "Different circumstances now. It's not just an adventure anymore."

"Life or death."

"Which means we have to be smart, think ahead," I said. "We have to go as hard and as far as we can every day."

Sampson was silent a moment. "Agreed," he said finally. "We can't afford the luxury of four more days."

"Can we do the whole thing in two days?" I said.

"Three," Sampson said. "I asked the hired hand, and he said with this water level and this amount of daylight, the best you could do from back at Gordon Creek was four days. Maybe two days from here if we get lucky and don't have to drag the raft."

Though the rain had lightened up again, the clouds on the other side of the river were getting lower and lower.

"This weather looks like it's settling in," I said. "If so, it could keep that helicopter out of the sky tomorrow and we could head downstream early, try to get to Big Salmon Lake. There may be people there camping who have a satellite phone we can use."

Sampson brightened. "Bauer said there are horse campers up there all the time."

"I remember," I said, getting up. "Feel like a shot of bourbon to calm the nerves?"

Sampson smiled. "I was actually thinking more like two shots of bourbon."

85

AROUND TWO THE FOLLOWING AFTERNOON, in a relentless drizzle, Raphael Durango was wearing rain gear as he climbed down off his horse and did a few deep knee bends to get the kinks out. His four men were similarly dressed but hobbled by the long hours in the saddle. It took a dozen stiff steps before they were walking easily.

They helped unload the mules, taking care of their personal canvas duffels first. They set their bags aside while Tim, Bauer's nephew, checked their outfitter's tent down by an old ranger cabin at the east end of Big Salmon Lake, not far from the banks of the South Fork of the Flathead River.

"We'll get your supplies into the tent and you'll be good to go whenever you're ready," Tim said, helping them carry two folded rafts to the riverbank for inflation.

"You're leaving today?" Durango said.

"Like I said last night, my wife's about to pop with our first kid," Tim said. "I promised her once you were set up, I'd turn right around and hoof it for home."

This is the only reason I am letting you live, Tim, Durango thought as he smiled at the younger man. *If my sister were here, you'd be six feet under.*

"Good luck, then," Durango said once they had the provisions squared away and the mules readied and Tim had gone over the grizzly-country protocols for food and trash. He held out a thick wad of hundred-dollar bills. "Here's a tip from all of us. Buy your wife and baby something nice."

Tim stared dumbly at the money the cartel man was holding for a few seconds before reaching out a shaky hand to take it. "That's not necessary, sir, but it sure will be appreciated. Thank you."

"We thank you for bringing us in here on such short notice," Durango said. "See you in a few days. We'll call when we near the pullout."

"Sounds like a plan," Tim said, stuffing the money in his jacket pocket and climbing back on his horse. He waved and was soon out of sight, heading back down the trail.

"Get the rafts inflated and assemble your weapons," Durango said to his men. "I'm calling Emmanuella."

While two of his men opened the duffels and retrieved the components of five AR rifles, the others pumped up the rafts. Durango walked off with the satellite phone. When he was out of his men's hearing, he texted his sister. A few moments later, he got a return text with a phone number, which he called.

"Where are you?" Emmanuella said.

"A place called Big Salmon Lake, getting ready to sit in ambush for Cross and Sampson," he said. "As far as we know Butler and his men are not with them. Do you have Cross's signal still?"

"They're three miles upriver of you, in the middle of Murphy Flat," she said. "And don't let your guard down, Raphael. I'm telling you, Butler or some other Maestro soldier is there somewhere. I can feel it."

Durango rolled his eyes. Emmanuella always "felt" things when she did not have facts to support her position.

"We'll keep a lookout," he said. "In the meantime, what do you want me to do if Butler is not with Cross and his friend? Let them go by? Engage? Cross is going to remember me."

"Obviously," she said, then paused. "How remote are you, really?"

"Like, deep Sierra Madre–remote. We haven't seen any-one else in a day and a half."

"No one camping at that lake you passed coming in?"

"No one we saw. The weather's getting shitty, raining, cold."

She was quiet again for a moment. "Cross has too much influence over Marco."

Durango frowned. His half brother was in a supermax prison; how much influence did *Marco* have anymore? None that he could see. But he said, "Okay?"

"And even if he's not turning Marco against us, I don't like thinking of Cross allied with Maestro," she said. "It keeps me up at night. Worried for our survival."

"I can't read minds, Emmanuella. What do you want me to do?"

"Kill them both, brother," she snapped. "And make sure they'll never be found."

He grinned a little and said, "That part's easy. We'll just cover their bodies in bacon grease and leave them for the grizzly bears, the wolves, and the ravens."

CHAPTER

86

IT WAS NEARLY FOUR P.M. on our second full day on the river. The rain was letting up. The skies were clearing.

We'd floated almost nine river miles and were nearing Big Salmon Lake. I was rowing while Sampson peered downriver, searching for any sign of the helicopter or of people camped there.

Near the confluence of Big Salmon Creek, I brought us in on the west bank. We pulled our raft high out of the water and climbed farther up the bank to see a white outfitter's tent by an old cabin surrounded by scattered trees. We scanned the area, saw no one.

"Hello!" I shouted. "Hello!"

We waited and heard no one. Sampson ran over to the wall tent, looked inside, then shook his head at me. He tried the old Forest Service cabin. No luck.

John returned, said, "We can camp here and hope someone comes along with a satellite phone, or we can keep going and get three or four more miles downriver before dark."

"Let's keep going," I said. "We could overtake someone ahead of us who has a satellite phone. At the very least, we'll be closer to the pullout."

Sampson nodded. "My turn to row."

"I'm not arguing," I said, massaging my sore shoulders.

A few minutes later, we pushed off with the sun warming our bones after the long day in the rain. We passed Big Salmon Creek and entered a thousand-yard straight with high rock walls on both flanks.

We rounded the far bend about twenty minutes later and found ourselves in a lazy S. In the middle of the S, about two hundred yards away, two blue rafts similar to our own and loaded with gear were pulled up on a gravel beach.

"I'm not seeing anyone," I said, peering through my binoculars.

"Someone is on that sandy hill above the rafts," Sampson said.

I looked, saw a man up there, and threw my binoculars on him. He had his hand to his brow and was looking our way. Then he dropped his hand and I caught his face.

"Son of a bitch!" I hissed to Sampson. "That's Raphael Durango! Emmanuella Alejandro's brother! Get us out of sight!"

Sampson started rowing maniacally toward the east shore while I went for the Ruger. I no sooner had it in my hand when I heard a familiar buzz.

"Helicopter!" I said.

Before John could reply, I saw it coming from half a mile

downriver. The same chopper from the day before, the same spiderwebbed windshield on one side.

"We're toast!" Sampson yelled. "Get in the river!"

We were both about to jump over the side and swim for shore when the helicopter suddenly swung toward that hill. Two men hung out either side of the helicopter and started shooting at Durango and another man, both of whom started shooting back with their own automatic weapons.

Then more shots came from the other side of the river and I could see three cartel men there with machine guns, all firing at the helicopter.

"What do we do?" Sampson said.

"Keep going!" I said. "They're occupied!"

"You're insane," John said, but he spun the raft so his back faced downriver and started to pull hard on the oars to take full advantage of the current.

We gathered speed. As the battle raged between the helicopter gunmen and the five cartel men trying to bring them down, I scrambled past Sampson to the rear of the boat and got the Ruger set up over the top of our gear.

We were sixty yards from the middle of the S when the man with Durango was hit. The helicopter swung about over the river and hovered, nose facing west toward the three cartel gunmen.

The belly of the helicopter was no more than eighty feet overhead when we passed under it and went by the rafts. The big black man hanging out the left side and the smaller Latino on the right opened fire on the three cartel men on the other bank.

I thought about shooting up at one of them. I thought

about shooting the rafts as well. But I did not want to attract attention. We floated beyond them as the battle raged.

The cartel men emptied their weapons at the helicopter with Durango doing the same from the east side of the river.

I could hear metal smacking metal and saw the Latino gunman above me flinch hard and disappear inside the helicopter, which banked away, then flew back at Durango. The big black guy in the chopper and the cartel boss were firing at each other.

When a chunk of the windshield gave way, the helicopter finally pulled off and headed straight west, up and over the nearest mountain. Looking back through my binoculars from a hundred and fifty yards downstream, I saw Durango stare after us and then disappear, running downhill toward the rafts.

CHAPTER

87

WE ROUNDED ANOTHER BEND IN the river. Sampson was sucking wind from rowing so hard.

"Gotta rest," he said, gasping.

"You rest. I row," I said. "Durango saw us. He's coming after us."

Sampson moved off the rowing bench and let me take his place. I put my back into it and got us going at a good clip downstream before I said, "I think those were M's men in the helicopter."

"Yeah, coming back after us. But Durango and his men were too good to pass up."

"It cost them. That helicopter's like swiss cheese."

"So how did both of them find us? And how did the cartel know to wait in ambush for us there?"

"Like I said, we didn't remove our phone batteries a

couple of times, maybe that's it," I theorized, sweat pouring off my brow as I kept rowing.

"Maybe, but it doesn't explain Durango and his boys. He knew we were coming downriver."

I wrestled with that for a moment before it dawned on me and I stopped rowing to look down at my belt. "It has to be," I said, yanking it off and tossing it to John.

"What has to be?" he asked as I started rowing again.

"The GPS transmitter Mahoney made me put in that belt. Durango had to have known I was wearing it when he ran a wand over me. He probably got its frequency."

"Which means they can still track us," Sampson said, cocking his arm to pitch the belt.

"Don't," I said.

Before he could ask why, we both heard a roar ahead of us.

"We've got quicker water coming at us. Spin the raft around and slow us down. You're going to want to see where you're going."

As I turned the raft, I said, "Look on the OnX map. I remember seeing creeks coming into this stretch on both sides."

Sampson studied the app on his phone and said, "Helen Creek on the east and Snow Creek on the west. Both about four miles downstream."

"Gets dark soon, but we'll make it. Which side has more cover?"

"Snow Creek," he said.

"Good," I said as the current began to quicken and the roar of the first rapids intensified. "Now get that transmitter out of my belt and find my empty Nalgene bottle."

Two hours later, with the sun gone behind the mountains

and the shadows lengthening, I took the Nalgene bottle with the transmitter inside and set it in the fast water. It quickly disappeared from sight downstream.

We dragged the raft fifty yards into the woods there, went back to the tree line with our guns, and waited. I figured they'd come through before dark, and we'd have a chance to turn the tables on them.

But I could barely see my hands much less the front bead of my shotgun when I heard voices in Spanish and the sound of oars in the swift water. The raft made squeaking noises brushing rocks, but I could not see it.

Then Sampson whispered, "Night vision."

Peering toward the river through my binoculars, I made out the telltale green glow of four pairs of night-vision goggles before they vanished and we heard their raft and oars headed downriver, chasing a Nalgene bottle.

CHAPTER

88

IT HAD TAKEN EVERY BIT of Matthew Butler's flying skills to get the bullet-riddled Jet Ranger over the mountains, across Swan River Valley, and to the remote clear-cut in the national forest. He landed the helicopter behind a huge pile of logging slash, which made it impossible to see from the logging road where they'd left the Land Cruiser.

"That's it," he said as he shut down the engine and then rocked his head back in relief. "I am never going up in this shitcan ever again. No matter what M says."

"He's going to say a lot," Big DD said. "He owns it now."

"His damn idea," said Vincente, who had a blood-coagulant patch pressed to the back of his right forearm, which had been slashed by a piece of flying metal when one of Durango's bullets ricocheted off the door frame. "He wanted us up there."

Butler said, "He did. Let's wipe the chopper down. Every-thing inside."

"They'll find my blood no matter what we do," Vin-cente said.

"Don't matter, JP," Big DD said, pulling out bleach wipes and starting on the dashboard. "You're already dead."

"That's who we are," Vincente said. "The living dead."

Butler wiped down the control panel and the stick, climbed out, and started on the pilot seat. Twenty minutes later, they were hiking back to the vehicle and he allowed his mind to think forward, to anticipate once more.

He knew M well enough to understand that they wouldn't be leaving Montana anytime soon. His boss had been right. Butler had thought following Cross to find the cartel men was a ludicrous idea, but M's instincts were correct. Which meant he'd want them all killed, which meant they needed a new plan.

They reached the Toyota before dark and drove the log-ging road three miles to an improved dirt road that they drove for eleven miles to Highway 83. It was pitch-black out and moonless when they pulled up to the Swan River Lodge, whose sign still bore traces of its former life as a Super 8 motel.

There were three or four other vehicles parked in the lot but none by their three rooms on the bottom floor. Butler had Big DD and Vincente unload the gear, went to the far-right room, and knocked twice and then three times.

A few moments later, the door opened, and he slipped inside. The door shut behind him. He turned to see Alison Purdy standing there, studying him with eyes that had dark bags beneath them.

"Did you get them so we can get the hell out of this dump?"

He shook his head. "We're lucky we're alive after getting into it with five cartel men. We took out at least one if not two, but they hammered the chopper good. It's no longer airworthy."

"M is not going to want to hear that," she said, limping over and climbing on the bed next to a night table with five different prescription bottles on it.

"Which is why I need options," Butler said. "Did you call that shop in Bigfork?"

"And bought them," she said, nodding. "They're in the other rooms, charging."

He felt relief. "How'd you pull that off?"

"Offered them a delivery fee they could not refuse. The van pulled in three hours later, right before dark."

"And how far can they really go?"

"Twenty-five miles a charge, max."

Butler thought about that. "Headlamps enough?"

"I had all four mounted with extra lights."

He smiled and then frowned. "Why four?"

"Because I'm going with you."

"Oh, no, you're not."

"Oh, yes, I am," Purdy said. "You've tried twice without me and failed both times. You don't want a third fail. You don't want to strike out and have to tell M, do you?"

Butler felt his chest constrict. "What about the leg?"

"I don't have to do a thing with that leg if I don't want to. Now, get some food and some sleep. To be up there in time, I figure we need to be gone by five a.m. 'And thank you, Alison, for your resourcefulness and ingenuity,'" she said with a smile.

Butler smiled back. "I appreciate the option, Alison."

"Glad to be of service," she said.

He left her room, went out in the Land Cruiser, and used the satellite phone.

When M answered, Butler gave it to him straight, listened to his self-congratulatory reaction to their finding the cartel by looking for Cross, and endured the inevitable barrage of anger that followed news of the helicopter's current state.

"You cost us at least a half a million dollars!" M roared.

Butler said, "With all due respect, the helicopter was your idea. And it's not like you can't afford the penalty."

"It's the principle," M replied in a seething tone. "They should all be dead now."

"But they're not. And the helicopter can't fly. Or at least, I won't fly it again."

For several moments, M was silent. Then he said, "You have options?"

"Two," Butler said. "First one, we sit on the pullout and trailhead where Cross and the cartel men will have to take their rafts out of the river. But that almost guarantees witnesses."

"And option two?"

"We get a good six or seven miles up the trail that parallels the river to a pinch point and rapids below Black Bear Creek," Butler said. "Do you see it on your satellite image? Anyone on the river has to get through that spot."

"I see it," M said after a few moments. "It does look like a good place for an ambush, but it's rugged country all the way up. How are you planning to get in there seven miles with that much elevation gain without a helicopter? Hiking? Horses?"

"E-bikes," Butler said. "Purdy bought four of them today."

89

SAMPSON AND I WOKE UP at four thirty in the morning. It was cold as we wolfed down freeze-dried scrambled eggs and drank coffee while again studying the river on the OnX maps.

We had decided the night before that our best chance for survival was to get down and off the river as fast as possible. But we also understood that the cartel was downstream somewhere and perhaps M's men were as well.

Sampson pointed to a spot about five river miles below our campsite, north of Black Bear Creek, near mile marker 63. "I've read about this. Biggest rapids on the float. Gets tight and fast before it finally spills out into calmer water. If I were Durango and I'd caught up to that Nalgene bottle and now knew you and I didn't come through those narrows yet, I'd be up on the cliffs above the rapids or just below them."

"It is the likeliest place if they've found the bottle and the transmitter," I agreed. "And it's upriver enough that no one will hear the shots."

Sampson nodded. "And we'd be distracted getting through the rapids, unable to defend ourselves in an attack from above."

"We could get out here above the rapids at mile marker sixty-four, say, find one of the bridle trails, and walk out the last six miles," I said. "But we risk running into them."

"True," Sampson said, looking at the map and then over at the raft and gear. "But then again, maybe we want to run into them."

"Explain that."

John was quiet and then gave me a more in-depth description of his evolving idea, which I could see was the most aggressive alternative to running the rapids beneath the guns of the cartel men and possibly M's people. His plan also gave us a semblance of control and the element of surprise.

"I like it," I said. "It's the way we want to go."

While I packed my headlamp light, Sampson tested the linchpin of what lay ahead of us. He cut ten inches of rope and tied it between two saplings about an inch below the wick of one of the candles we'd brought in our emergency kits.

John lit the candle, checked his watch, and then joined me ferrying the raft to the river and our gear to the raft. On each trip he checked the candle and his watch.

Thirty-two minutes after he lit the candle, the rope burned apart.

"There it is," he said. "Thirty-two minutes to the inch."

"As long as the candle doesn't go out," I said, putting our dry bags into the raft.

"As long as I shield the flame, it won't."

Sampson and I were packed and pushing away from shore at the crack of dawn. Mist rose off the river in the cold morning air.

Near mile marker 67, a herd of cow elk with a massive bull trailing waded the river right in front of us, an awesome experience that kept us out of our anxious thoughts for the next three hours. Then, around ten that morning, masked by flotsam in a back channel, Sampson spotted the blue top of my Nalgene bottle. I got out and retrieved it, saw the transmitter still inside.

"They must have missed it and kept going," I said, starting to unscrew the lid.

"What are you doing?" Sampson asked.

"Tossing the transmitter."

"Don't," he said. "I think it could help us."

At eleven a.m., below mile marker 66 near Hodag Creek, we pulled the raft over but did not drag it up the bank. Sampson jumped out and tied the front end to a sapling some ten feet from the water's edge.

The raft swung on the current and stayed pinned to the bank, the rope stretched taut. I waded over next to it and found the life preservers, rain gear, and extra clothes.

I stuffed the arms and legs of the rain gear with the clothes and used the life vests to fill out the torsos. I even took the wool balaclavas we'd brought in case we faced a snowstorm, stuffed them with leaves and sticks from bushes along the shore, and fixed them beneath the jacket hoods.

Sampson stayed dry up on the bank, arranging the candle next to the rope and shielding it from the wind with layers of aluminum foil that he weighted in place with rocks.

It was almost noon when I finished with the dummies and Sampson lit the candle, with the rope four inches below the wick.

"Roughly two hours until it burns through," Sampson said. "If the raft doesn't snag or go up on a gravel bar, it should take a good hour for it to reach the rapids."

"So at least three hours before we see it," I said. "Should be more than enough time for us both to get where we want to be."

CHAPTER

90

TWO HOURS LATER AND A mile and a half downriver, Raphael Durango and his three remaining men were in the same positions they'd been in for most of the morning.

Durango and one man were tucked in a small pocket of timber on the west side of Black Bear Canyon some three hundred yards below the rapids and two hundred vertical feet above the river. The position gave them a better view of the narrows upstream.

His other two men were on the opposite side of the river drainage at a similar elevation but upriver another hundred and fifty yards. Due to the bend above the rapids, they would not see the raft until it was sweeping into the final approach to the whitewater.

Durango would signal them when he saw the raft. Cross

and Sampson would be caught in the crossfire as soon as they entered the narrows.

After they disposed of the bodies and the raft, Durango could start home to Mexico knowing that he'd laid waste to many of his enemies and—

His satellite phone buzzed, alerting him to an incoming text. He did not have to look to know who it was from. Only one person knew the number.

Durango told his man to keep an eye on the river and whistle if he saw the raft coming. Then he climbed farther up the slope, much of which had burned at some point in the past decade, leaving a patchwork of living trees alongside scorched trunks.

He looked at the text, saw the new phone number, and called it.

"They're not moving," Emmanuella said. "It's been almost two hours."

"I'm watching the signal too, sister," he said.

"I still don't understand how you got by them last night."

"The only thing I can figure is my battery was low and wasn't picking up the signal in the deeper parts of the canyon. And we never saw their raft even with the goggles."

"But you're seeing their signal now?"

"I'm on the spare battery. The signal's strong."

"Conditions?"

"Bright sunshine earlier, but now it looks like it's about to rain again."

"No one will hear the shots?"

"We're miles from the takeout," he said, feeling irritated at being micromanaged.

"What about Butler and his men? You said it was him. Or have you reconsidered?"

"It was him," he shot back as the first raindrops of the day fell. "I got a good look. And we've seen no helicopters today."

"I said they'd be there," she said, sounding superior. "M's men."

Durango rolled his eyes but said, "You also said M was allied with Cross."

"Isn't he? Butler attacked you when you were about to ambush Cross and Sampson. Cross got by you while you defended yourself. Or isn't that the story?"

Feeling even more like he was being interrogated, Durango said, "That's one version of the story. Another says that Maestro's men were flying up there to kill Cross, but they recognized me and decided to take us out first."

There was silence before Emmanuella said in a tighter voice, "In the end, it doesn't matter. But I'd advise you to keep an eye out for that helicopter, just in case Cross and Sampson are in touch with Maestro and asking for help."

"I'll text you when it's over," he said.

"You'll call me when it's over, half brother. And I want to see pictures."

"Pictures of what?"

"The bodies," Emmanuella said as the rain around Durango became a patter. "And get your men ready. Cross and Sampson are finally moving again."

CHAPTER

91

EVEN THOUGH HIS GORE-TEX gear was back in the raft stuffed with most of his warm clothes, and John was getting wetter by the moment, he welcomed the rain. He'd been walking for nearly three hours by then, much of it traversing steep hillsides on game trails through loud and crunchy dry grass and brush that was crisscrossed with downed, scorched tree trunks.

But the rain, light and steady for almost an hour now, had deadened the sound of his passing. And he'd decided to climb a little higher to find the bridle path that led north, a clearer way through the patchwork of burned-over land and strips of standing trees, which made the going quieter still.

To Sampson's left and diagonally downhill, the river was about to turn hard right into the rapids. If John paused, he could hear the light roar of the whitewater coming from around the point of the turn, which was just ahead of him, no more than a few hundred yards away.

He stopped in a large patch of timber, put the .375 Ruger against a big ponderosa pine, and rubbed his stomach and thigh scars a moment before picking up his binoculars. He looked upriver and still saw no sign of the raft.

That rope had to have burned through before the rain began, Sampson thought. *But it's five minutes to three now. I should be seeing the raft, and I'm not.*

He turned the binoculars on the opposite side of the river, hoping to spot Alex. The last time he'd seen his oldest friend was two hours before, when Sampson was crossing Black Bear Creek and Alex was climbing the north side of the Slick Creek drainage.

He scanned along the steep hillsides and through the burned-over forests at roughly his same elevation. There was another bridle trail somewhere over there and he hoped Alex had thought to use the easier path as well.

But try as he might, Sampson could not find Cross. After several minutes of searching and another quick glance upriver, he lowered the binoculars and hiked on toward the big rock formation above the river bend.

That cliffy area was farther than it appeared at first because the bridle path followed the contours of the hill deep into draws and around outcroppings. Nearly thirty minutes passed before the trail wound into a denser stand of trees ahead of that large rock formation.

Sampson stopped in dark shadows, waiting for his eyes to adjust. He could hear the swift water but was unable to get more than glimpses of it through the woods that lined the steep slope above the rapids. He picked up the binoculars and peered as far down the trail as he could, looking for the silhouette of a man.

When he was sure there was no one, he took two steps and peered through the binoculars again. He saw where the rock formation began, jutting out over the river forward and to his left another fifty yards. The horse trail went more to his right and north through the trees, disappearing over a gap in the ridgeline maybe seventy yards away.

Sampson picked apart every tree and bush, but he could not place a man on the ridge or the ledge at the top of the rock formation. He was about to take another step when he heard a shriek of laughter come from well behind him and down on the river, somewhere in the long straight before the bend above the rapids.

Then he heard another shriek of fear and joy, followed by children screaming and yelling, "Here we go, Mom! Here we go, Dad! Into the jaws of death!"

CHAPTER

92

ON THE WEST SIDE OF the river, I was gasping for air after getting caught in a nightmare of blown-down charred trees and having to climb straight up a nearly sheer face to escape and find the bridle path we'd seen on the OnX maps.

It was lightly raining and cool with a slight breeze, but I was sweating like a horse when I finally found the trail and began to ease down it, heading north with the ten-gauge pump-action shotgun held at port arms, peering with the binoculars across the open burns and through the groves that survived the fire.

By then, three hours into my hike, I was almost in line with the rapids but several hundred vertical feet above the narrowest point of the canyon. My pace slowed to a creep.

Every few feet, I paused to use my binoculars to look back upriver through the light rain, then down the trail, then down through the trees toward the narrows. No sign of men I could see. And the lack of tracks in the muddy trail said it had been a few days since a horseman rode through there. I wondered whether Sampson was having better luck on the other side of the river and began to question our plan to split up.

Where the hell are Durango and his men? It would make sense they'd wait for us here. Maybe they're farther north? But how much farther? And where's our raft? It should have been here by—

I stopped short, staring at the trail ahead of me and the mud and the tracks of a huge animal that had left the trees and walked right up the path, heading in the same direction as me. I took a few more steps and saw the tracks were fresh. Very fresh. There was hardly any rainwater in the deep, oval tracks, which looked almost like an old-time catcher's mitt had been pressed deep into the mud—an old-time catcher's mitt equipped with claws that were as long and as thick as my fingers.

My throat constricted. I'd never seen anything remotely like those tracks before, but I knew in my gut what had made them.

Then I smelled something putrid in the air and knew for certain, because Bauer, the packer who'd brought us into the wilderness, had told us they often "stink to high heaven" from eating rotting carcasses, animals they'd either killed themselves or blundered onto.

"That's a grizzly bear," I muttered. "A big one. He's got to be right here in front of me somewhere."

For several moments I did not know what to do. If I kept moving, I might run into one of the cartel men, but given the freshness of the tracks, I was more likely going to walk up on a six-hundred-pound apex predator with a reputation for extreme nastiness.

No matter what I did, I could not calm my heart, and I felt nauseated as I peered ahead with my binoculars. I saw nothing moving directly ahead of me, but when I turned the glasses back upriver, I caught a flash of blue that became our raft, a half a mile away, spinning slowly in the current, bouncing into rocks, but moving steadily closer.

From this far, those dummies look real, I thought, smiling. *If the cartel men are ahead of me, I'm going to know it the second the raft drops into the rapids and—*

A shriek of laughter cut my thoughts. I heard it again before kids started screaming, "Here we go, Mom! Here we go, Dad! Into the jaws of death!"

I moved the binoculars to the river much closer to me, seeing a family of four wearing camouflaged rain gear and riding in a dark green raft. They were coming toward the rapids, a hundred yards from the bend, a young boy and a girl forward, the dad at the oars, the mom behind him.

"Into the jaws of death!" the father bellowed.

The mom shrieked again and they all started laughing.

How did I miss them? The rain? The camouflage? Looking too far upriver for our raft?

I had a feeling it was all three of those reasons before I realized they were heading into the narrows. I began to panic.

What if the cartel men or M's men see the raft and just start blazing?

Part of me wanted to start sliding down the slope toward the narrows to try to warn the family off. But there was no time. I would not make it before they hit the tight spot.

Another part of me wanted to shoot my gun and yell from there, but then whatever flavor of bad guy was waiting to my north would know my position, and the element of surprise we'd planned and worked for would be gone.

Before I could come to a decision, it was too late. The dad was hauling on his oars, sweeping them hard toward the west bank of the South Fork, then let the nose of the raft drift into the bend. The kids started screaming like roller-coaster riders.

I watched the family and the raft vanish from sight into the rapids far below me and felt like I'd just seen them go to their doom.

CHAPTER

93

FIVE HUNDRED YARDS DOWNRIVER AND on the same west side of the South Fork, Matthew Butler and J. P. Vincente were separated by fifty yards and moving steadily south, keeping the muddy bridle trail between them.

They wore camo. Thermal-imaging goggles hung around their necks.

Even though it was daylight, every ten yards or so, Butler would lift the goggles and peer through them, looking for the heat signatures of men in the trees ahead of him. If Durango and the cartel men were waiting in ambush for Cross and Sampson, Butler felt in his bones that they would be up ahead, between him and Vincente and those rapids.

They'd stashed their e-bikes and Alison Purdy's off the trail a mile back. She'd limped with them up the path until fifteen minutes ago, when Butler had sent her out on a point above the river, roughly seven hundred yards downstream of the narrows.

Seven hundred yards is a long shot for anyone, but Purdy carried a soft case for a .28 Nosler sniper rifle that Butler had stashed in the Land Cruiser along with several other weapons. The thief was a small woman and the Nosler a hard, flat-shooting weapon.

But the custom rifle came with an integrated tripod, an adjustable elevation turret, and a muzzle brake, which cut the recoil in half. With that setup, even Purdy could reach out and kill a man at close to a mile if need be.

He'd left her with orders to shoot whenever she felt she had one of the cartel men in her sights. And she'd play mop-up in case Cross and Sampson somehow managed to get past Butler, Vincente, and Big DD, who was working his way up the bridle path on the opposite side of the river.

"How are you making out there, Cap?" Dawkins whispered in Butler's earbud a few minutes later.

"They've got to be right here ahead of us," Butler said.

"Same on this side. I can't be more than four-fifty out from the rapids."

"Any thermal reads?"

"Negative, but there are ravines and folds where a man could hide without…we have a raft in the river bend!"

"I see them too," Purdy whispered.

"Vincente, flank to the outside and advance," Butler said. "I'm river-bound. If the cartel is here, they'll start shooting any second."

"Roger that," Vincente said.

Purdy said, "Wait, there's four in the raft."

"Four?" Butler said, moving fast to where he could see

more of the river. He trained his binoculars on the narrows and saw four people in a dark green raft coming into the whitewater, bouncing off one rock, hanging up a moment on another, spilling down a chute that threw a wave of water up and over two kids in the bow.

"Don't shoot!" he warned. "It's not Cross. Repeat, not Cross. Let them go by."

CHAPTER

94

UPRIVER SEVERAL HUNDRED YARDS, Raphael Durango did not hear the shrieking family of four, but he'd caught glimpses of them before they floated around the river bend fully into his view and plunged into the rapids.

He'd given no signal to his two men on the east side of the South Fork and told the man with him to stay put until the family was well past their position. Cross and Sampson were still somewhere upstream. But they couldn't be far. Emmanuella was right. The transmitter in Cross's belt had started moving more than an hour ago. *They should have been here by—*

Durango shifted the binoculars, trained them farther south, and caught a glimpse of a blue raft and two figures in it, hooded and hunched over in the rain. "Here we go," he said to the man with him. "Move up, find a place you can shoot down on them as they go past."

The man nodded, scrambled out of their dry ambush spot to the bridle trail, and began to run south. Durango picked up his AR rifle and walked a few feet into a large opening in the trees. He set the gun down and started waving an orange handkerchief with his left hand while training his binoculars at the bend above the whitewater.

"C'mon, Cross; c'mon, Sampson," he muttered, his stomach fluttering in anticipation of action. "It's going to be a fiesta just for two." The second he saw the raft's blue nose enter the rapids, Durango dropped the orange scarf and snatched up his rifle.

This will be over in seconds and we'll get the hell out of here and go back to Mexico where we belong.

CHAPTER

95

UPRIVER ON THE WEST SIDE of the canyon, Sampson watched and heard the family of four screaming with delight as the raft bounced off a rock at the top of the whitewater section, then slid off and down into a steep chute that threw a wave over the boy and the girl in the front.

Sampson knew that as rapids went, the one below him was relatively mild. At least when compared to the big, dangerous, rolling ones on the Salmon River in Idaho. And the dad appeared capable and comfortable with his oars. After that first jarring hit off the rock and the bounce and spray at the bottom of the chute, he expertly piloted the raft through the rest of the rapids, and within minutes they were out of it and floating a little slower across deeper water. Sampson could hear their laughter fading when he spotted their blue raft coming downriver with Alex's dummies, looking for all the world like two fishermen with their hoods up in the rain.

What amazed Sampson was how, after a spin or two up-river, the raft had stabilized and floated nose-first in the quickening current down the last straight before that right-hand bend into the rapids. But the raft got sideways coming around the turn, smashed off the far bank, and went right up on top of the rock in the tight spot, where it hesitated and shuddered.

Sampson was sure the raft was going to take on water and capsize, but it slid off and careened into the chute. Water sprayed up over the bow, and John took off, running north along the trail and over that gap in the ridgeline.

Now he could see almost a mile to the north, with a commanding view of the burned slopes and pockets of live trees ahead of him, the canyon and river below, and the mountain ledges, steep pitches, and benches above it.

Sampson moved through the rain another fifteen yards and threw the .375 Ruger over the top of a downed tree trunk. Once he had the bear gun solidly in position, he glanced back down at the rapids and saw the raft and the dummies still bouncing and careening through the churning whitewater. He picked up his binoculars to scan the hillsides on both sides downriver and almost immediately saw a man high on the west side, four hundred yards away. The man waved an orange cloth, dropped it, and picked up an AR rifle.

That looks like Durango! Sampson let go of the binoculars and started to get behind the .375, knowing it was a long shot for a bear gun shooting a heavy bullet. But then he caught movement some two hundred yards straight north of his position on his side of the river.

A second man with an assault rifle emerged from the woods there and ran out toward a drop-off in the terrain. Then a third man with an AR appeared on the opposite side of the river, a good hundred yards closer than Durango. That man started shooting down at the raft. So did the guy on Sampson's side of the South Fork. Snugging the stock of the Ruger into his shoulder, he moved the scope onto that gunman.

He thumbed off the safety and got the crosshairs on the cartel man's chest a split second before the gunman jerked and arched as a well-placed bullet blew through him. It exploded out the cartel man's left side, throwing a heavy blood spray into the air before the sound of the shot finally carried from far downriver.

The dead narco tumbled down the slope toward the river.

96

I HAD BEEN MOVING CAUTIOUSLY north ever since the family went into the narrows, praying to God I'd see one of the cartel men instead of the monster grizzly bear that was stalking in the forest somewhere ahead of me.

The beast's tracks were no longer on the trail, but I'd seen where it'd left it, pressing down grass and snapping brush and branches as it headed diagonally northeast toward the river. It wasn't until I stopped to watch our raft go around the bend and into the narrows that I saw movement that became a man carrying an AR rifle about a hundred and fifty yards ahead of me.

His attention was off the trail toward the river and for a second, I thought for sure he'd seen the bear. But then he darted into the trees where he'd been looking.

I took a few more steps and picked him up again, moving

through the woods toward a ledge high above the South Fork. He walked out onto the ledge, aimed toward the river bottom, and let go a burst of gunfire.

Someone across the river on the east side opened fire with another automatic weapon. I'd just found the second shooter in my binoculars when a shot from way downriver buckled him.

The narco on my side seemed puzzled by that shot but fired at the raft again. Thanking God for the rain, the green khaki clothes I wore, and the gunman still shooting, I stooped over and ran at him.

He stopped firing and I came to a halt on the backside of a big ponderosa pine tree about fifty yards from him, close enough to hear the action on his rifle clank open when he ran out of bullets.

Footsteps! He's coming to the trees to reload!

I saw him slip off the ledge, still moving, head down, fumbling to eject and load a new clip. With his attention there and my shotgun still shouldered, I managed to close another fifteen yards on the narco. I stopped and whistled softly his way.

The gunman glanced and saw me with the shotgun aimed at him from thirty-five yards. No way I could miss.

"Drop it or you're a dead man," I said in Spanish.

He hesitated, then dropped the AR and the clip.

"Back out on the ledge," I said, waving the shotgun's muzzle that way.

He hesitated for a moment before trudging back onto the ledge with me paralleling him, the shotgun's bead never leaving his center of mass. After taking two steps out into the open, he halted and looked at me.

"On your belly," I said. "Hands behind your head."

He lay down and complied. I took my first step onto the ledge, glanced left about forty yards, and saw that the fifteen-foot-wide ledge met a vertical rock wall there, eight feet at the top and maybe six feet wide.

The wall was shielding me and the narco from that weapon far downriver. I went quickly to the cartel man, put my boot on his back, and used extra zip ties Sampson had brought on the trip to bind his wrists.

Done, I peered across the river through the rain, trying to spot Sampson. But I wasn't seeing him or any movement whatsoever despite the machine-gun fire that had to have echoed through the entire canyon.

"Don't move," I told the gunman and turned toward the woods, meaning to retrieve his AR rifle and clip.

Raphael Durango was coming through the trees, not twenty yards away, and aiming a rifle at me.

"Drop the gun, Cross," he said. "It's over."

CHAPTER

97

WE HAD SEEN EMMANUELLA ALEJANDRO'S half brother the day before at a distance. But now, up close, I could see that Durango was a far different man than the one who'd appeared on a bench next to me in Mexico City a few weeks ago.

Back then, his lively eyes had roamed all over me, his expression a study in confidence and mild amusement. Now, Durango's eyes had gone dark and flat, the telltale sign of a man who's flipped the off switch to his humanity and gone asocial.

Going asocial is what stone-cold killers do before they strike. They lose compassion, dehumanize themselves and their prey. There's little reasoning with them once it happens.

I set down the shotgun. He came to the edge of the trees, not ten feet from me, one eye behind the rifle scope, the other wide open and blank.

"Back up," he said. "Let's see if Emmanuella is right about you."

I looked at him, puzzled. "Right about what?"

"She thinks you're allied with Maestro."

I glanced over my shoulder at the edge of the ledge about fifteen feet behind me. It looked like a long fall beyond it. "What would backing up prove?" I asked.

Durango's expression never changed. "If M's sniper knows you, he won't shoot you when you appear in his sights."

"You think M is here?"

"I think his men are," he said in a monotone, taking another step. "Maestro guns below us on the river, you above us on the river, working a squeeze play with your dummies in the raft, getting us to expose ourselves. How many men does M have there?"

"I have no idea who is or is not downriver."

"Back up, Dr. Cross," Durango said. "Let's see."

"And if the sniper doesn't shoot me?"

He smiled coldly. "I'll shoot you myself. It's what my sister wants. Now, back up."

I glanced to my right, saw that wall of stone at the far end of the ledge, knew it would cover me only a few more feet. I took one step back, then two.

Durango followed me, staying in point-blank range. His smile disappeared and he went reptilian once more.

"Almost there," he said. "Two more steps, Dr. Cross, and we'll know your fate."

I stared at him, swallowed, and shakily reached my right

foot back six inches, sure now that I would be in view of the shooter downriver.

I stepped back again with my left foot and heard a tremendous *kaboom!* along with the sonic whoosh of the three-hundred-grain Alaskan bullet that ripped past my left ear and smashed into the forehead of the half brother of Emmanuella and Marcus Alejandro.

The top of Durango's head erupted. Blood spattered with the wind and fell with the rain. He collapsed lifeless on the ledge, a bloody groove dug so deeply into his skull that it looked like the hull of a small canoe had blasted through it.

Shaking head to toe and knowing I was still exposed, a target, I moved fast around him and over his man, who was whimpering at the blood and gore all over him.

Once I knew I was behind that wall of rock and safe from the sniper downstream, I looked back across the river and saw Sampson standing just inside the tree line opposite me with his bear gun thrown overhead in victory.

CHAPTER

98

ALEX PUMPED HIS FIST AT SAMPSON.

Big John's heart slammed in his chest, and he grinned wildly as he started to lower the Ruger. A bullet smacked into the tree right next to him. It threw bark and splinters into the air before the report of the big-bore rifle came again from far downriver.

They're onto me now!

Sampson spun around and ran deeper into the trees and shadows until he was sure he could not be seen. When he finally stopped and looked back with his binoculars, he could make out Durango's corpse and the other narco struggling to sit up with his hands zip-tied behind his back.

Alex was nowhere in sight. He had to be moving north, hunting the sniper.

It's a good thing, Sampson decided before starting north

himself. *We're not hanging back. We're taking the fight to them on our terms.*

But that didn't mean acting foolhardy. Sampson forced himself to move at a much slower pace, stopping constantly to scan the way ahead and peer downriver at the west flank of the canyon, trying to spot the sniper attempting to kill him.

As he walked on, he did simple subtraction and geometry.

The day before, there'd been five men with Durango. One died in the S below Big Salmon Lake, shot from the air by one of M's men.

Another had died just a few minutes ago on Sampson's side of the river, killed by the sniper. Alex had left one of them subdued on the ledge on the east bank. And Durango was dead. That meant there were at least two more narcos to deal with.

It also meant Maestro had sent men up here as well, the sniper, certainly, and probably more. There'd been three men in that helicopter both times they'd seen it.

Is one of them the sniper? Or is this a new player?

As Sampson kept pushing north, he realized he had to act as if there were two cartel gunmen and three or even four of M's men in the six miles of rugged terrain between him and the trailhead and civilization.

When he was forced to cross open ground, Sampson hung back in the shadows until he could see exactly where the bridle trail met the far woods. Then he ducked down and sprinted in a straight line to that spot, getting back in the trees as quick as he could.

The first time he did it, he knew not even the best sniper in the world could hit a running man at that long a distance.

But with every step he was getting closer, closing the gap on the shooter's limits, making himself more and more a viable target.

Sampson had gone three hundred yards north when he looked down into the canyon and saw the wreckage of their raft, deflated and wrapped around a log that had fallen in the river. Downstream, a few of their brightly colored dry bags were floating north, along with their cooler.

Far ahead of the last of their gear, more than a mile off now, he made out the other raft with the young family in it, heading toward the takeout and the trailhead.

They had to have heard all the shooting. They'll report it, won't they?

From a thick patch of trees not a hundred yards in front of him, the air was split by a burst of machine-gun fire followed by a second burst from another angle. Sampson took cover in time to hear two men screaming in agony in Spanish.

Two pistol shots silenced their pain.

CHAPTER

99

I WAS BACK ON THE bridle trail, moving slowly north, when I heard the shooting from the other side of the canyon, two bursts of automatic-weapon fire and then a single shot that sounded like a pistol.

My stomach turned over. Had I just listened to John's death?

I wanted to cut back toward the river and use my binoculars to see if I could spot Sampson again, make sure he was still standing. But then a branch cracked uphill and to my left, deeper into the patch of timber I was traversing.

The crack was followed by crashing.

My mind screamed: *It's the bear!*

On our long horseback ride into the Bob Marshall, Bauer had told us to never try to outrun a grizzly bear, to stand our ground. But my gut told me to get downhill.

I stepped off the path and side-slid down the steep embankment. The crashing came louder and closer. Four feet down, I hit level ground, pinned my left side to a tree trunk, got the shotgun up, and pointed at the noise, with only my upper chest and head exposed above the level of the path.

Three big mule-deer bucks exploded from the thicket and charged downhill. They vaulted over the trail in front of me and bounced down the slope and out of sight.

My clothes were soaked from rain and sweat. The wind had picked up.

I tried hard not to shiver as I lowered the shotgun and peered uphill with my binoculars, looking for the source of the loud crack that had spooked the deer, looking for the big grizzly I knew was prowling somewhere in the area.

Almost five minutes passed before I caught a flicker of movement; it was followed by the soft snapping and popping of brush that at seventy-five yards became the torso and legs of a man—a skilled and trained man, by the way he fluidly moved in an athletic stance, his head swiveling, his gun held like a commando and clipped to a SWAT-style chest harness.

I recognized him. He was the same burly Hispanic who'd been hanging out the side of the helicopter during the first attack, the one who'd shot at us.

Somehow, I knew I would not get the drop on him the way I had Durango's man. I had no choice. I had to kill him or be killed.

Carefully, I lowered the binoculars and tried to raise the shotgun up just as slowly.

But he was a pro and must have caught movement.

Bolting and scrambling across the hill, he fired a sweeping burst, left to right, that broke branches and ripped into trees, including the one I was leaning against. I kicked my feet out and fell hard on the gun and my binoculars and the forest floor, knocking the wind from my lungs.

Stifling a groan, I tried to get to my knees. But another burst of gunfire clipped the trail above me, sending dirt and rocks down on my head.

I rolled over on my back, still fighting to breathe and holding the shotgun close to my chest, the muzzle above my head. The shooting stopped.

Given the circumstances, I was outgunned, but I did not reach for the pistol at my left hip. I didn't want him to hear anything but the rain falling and the wind blowing as I stayed perfectly still and prayed that I'd dropped from sight so fast and so close to where he'd been aiming that he'd think I was dead already.

The ache in my diaphragm had faded by the time I heard him moving down the hill in my direction, no doubt his gun up, sweeping the area where he'd last seen my head and chest.

When I heard him get close, I looked back and up to where the embankment met the trail. Then I adjusted the butt of the shotgun's stock against my belt and tilted the muzzle up a good thirty degrees before relaxing my head against the embankment.

I did not want to but I closed my eyes so I could listen better. A full minute passed before I heard a boot make a squishing and sucking noise as it settled into the mud up on the path, which was no more than five feet wide. I took a deep breath and let out a quarter of it before settling.

Ten seconds later, another boot squished and sucked mud, then another.

He's coming with confidence, I thought, only to have him stop for twenty seconds, then thirty seconds. I wanted to breathe, to sniff in just a little more air, but I was scared he was close enough to see my boots and lower pants now. Any twitch and he'd shoot.

Forty seconds.

My grip on the shotgun in that odd position began to slip. I was going to have to breathe. I was going to have to—

Squish. Suck.

Fifty seconds.

Squish. Suck.

I opened my eyes to slits, saw him appear over the top of the embankment.

His gun was pinned to his cheek and aimed at me, looking for signs of life, when I squeezed the trigger on a load of double-aught buckshot.

100

ON THE EAST SIDE OF the river, Sampson had not moved position since the two bursts of machine-gun fire and the two pistol shots had gone off in the thick patch of trees a hundred yards north of his position. He was lying prone over the top of a hummock of dirt, looking through binoculars at scattered live trees and standing burned trunks between him and the heavier timber.

He started at automatic-weapon fire from across the river, his heart racing, his stomach souring. Alex was engaged.

Sampson turned his binoculars westward and focused on the big piece of timber where he guessed the shooting had come from. A second burst of gunfire confirmed it.

Sampson tried to dissect the woods opposite him but could make out nothing. He swung the binoculars back to study the timber patch out in front of him.

He went back and forth this way for ten minutes before hearing a single blast that sounded more shotgun than rifle. When he looked over there, his grin surfaced and then broadened with every second that passed without automatic gunfire.

Sampson shifted the binoculars back to his side of the river, to where the trail met the woods a hundred yards out, and saw nothing. He panned them slowly left and locked.

Right there, not sixty yards away, stood the mammoth black guy who'd ridden shotgun during the first helicopter attack. How had he not heard him? How had he not seen him?

Sampson was six nine and weighed two hundred seventy-five pounds, but this guy was big too, six foot six easy and pushing the upper two hundreds.

Massive. Solid muscle. A Goliath.

And Goliath was dressed and equipped for modern war, right down to the black clothes, the black gun, the Kevlar vest, and the goggles he wore.

Those can't be night-vision, Sampson thought. *They've got to be thermals.*

Goliath started to swing his head.

He's going to peg my heat signature in this rain!

Sampson dropped the binoculars and shifted to get behind the bear gun. He moved too fast. M's man jerked his head Sampson's way.

Before Sampson could flip off the safety on the Ruger, Goliath leaped sideways and started sprinting downhill off the trail and in an arc through the trees, firing short bursts at John. Rounds smacked the front side of the hummock and blew mud in his face.

Sampson swung the barrel of the bear gun after the

running man. He fired and missed, hitting a stump just behind the giant.

Ducking down, John ran the bolt on the .375 just before Goliath responded with another burst that chewed up the front of the hummock he was hiding behind.

When Sampson peeked again, Goliath was still running like hell and across the hill. When John had first seen the giant, he had been at Sampson's eleven o'clock. Now he was at ten o'clock and showed no signs of slowing.

Sampson swung the gun after him, fired, and missed again. Nine o'clock.

What's he doing? Where's he going?

Sampson ran the bolt a third time, looking past the running Goliath all the way to seven o'clock, and understood. There was a ridge about seventy yards out that climbed and ran west toward the river. He was going for higher ground.

Sampson knew he'd have to reload after this next shot and wanted to make it count before Goliath could get the advantage and shoot down on him.

Keeping both eyes open, John swung the .375 after the running giant a third time, found the man's left side in the sights, moved the crosshairs just ahead of Goliath, and tapped the trigger. The bear gun roared.

The heavy bullet hit the giant in the ribs below his shoulder.

Dead before he knew it, Goliath did a twisting somersault, bounced off the trunk of a burned tree at the base of the ridge, and crashed to the ground, unmoving.

CHAPTER

101

I PUMPED THE ACTION ON the ten-gauge, got upright on wobbly legs, and looked over the top of the embankment at the dead guy on the trail. He was on his back and unrecognizable.

His eyes were gone. His face looked like hamburger ground by buckshot fired at point-blank range.

I climbed the embankment, trying to breathe slow and calm the adrenaline, and squatted by the dead man, meaning to search him for identification. But then I noticed he had an earbud in and a tiny bone-conduction mike taped to the hinge of his left jaw.

I rolled him over, found a small Motorola radio clipped to his belt at the small of his back, and took it. I popped out the earbud, wiped the blood off it, and stuck it in my own ear, hoping to listen in on whoever else was in the woods hunting us.

Across the river, an automatic weapon fired a short burst. A second later, a rifle shot went off. Another burst. A second rifle shot. Another burst.

The third rifle shot sounded different, abrupt, as if it had connected, and it went unanswered long enough that I allowed myself a smile. If that was the bear gun I'd heard, Sampson was still alive.

"Big DD? Do you copy?" came a male voice through the earbud. "Vincente? Do you copy? If you can't talk, tap twice."

Figuring the dead man at my feet was Vincente, I carefully peeled off the tape holding the microphone and tapped it twice.

"Good man," the voice said. "Big DD? Come back?"

The radio stayed silent for several seconds before a woman answered, choking, "He's gone, Butler. I saw him hit. I...I see Sampson! He's moving in that open timber! He's going to Dawkins's body!"

"Where?" Butler demanded.

"Face the river, Cap. Two hundred vertical up, at your one o'clock, he's heading toward the base of that ridge."

"If you can see him, shoot him, Purdy!"

The big gun went off from downriver.

"Missed," Purdy said, sounding disgusted.

"I have him now!" Butler said.

Three rapid shots went off from a lighter rifle, not far away, less than a hundred and fifty yards from me, over a brushy knoll toward the river, out there in the open where the fire must have burned hottest.

"All misses," Purdy said. "He's behind those trees now."

"You take left. I'll take right. He moves, kill him."

"Roger that."

I was already running; I went down the trail and out into the burn, then cut into the wet high grass and brush growing on the knoll. The rain picked up, giving me more sound cover as I lifted the shotgun and slowed.

"Send one, Purdy," Butler said. "See if it spooks him out."

I angled slightly to my right, crouched, and crept around the top of the knoll. The bigger gun went off a good four hundred yards to my left.

"Gonna move," Butler said. "Get a better angle on him."

I heard him in the earbud and also with my free ear. I took three quick steps and saw him below me, no more than thirty yards. Butler was facing away from me, lying prone behind a scoped AR rifle at the edge of a drop-off above the river bottom.

When he got to his feet and turned, I had the shotgun pointed at his head.

"Drop the gun or I'll make your face look like Vincente's," I said.

CHAPTER

102

BUTLER STARED AT ME IN disbelief, then set his rifle down.

"The pistol too," I said. "Remove it with your thumb and index finger. Slow."

He straightened up and did as I asked, tossing the pistol.

"Hands behind your head and move away from the weapons, Mr. Butler," I said, gesturing to his right with the shotgun.

Again, he complied, walking six feet to his left, his eyes never leaving mine. "How do you know my name?"

"I listen well. But it doesn't matter. M sent you and your men to kill us."

"I was against it, but he's sick of you."

"Is he, now?" I said. "Who is he, anyway? M? And what exactly is Maestro?"

Butler almost smiled. "That's the beauty and brilliance of

this movement. No one at my level of Maestro operations knows who he is. No one at my level wants to know."

Before I could reply, the big gun downriver fired. The shotgun was blown from my hands.

Butler started to lunge for his weapons, but I was already going for my pistol on my right hip. But it was on the other hip!

I came up with the bear spray instead.

Rather than risk a cloud of pepper gas to the face, Butler spun and leaped over the drop-off. He disappeared before I could get the pistol out of the holster on my left hip.

I ran forward and saw he'd dropped a few yards, landed on his feet, and was now sprinting and weaving pell-mell down the mountainside away from me, heading northeast toward a ravine and the river a few hundred yards beyond it.

I thought about shooting at him but realized it would have been a Hail Mary at best with a pistol. And that sniper was still to my left somewhere, which caused me to go down on my belly behind some rocks. I watched Butler get farther and farther away from me, listened to him grunt and gasp with effort in my earbud.

"Bug out, Purdy," he said. "Repeat, bug out."

"I'm gone, Cap," Purdy said.

I cringed, expecting one last shot from her in my direction. But none came and Butler put even more ground between us, still running at the same angle toward that cut in the mountainside.

And then I saw why through my binoculars. Beyond the ravine several hundred yards and pulled up on the far bank of the river, there was a blue raft just like ours, probably Durango's. Butler was headed straight for it.

He was a solid two hundred and fifty yards from me when he disappeared over and into the draw. With no idea how deep or how brushy the ravine might have been, I kept my focus on the far side of it in direct line with the river and the raft.

Twenty seconds went by and then, to my shock, I saw M's man sprinting up the other side of the draw, moving even faster than he'd gone down into it.

He got halfway up and twisted to look over his left shoulder, not back and up at me but down into the ravine.

I could see terror weave through every inch of him.

My own emotions shifted from puzzlement to horror when a massive silver-backed bear charged up out of the draw.

Butler ran even harder.

But the big male grizzly made up the ground between them with blinding speed. He lunged at Butler's back and knocked him to his knees.

M's man tried to scramble away, but the bear was on him now, cuffing him about the back and neck with his front paws and claws.

Even from that distance, even through the rain and the wind, I could hear Butler screaming as the bear flipped him over and went for his stomach.

CHAPTER

103

Washington, DC

NANA MAMA LOWERED HER HEAD and said grace before Sunday dinner.

"Heavenly Father, we thank You for this meal and our family and our friends," she said. "We are grateful for the lives and gifts You've given us and most of all for the love we have for each other and for You. We are blessed, Lord. Truly blessed."

"Amen," I said.

"Amen," said Bree and the rest of our family, plus Sampson, Willow, and Ned Mahoney.

Bree squeezed my hand and I squeezed back. We'd been doing a lot of that since I'd come home from Montana.

Between what she'd gone through in Paris and what Sampson and I had endured in the Bob Marshall Wilderness, we were highly aware of the thin line between life and death and how arbitrary that line could sometimes be.

"Dad?" Ali said. "Did the biologists find the bear yet?"

"Not yet," I said, stabbing a thigh from a roast chicken in mustard sauce from a platter.

Sampson said, "And I kind of hope they don't."

"Me too," I said.

"Even if he's a man-eater?" Ali asked.

"Even if he's a man-eater."

My grandmother put her knife down hard on her plate. "No more talk about man-eaters at Sunday dinner, please."

We all shrank back a little. Hell hath no fury like Nana Mama when she thinks one of her meals is not being fully appreciated.

I looked at John, then her, and nodded sheepishly before digging in. As usual, the food was excellent, and we all fell silent as we ate except for a few moans brought on by the perfect tang in the mustard sauce and the sweetness of the saffron rice Nana had made to go with it. But I could not keep my thoughts from drifting back to the aftermath of our trip into the Montana wilderness.

After seeing the bear kill Butler and drag him back into the ravine, I signaled to Sampson to head for Durango's raft a half a mile beyond it.

I made a long circle around the ravine to get to the raft myself. Along the way, I found a sniper rifle stashed by the trail along with two electric bikes and evidence of a third one missing. I marked the spot on my OnX map and left it all where I'd found it.

Sampson and I were off the river three hours later and hustling down the path to the trailhead to report what had happened. The first Flathead County Sheriff's deputies were already on the scene when we finally got to the parking lot.

The family we'd seen run the rapids had already called to report the gunfire. We told the deputies to bring in the Montana Bureau of Investigations and the FBI and to be looking for a woman riding an electric bike coming off the trail system.

On our way to Kalispell to make formal statements, we called home to tell everyone we were safe and out of the woods two days early. Mahoney came out on the very next flight to oversee the investigation and the retrieval of the various bodies strewn along both sides of the river. The three of us went back in by helicopter the next morning. A larger team rode in on horseback.

The narco I'd left bound at the wrists walked right into them. He was suffering from dehydration and terrified of bears, and he was immediately taken into federal custody.

A group of U.S. Fish and Wildlife investigators came in later that day. Armed with high-powered rifles and dart guns, they'd gone into the ravine to retrieve Butler's remains. They found what was left of him buried under a pile of dirt and rocks near another pile of dirt and rocks the grizzly had put over a rotting mule deer carcass. The Fish and Wildlife investigators believed the tracks I'd seen well south of the ravine belonged to the same bear on his way back to eat the mule deer, which he'd probably buried days before.

They also believed Butler had charged right into the draw where the grizzly was preparing to feast. The bear went territorial on him and attacked.

"Alex?" Nana Mama said.

I looked up at her. "Nana?"

"She asked you three times if you liked the meal," Bree said.

"Shows how good it is," I said.

"It's so good," Mahoney said.

"Best I've had in a long time," Sampson said. "Right, Willow?"

His daughter nodded. "Can I have my dessert now?"

My grandmother smiled as she got up. "You can. Who else wants ice cream?"

104

AFTERWARD, BREE AND I WENT out on the front porch with Sampson and Mahoney. The mid-September evening was beautiful— hardly any humidity in the warm air, and the sounds of the city were somehow soothing, familiar and forgiving in a way the wilderness sounds had not been.

"We have DNA matches on Butler, Vincente, and Dawkins," Mahoney said.

"Let me guess," Sampson said. "They're all dead men."

Ned nodded. "Matthew Riley Butler was a DIA interrogator, supposedly blown to bits in an IED explosion in Iraq six years ago. Jesus Pedro 'JP' Vincente was a Green Beret who purportedly died in a firefight in northern Afghanistan four years ago. David 'Big DD' Dawkins was with SEAL Team Four. He supposedly died five years ago by rocket-propelled grenade during a secret incursion into Somalia. His body was never recovered."

"What about the helicopter they used?" Bree asked. "I heard they found it."

Mahoney nodded. "In a clear-cut about twenty air miles from where they attacked you. Shot to hell. Used to belong to a helicopter service north of there. The owner claims it was bought sight unseen and paid for in cryptocurrency by Matthew Butler, whom he identified from pictures. We're trying to track the crypto back to the buyer."

I said, "I know who the buyer was. M. He's behind all of it."

"You believe what Butler told you before he ran?" Sampson asked. "That he had no idea who M actually was?"

"I go back and forth," I said. "But it makes sense when I remember that he called what they were doing a 'movement.'"

"Suggests an ideology," Mahoney said. "Fanaticism."

"Yes," I agreed. "With independent cells acting without knowledge of others but all under Maestro's and M's direction."

"I can see some of that," Sampson said. "But from Manitoba?"

Mahoney said, "We had Canadian Mounted Police check out the location. Middle of nowhere, six miles from the nearest building."

Bree frowned. "But you were saying there could be other teams like Butler's? That M could send other teams like that after you? From wherever?"

I nodded unhappily. "Butler said M was sick of me and John. Butler said he disagreed with M, but that's why he was there."

Sampson said, "With M paying a half a million for a helicopter on short notice to make it happen, I'm thinking we've gone and pissed M off again. I'm thinking things are not over between us."

I wanted to believe otherwise, but I said, "Not by a long shot, I'm afraid."

CHAPTER

105

Northeastern Massachusetts

SET UP LIKE AN AMPHITHEATER with six stacked rows of work-stations, the operations room was kept intentionally dim so the fifteen men and women working at their individual computers could clearly see the cinema-size screen mounted high on the front wall.

The big display was filled with a feed from a camera aimed from several hundred yards away at a small private jet parked on the tarmac of an unidentified airport.

On the top row of the amphitheater, a tall man in his forties with longish dark hair and a clipped salt-and-pepper goatee watched the screen intently, his arms crossed.

He adjusted the microphone on his headset. "Can we zoom in, Edith?"

To his right, Edith, a harried-looking brunette in her

fifties, adjusted her eyeglasses before giving her keyboard a command.

The screen magnified, showing the Citation Jet and two men in dark sunglasses climbing down the gangway. Both carried machine pistols.

On the screen, a third, smaller, person loaded luggage into the hold from a cart. Finished, the handler shut the hold and, with a nod to the armed men at the bottom of the gangway, pushed the empty cart out of view.

"That was smoothly done, Mr. Vance," the tall man remarked to the beefier man standing a few feet away from him.

"Flawless, Mr. Malcomb," agreed Steven Vance, the CEO of Paladin Inc.

Ryan Malcomb, his tech-genius partner, was now tapping his fingers on the back of an unoccupied chair at one of the workstations.

A woman with a buzz cut on much of the left side of her head and the hair on the right dyed purple said, "They've got their flight plans cleared."

"Excellent," Ryan Malcomb said.

A younger man two rows down said, "Escalade's at the gate."

A few minutes later, a black Cadillac SUV rolled onto the scene and stopped near the gangway. Three more armed men climbed out.

One of them opened the right rear door and a woman exited. Dark pantsuit. Dark glasses. Jet-black hair. A stunning beauty.

Vance said, "Edith, make sure it's not a body double."

Edith adjusted her glasses and typed again, freezing the

woman in a frame and setting it to one side of the big screen. A biometric model appeared and settled over the woman's face.

"Twenty-four-point match," Edith said. She had a British accent. "It's her. Emmanuella."

The cartel chief climbed after two of her bodyguards into the eight-person jet. Two more bodyguards followed her inside.

The door was pulled up. The Cadillac drove away. The jet began to taxi.

It got no more than thirty feet toward the runway when it exploded in a fireball.

The entire room stayed dead silent for several beats.

Malcomb broke the tension, saying, "Well done, little burglar."

"Thank you, M," Alison Purdy replied in his ear. "My great pleasure."

"Mine too," M said, and he began to clap.

Starting with Vance and then Edith, one by one every person in the room stood to clap as Malcomb called out, "Brilliantly done! All of you! The dream we shared is now manifest. The Alejandro cartel is no more. This battle against the darkness is over. The forces of Maestro have triumphed!"

As the others in the room cheered and hugged, Edith said, "Do you wish to notify Alex Cross, M?"

Malcomb's expression tightened a little before he smiled and shook his head. "I'm sure Dr. Cross will find out soon enough, Edith."

ABOUT THE AUTHOR

JAMES PATTERSON is one of the best-known and biggest-selling writers of all time. His books have sold in excess of 400 million copies worldwide. He is the author of some of the most popular series of the past two decades – the Alex Cross, Women's Murder Club, Detective Michael Bennett and Private novels – and he has written many other number one bestsellers including non-fiction and stand-alone thrillers.

James is passionate about encouraging children to read. Inspired by his own son who was a reluctant reader, he also writes a range of books for young readers including the Middle School, Dog Diaries, Treasure Hunters and Max Einstein series. James has donated millions in grants to independent bookshops and has been the most borrowed author in UK libraries for the past thirteen years in a row. He lives in Florida with his family.

Have you read them all?

ALONG CAME A SPIDER

Alex Cross is working on the high-profile disappearance of two rich kids. But is he facing someone much more dangerous than a callous kidnapper?

KISS THE GIRLS

Cross comes home to discover his niece Naomi is missing. And she's not the only one. Finding the kidnapper won't be easy, especially if he's not working alone . . .

JACK AND JILL

A pair of ice-cold killers are picking off Washington's rich and famous. And they have the ultimate target in their sights.

CAT AND MOUSE

An old enemy is back and wants revenge. Will Alex Cross escape unharmed, or will this be the final showdown?

POP GOES THE WEASEL

Alex Cross faces his most fearsome opponent yet. He calls himself Death. And there are three other 'Horsemen' who compete in his twisted game.

ROSES ARE RED

After a series of fatal bank robberies, Cross must take the ultimate risk when faced with a criminal known as the Mastermind.

VIOLETS ARE BLUE

As Alex Cross edges ever closer to the awful truth about the Mastermind, he comes dangerously close to defeat.

FOUR BLIND MICE

Preparing to resign from the Washington police force, Alex Cross is looking forward to a peaceful life. But he can't stay away for long . . .

THE BIG BAD WOLF

There is a mysterious new mobster in organised crime. The FBI are stumped. Luckily for them, they now have Alex Cross on their team.

LONDON BRIDGES

The stakes have never been higher as Cross pursues two old enemies in an explosive worldwide chase.

MARY, MARY

Hollywood's A-list are being violently killed, one-by-one. Only Alex Cross can put together the clues of this twisted case.

CROSS

Haunted by the murder of his wife thirteen years ago, Cross will stop at nothing to finally avenge her death.

DOUBLE CROSS

Alex Cross is starting to settle down – until he encounters a maniac killer who likes an audience.

CROSS COUNTRY

When an old friend becomes the latest victim of the Tiger, Cross journeys to Africa to stop a terrifying and dangerous warlord.

ALEX CROSS'S TRIAL
(with Richard DiLallo)

In a family story recounted here by Alex Cross,
his great-uncle Abraham faces persecution, murder
and conspiracy in the era of the Ku Klux Klan.

I, ALEX CROSS

Investigating the violent murder of his niece Caroline,
Alex Cross discovers an unimaginable secret that could
rock the entire world.

CROSS FIRE

Alex Cross is planning his wedding to Bree,
but his nemesis returns to exact revenge.

KILL ALEX CROSS

The President's children have been kidnapped,
and DC is hit by a terrorist attack. Cross must
make a desperate decision that goes against
everything he believes in.

MERRY CHRISTMAS, ALEX CROSS

Robbery, hostages, terrorism – will Alex Cross make it
home in time for Christmas . . . alive?

ALEX CROSS, RUN

With his personal life in turmoil, Alex Cross
can't afford to let his guard down.
Especially with three blood-thirsty
killers on the rampage.

CROSS MY HEART

When a dangerous enemy targets Cross and his family,
Alex finds himself playing a whole new game of
life and death.

HOPE TO DIE

Cross's family are missing, presumed dead. But Alex Cross will not give up hope. In a race against time, he must find his wife, children and grandmother – no matter what it takes.

CROSS JUSTICE

Returning to his North Carolina hometown for the first time in over three decades, Cross unearths a family secret that forces him to question everything he's ever known.

CROSS THE LINE

Cross steps in to investigate a wave of murders erupting across Washington, DC. The victims have one thing in common – they are all criminals.

THE PEOPLE VS. ALEX CROSS

Charged with gunning down followers of his nemesis Gary Soneji in cold blood, Cross must fight for his freedom in the trial of the century.

TARGET: ALEX CROSS

Cross is called on to lead the FBI investigation to find America's most wanted criminal. But what follows will plunge the country into chaos, and draw Cross into the most important case of his life.

CRISS CROSS

When notes signed by 'M' start appearing at homicide scenes across the state, Cross fears he is chasing a ghost.

DEADLY CROSS

A shocking double homicide dominates tabloid headlines. Among the victims is Kay, a glamorous socialite and Cross's former patient – and maybe more. But who would want her dead, and why?

Also by James Patterson

THE WOMEN'S MURDER CLUB SERIES

1st to Die • 2nd Chance (*with Andrew Gross*) • 3rd Degree (*with Andrew Gross*) • 4th of July (*with Maxine Paetro*) • The 5th Horseman (*with Maxine Paetro*) • The 6th Target (*with Maxine Paetro*) • 7th Heaven (*with Maxine Paetro*) • 8th Confession (*with Maxine Paetro*) • 9th Judgement (*with Maxine Paetro*) • 10th Anniversary (*with Maxine Paetro*) • 11th Hour (*with Maxine Paetro*) • 12th of Never (*with Maxine Paetro*) • Unlucky 13 (*with Maxine Paetro*) • 14th Deadly Sin (*with Maxine Paetro*) • 15th Affair (*with Maxine Paetro*) • 16th Seduction (*with Maxine Paetro*) • 17th Suspect (*with Maxine Paetro*) • 18th Abduction (*with Maxine Paetro*) • 19th Christmas (*with Maxine Paetro*) • 20th Victim (*with Maxine Paetro*) • 21st Birthday (*with Maxine Paetro*)

DETECTIVE MICHAEL BENNETT SERIES

Step on a Crack (*with Michael Ledwidge*) • Run for Your Life (*with Michael Ledwidge*) • Worst Case (*with Michael Ledwidge*) • Tick Tock (*with Michael Ledwidge*) • I, Michael Bennett (*with Michael Ledwidge*) • Gone (*with Michael Ledwidge*) • Burn (*with Michael Ledwidge*) • Alert (*with Michael Ledwidge*) • Bullseye (*with Michael Ledwidge*) • Haunted (*with James O. Born*) • Ambush (*with James O. Born*) • Blindside (*with James O. Born*) • The Russian (*with James O. Born*)

PRIVATE NOVELS

Private (*with Maxine Paetro*) • Private London (*with Mark Pearson*) • Private Games (*with Mark Sullivan*) • Private: No. 1 Suspect (*with Maxine Paetro*) • Private Berlin (*with Mark Sullivan*) • Private Down Under (*with Michael White*) • Private L.A. (*with Mark Sullivan*) • Private India (*with Ashwin Sanghi*) • Private Vegas (*with Maxine Paetro*) • Private Sydney (*with Kathryn Fox*) • Private Paris (*with Mark Sullivan*) • The Games (*with Mark Sullivan*) • Private Delhi (*with Ashwin Sanghi*) • Private Princess (*with Rees Jones*) • Private Moscow (*with Adam Hamdy*) • Private Rogue (*with Adam Hamdy*)

NYPD RED SERIES

NYPD Red (*with Marshall Karp*) • NYPD Red 2 (*with Marshall Karp*) • NYPD Red 3 (*with Marshall Karp*) • NYPD Red 4 (*with Marshall Karp*) • NYPD Red 5 (*with Marshall Karp*) • NYPD Red 6 (*with Marshall Karp*)

DETECTIVE HARRIET BLUE SERIES

Never Never (*with Candice Fox*) • Fifty Fifty (*with Candice Fox*) • Liar Liar (*with Candice Fox*) • Hush Hush (*with Candice Fox*)

INSTINCT SERIES

Instinct (*with Howard Roughan, previously published as* Murder Games) • Killer Instinct (*with Howard Roughan*)

THE BLACK BOOK SERIES

The Black Book (*with David Ellis*) • The Red Book (*with David Ellis*)

STAND-ALONE THRILLERS

The Thomas Berryman Number • Hide and Seek • Black Market • The Midnight Club • Sail (*with Howard Roughan*) • Swimsuit (*with Maxine Paetro*) • Don't Blink (*with Howard Roughan*) • Postcard Killers (*with Liza Marklund*) • Toys (*with Neil McMahon*) • Now You See Her (*with Michael Ledwidge*) • Kill Me If you Can (*with Marshall Karp*) • Guilty Wives (*with David Ellis*) • Zoo (*with Michael Ledwidge*) • Second Honeymoon (*with Howard Roughan*) • Mistress (*with David Ellis*) • Invisible (*with David Ellis*) • Truth or Die (*with Howard Roughan*) • Murder House (*with David Ellis*) • The Store (*with Richard DiLallo*) • Texas Ranger (*with Andrew Bourelle*) • The President is Missing (*with Bill Clinton*) • Revenge (*with Andrew Holmes*) • Juror No. 3 (*with Nancy Allen*) • The First Lady (*with Brendan DuBois*) • The Chef (*with Max DiLallo*) • Out of Sight (*with Brendan DuBois*) • Unsolved (*with David Ellis*) • The Inn (*with Candice Fox*) • Lost (*with James O. Born*) • Texas Outlaw (*with Andrew Bourelle*) • The Summer House (*with Brendan DuBois*) • 1st Case (*with Chris Tebbetts*) • Cajun Justice (*with Tucker Axum*) • The Midwife Murders (*with Richard DiLallo*) • The Coast-to-Coast Murders (*with J.D. Barker*) • Three Women Disappear (*with Shan Serafin*) • The President's Daughter (*with Bill Clinton*) • The Shadow (*with Brian Sitts*) The Noise (*with J.D. Barker*) • 2 Sisters Detective Agency (*with Candice Fox*) • Jailhouse Lawyer (*with Nancy Allen*)

NON-FICTION

Torn Apart (*with Hal and Cory Friedman*) • The Murder of King Tut (*with Martin Dugard*) • All-American Murder (*with Alex Abramovich and Mike Harvkey*) • The Kennedy Curse (*with Cynthia Fagen*) • The Last Days of John Lennon (*with Casey Sherman and Dave Wedge*) • Walk in My Combat Boots (*with Matt Eversmann and Chris Mooney*) ER Nurses: True stories from the frontline (*with Matt Eversmann*)

MURDER IS FOREVER TRUE CRIME

Murder, Interrupted (*with Alex Abramovich and Christopher Charles*) • Home Sweet Murder (*with Andrew Bourelle and Scott Slaven*) • Murder Beyond the Grave (*with Andrew Bourelle and Christopher Charles*) • Murder Thy Neighbour (*with Andrew Bourelle and Max DiLallo*) • Murder of Innocence (*with Max DiLallo and Andrew Bourelle*) • Till Murder Do Us Part (*with Andrew Bourelle and Max DiLallo*)

COLLECTIONS

Triple Threat (*with Max DiLallo and Andrew Bourelle*) • Kill or Be Killed (*with Maxine Paetro, Rees Jones, Shan Serafin and Emily Raymond*) • The Moores are Missing (*with Loren D. Estleman, Sam Hawken and Ed Chatterton*) • The Family Lawyer (*with Robert Rotstein, Christopher Charles and Rachel Howzell Hall*) • Murder in Paradise (*with Doug Allyn, Connor Hyde and Duane Swierczynski*) • The House Next Door (*with Susan DiLallo, Max DiLallo and Brendan DuBois*) • 13-Minute Murder (*with Shan Serafin, Christopher Farnsworth and Scott Slaven*) • The River Murders (*with James O. Born*) • The Palm Beach Murders (*with James O. Born, Duane Swierczynski and Tim Arnold*)

For more information about James Patterson's novels, visit www.penguin.co.uk

From America's most beloved superstar
and its greatest storyteller – a thriller
about a young singer-songwriter on the
rise and on the run, and determined
to do whatever it takes to survive.

Read on for an exclusive extract...

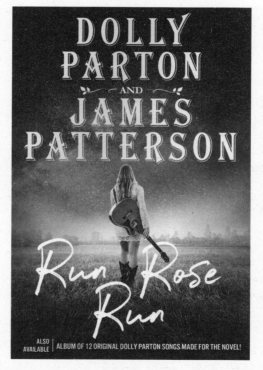

ALSO AVAILABLE | ALBUM OF 12 ORIGINAL DOLLY PARTON SONGS MADE FOR THE NOVEL!

**Available in hardback from March 2022, along with an album of
12 original Dolly Parton songs made for the novel!**

PROLOGUE

The Louis Seize–style mirror in the bedroom of suite 409 at the Aquitaine Hotel reflected for little more than an instant a slim, fine-featured woman: wide blue eyes, clenched fists, dark hair streaming behind her as she ran.

Then AnnieLee Keyes vanished from the glass, as her bare feet took her racing into the suite's living room. She dodged the edge of the giltwood settee, flinging its throw pillow over her shoulder. A lamp fell with a crash behind her. She leaped over the coffee table, with its neat stack of *Las Vegas* magazines and tray of complimentary Debauve & Gallais truffles, her name written in chocolate ganache flecked with edible gold. She hadn't even tasted a single one.

Her foot caught the bouquet of Juliet roses and the vase tipped over, scattering pink blooms all over the carpet.

The balcony was up ahead of her, its doors open to the afternoon sun. In another instant, she'd reached it, and the hot air hit her in the face like a fist. She jumped onto the chaise longue and threw her right leg over the railing, struggling to push herself the rest of the way up.

Then, balanced on the thin rail between the hotel and the sky, she hesitated. Her heart beat so quickly she could hardly breathe. Every nerve ending sparked with adrenaline.

I can't, she thought. *I can't do it.*

But she had to. Her fingers clutched the rail for another split second before she willed them loose. Her lips moved in an instant of desperate prayer. Then she launched herself into the air. The sun flared, but her vision darkened and became a tunnel. She could see only below her—upturned faces, mouths open in screams she couldn't hear over her own.

Time slowed. She spread out her arms as if she were flying.

And weren't flying and falling the same?

Maybe, she thought, *except for the landing.*

Each millisecond stretched to an hour, these measures of time all she had left in this world. Life had been so damn hard, and she'd clawed her way up only to fling herself back down. She didn't want to die, but she was going to.

AnnieLee twisted in the air, trying to protect herself from what was coming. Trying to aim for the one thing that might save her.

ELEVEN
MONTHS EARLIER

CHAPTER

1

AnnieLee had been standing on the side of the road for an hour, thumbing a ride, when the rain started falling in earnest.

Wouldn't you know it? she thought as she tugged a gas station poncho out of her backpack. *It just figures.*

She pulled the poncho over her jacket and yanked the hood over her damp hair. The wind picked up, and fat raindrops began to beat a rhythm on the cheap plastic. But she kept that hopeful smile plastered on her face, and she tapped her foot on the gravel shoulder as a bit of a new song came into her head.

Is it easy? she sang to herself.

No it ain't
Can I fix it?
No I cain't

She'd been writing songs since she could talk and making melodies even before that. AnnieLee Keyes couldn't hear the call of a wood thrush, the *plink plink plink* of a leaky faucet, or the rumbling rhythm of a freight train without turning it into a tune.

Crazy girl finds music in everything—that's what her mother had said, right up until the day she died. And the song coming to AnnieLee now gave her something to think about besides the cars whizzing by, their warm, dry occupants not even slowing down to give her a second glance.

Not that she could blame them; she wouldn't stop for herself, either. Not in this weather, and her probably looking no better than a drowned possum.

When she saw the white station wagon approaching, going at least twenty miles under the speed limit, she crossed her fingers that it would be some nice old grandpa pulling over to offer her a lift. She'd turned down two rides back when she thought she'd have her choice of them, the first from a chain-smoking lady with two snarling Rottweilers in the back seat, the second from a kid who'd looked higher than Mount Everest.

Now she could kick herself for being so picky. Either driver would have at least gotten her a few miles up the road, smelling like one kind of smoke or another.

The white wagon was fifty yards away, then twenty-five, and as it came at her she gave a friendly, graceful wave, as if she was some kind of celebrity on the shoulder of the Crosby Freeway and not some half-desperate nobody with all her worldly belongings in a backpack.

The old Buick crawled toward her in the slow lane, and AnnieLee's waving grew nearly frantic. But she could have stood on her head and shot rainbows out of her Ropers and it wouldn't have mattered. The car passed by and grew gradually smaller in the distance. She stomped her foot like a kid, splattering herself with mud.

Is it easy? she sang again.

No it ain't
Can I fix it?
No I cain't
But I sure ain't gonna take it lyin' down

It was catchy, all right, and AnnieLee wished for the twentieth time that she had her beloved guitar. But it wouldn't have fit in her pack, for one thing, and for another, it was already hanging on the wall at Jeb's Pawn.

If she had one wish—besides to get the hell out of Texas—it was that whoever bought Maybelle would take good care of her.

The distant lights of downtown Houston seemed to blur as AnnieLee blinked raindrops from her eyes. If she thought about her life back there for more than an instant, she'd probably stop wishing for a ride and just start running.

By now the rain was falling harder than she'd seen it in years. As if God had drawn up all the water in Buffalo Bayou just so He could pour it back down on her head.

She was shivering, her stomach ached with hunger, and suddenly she felt so lost and furious she could cry. She had nothing and nobody; she was broke and alone and night was coming on.

But there was that melody again; it was almost as if she could hear it inside the rain. *All right,* she thought, *I don't have* nothing. *I have music.*

And so she didn't cry. She sang instead.

Will I make it?
Maybe so

Closing her eyes, she could imagine herself on a stage some-where, singing for a rapt audience.

Will I give up?
Oh no

She could feel the invisible crowd holding its breath.

I'll be fightin' til I'm six feet underground

Her eyes were squeezed shut and her face was tilted to the sky as the song swelled inside her. Then a horn blared, and AnnieLee Keyes nearly jumped out of her boots.

She was hoisting both her middle fingers high at the tractor trailer when she saw its brake lights flare.